21ˢᵗ Century Seminars

where professionals grow

Continuing Education Credit

Social Workers, Marriage and Family Therapists, Educational Psychologists, and Professional Clinical Counselors: This course has been approved for 8.0 hours of continuing education self-study by the California Board of Behavior Sciences for LCSWs, MFTs, LEPs and, LPCCs. Provider # PCE 5317. Non-California residents must contact the licensing board in their respective states to determine if that state will honor the CE units earned through this course.

Play Therapists: This course qualifies for 8.0 hours of non-contact continuing education and training (Play Therapy Applications) for Registered Play Therapists (RPT) and Supervisors (RPT-S) through the Association for Play Therapy (APT) Approved provider 02-122. Our Play Therapy training hours are approved in the United States, Alaska, Hawaii, and where Association for Play Therapy CE credit is accepted.

Registered Nurses: This course qualifies for 8.0 hours of continuing education contact hours by the California Board of Registered Nursing for Registered Nurses. Provider #: 16196. Non-California residents must contact the licensing board in their respective states to determine if their state will honor the CE units earned through this course.

Non-licensed Professionals and Non-California Residents: Non-licensed professionals will receive a certificate of completion for 8.0 hours of training. Non-California residents must contact the licensing board in their respective states to determine if their state will honor the CE units earned through this course. Our Play Therapy training hours are approved in the United States, Alaska, Hawaii, and where Association for Play Therapy CE credit is accepted.

21st Century Seminars Presents

Termination That Works

With At-Risk Children and Adolescents

Four Steps That Build Resilience and Give
Hope to Challenging Populations

Over 70 Creative Interventions From The Beginning of
Termination To The Last Goodbye

From the Kidz in the Hood Series

Termination That Works With At-Risk Children and Adolescents

©2012, 21st Century Seminars, Inc.

Limited Photocopying Permission

Library of Congress Control Number: 2012943999

ISBN-13: 978-0-9858265-0-5

ISBN-10: 0985826509

Printed in the United States of America

Correspondence regarding this manual can be sent to:

21st Century Seminars, Inc.
1590 W. Rosecrans Avenue, Suite D-130
Manhattan Beach, California 90266

The Kidz in the Hood Series

The Kidz in the Hood Series is dedicated to giving mental health professionals effective tools to work with at-risk youth. Interventions in this series are culturally sensitive, research-based, and harness the power of resilience-building assets that help young people thrive.

Kidz in the Hood is a term of endearment that playfully describes at-risk children and adolescents from all walks of life...they are youth, who live in neighborhoods (hoods) that give them less than they deserve. There are hoods made of: danger and violence; grief and sorrow; substance abuse and addiction; separation and loss; abuse and family secrets; and the list goes on. There are the hoods of our inner cities, whose the kidz must learn to overcome poverty, peril and deprivation. And, there are the hoods of our affluent areas, whose kidz may have more than enough, but their emotional, physical, and psychological trauma is very real and very deep.

Kidz in the Hood are amazing, insightful, inspiring, fun...and deeply wounded. Building a relationship with one of these kidz can be both challenging and one of the most rewarding experiences a mental health provider can have.

The goal of the Kidz in the Hood series is to equip these brave souls with the tools needed to thrive and to overcome the hoods in which they live.

This training manual focuses on the importance of terminating treatment successfully.

Dedication

This book is dedicated to my 2010-2012 supervisees who made me better, stronger, and wiser:

Christie, Corbett, Desiree, Graciela, Jessica, Katie, Kristin, LaNesha, Latasha, Rionnisha, Sadaff, and...

Berenice, Claribel, Derek, Erin, Lauren, Maria, Samantha, Yesenia and Zachary...

All of you have paid it forward for those who will come after you.

Acknowledgements

To all the Kidz in the Hood, who have the courage to share your lives with those who have come alongside to help. Thank you for your inspiration...

And to my son, one of the most amazing kidz I know...I love you.

21st Century Seminars would like to thank the following individuals for their contributions to this training manual:

Bridgette Mitchell, LCSW, RPT-S, Director of Training

Fred at www.GoliathGraffix.com, cover design

Alain at www.Spanishenglishtranslations.com, translation

TABLE OF CONTENTS

INTRODUCTION

FOUR STEPS TO END TREATMENT SUCCESSFULLY

STEP TWO: Process The Range of Feelings About Termination 78

Interventions: 83

STEP THREE: Prepare Client To Manage Life After Termination 132

Interventions: 138

- My client's case hasn't been open that long. I don't think termination means that much to him. We are stopping just when we are starting. What is a proper termination in this case?
- How long should the termination process last?
- How many sessions do I devote to each of the 4 Termination Steps?
- What if I only have a couple of sessions to terminate?
- Counting down to termination each week feels awkward. What if my client drops out of treatment because we are so focused on termination?
- My client was inconsistent throughout treatment. I do not want her thinking she did something inappropriate to cause treatment to end. How do I address this?

- My client started opening up after I told him it was time to end. I'm afraid if I talk too much about termination he will stop sharing. How do I address this?
- May I offer extra sessions, accept a gift or see a client at unscheduled times during termination?
- After discussing termination, my client sent me a "friend" request on my social media page. How should I address this?
- Do I hug my client on the last session? What if my client hugs me?

CONTINUING EDUCATION INFORMATION

Interventions – At – A – Glance
Termination That Works With At-Risk Children and Adolescents

Age: Y= Young (5-6); M= Middle (7-11); Adolescents (12-18)   **Modality:** I= Individual; F=Family; G=Group

Step One	Provide psychoeducation about termination; allow for processing of cognitive distortions about why treatment is ending; reinforce ending date; put supports in place to pre-empt early termination from treatment.			
Intervention	**Goal**	**Age**	**M**	**Materials Needed**
Termination Script	Scripts to assist treatment providers with finding sensitive phrases for the termination announcement	5-18	N/A	Script included
Common Reactions as Treatment Ends	Psychoeducation handout for clients and parents. English/Spanish	5-18	I F G	English/Spanish handouts included
Letter to Parents	Sample letter to parents explaining termination. English/Spanish	5-18	I F	English/Spanish letters included
My Good-bye Calendar	Tracks sessions/weeks to termination	5-11	I F G	Calendar included
Countdown Tokens	Uses tokens to track sessions/weeks to termination	5-11	I F G	Template for tokens included
Termination Questionnaire	Client shades how much agrees/disagrees with statements kids make about termination. Non-threatening. Allows for a range of thoughts/feelings. Encourages engagement.	5-18	I F G	Questionnaire included. Pen, pencil or marker
Penny For My Thoughts Game	Flip a coin to play a board game. Fun and engaging.	5-11	I F G	Scissors, a penny coin. Template and worksheet included.
Termination Puzzle	Puzzle activity. Non-threatening, creative, fun	5-18	I F G	Puzzle included. Scissors. Pen or pencil.
Tic-Tac-Toss	Uses movement. Good for kinetic learners, language or cognitive difficulties.	5-11	I F G	3 sheets of paper. Pen or marker. Optional bean bag
Chips Away	Game using poker chips. Good for younger clients, language issues, or emotional restrictiveness	5-18	I F G	1 sheet of paper. At least 20 poker/plastic/wooden chips
The Matching Game	Card Game. Provider tries to match client's answers, then processes how answers are the same or different	5-18	I F G	Game cards included. Scissors.
Step-by-Step	Uses movement. Focuses on Step 1 themes. Good for kinetic learners. Activity can be used for all 4 termination steps. Engaging and non-threatening. Great for kids with language or cognitive challenges.	5-18	I F G	Pen, pencil, marker. Scissors. Stepping Stone template included.
Basketball	Good for kinetic learners. Focuses on Step 1 themes. Activity can be used for all 4-termination steps. Engaging and non-threatening. Great for all, especially kids with language or cognitive challenges.	5-18	I F G	Scissors, small container for basketball hoop and ball for shooting. Includes basketball court and cards
Tip the Scales	Uses scaling technique to engage client. Processing a range of thoughts and feelings. Encourages engagement	7-18	I F	Pen, pencil or marker. 6 small tokens (any small, flat object like a coin or paperclip)
My Story: Chapter 1	Narrative activity. Creative, expressive.	5-18	I F	Pen, pencil, crayons or markers. Book included
Step Two	Encourage feelings identification, exploration, verbalization and processing; educate how termination may trigger feelings of previous losses. Monitor counter-transference reactions			
Intervention	**Goal**	**Age**	**M**	**Materials Needed**
Feeling Faces Puppets	Stick puppets made of feeling faces. Fun and engaging, symbolic. Good for kids with limited vocabulary and language or cognitive challenges.	5-11	I F G	Scissors, 8 popsicle sticks, crayons or markers, glue stick or tape.
A-Mazing Feelings	Client explores feelings via a maze. Different mazes for older and younger clients. Encourages processing.	5-18	I F	Pen, pencil or marker
In Living Color	Creative art activity. Client uses colors to express feelings.	12-18	I F G	Colorful pens, pencils, crayons or markers.
Feelings Dice	Client rolls dice to match feelings. Creative, interactive, engaging.	5-18	I F G	Scissors. Dice templates included or use real dice

Intervention	Goal	Age	M	Materials Needed
Basketball	Kinetic activity using Step 2 themes. Can be used for all 4 termination steps. Engaging and non-threatening. Great for all, especially kids with language or cognitive challenges.	5-18	I F G	Scissors, small container for basketball hoop and ball for shooting. Includes basketball court and cards
Color The Feelings In	Projective. Client colors feelings that a child his/her age might feel. Safe, non-threatening.	5-11	I F G	Colorful pens, pencils or markers.
Step-by-Step	Kinetic activity using Step 2 themes. Can be used for all 4 termination steps. Engaging and non-threatening. Great for kids with language or cognitive challenges.	5-18	I F G	Pen, pencil, marker. Scissors. Stepping Stone template included.
The Feelings Puzzle	Problem solving game play. Non-threatening, fun.	5-18	I F G	Puzzle included. Scissors. Pen or pencil. Optional glue or poster board
My Feelings About Goodbyes	Explores how past good-byes impact current feelings about termination	7-18	I F G	Colorful pens, pencils or markers
Good and Not So Good	Uses the time tested "line down the middle of the page" activity to safely explore range of feelings about treatment	7-18	I F G	Colorful pens, pencils or markers. Optional magazine pictures
Feelings Target	Client throws clay bombs at a target to identify feelings. Kinetic, fun, engaging, interactive, playful	5-18	I F G	Targets included. Make darts out of wet clay, toilet tissue, cotton, or putty
My Collage- Reloaded	Takes a new spin on collaging. Creative, thoughtful, engaging, playful	7-18	I F G	Scissors. Glue stick, collaging materials
Color My Time in Counseling	Art activity. Uses colors to express a range of feelings. Encourages processing.	5-18	I F G	Paper. Colorful pencils, pens, crayons or markers
My Story: Chapter 2	Narrative Activity. Creative, expressive	5-18	I F	Pen, pencil, crayons or markers. Book included
Step Three	**Prepare client to maintain skills and manage life after treatment ends. Goal review; Build concrete problem solving and coping skills; Predict, Plan and Prepare for future challenges, anniversaries and trauma reminders. Encourage connection with caregivers, family and community supports.**			
Intervention	Goal	Age	M	Materials Needed
Guide to Promoting Resilience in Children and Adolescents	Information for Mental Health Professionals. Factors that build resilience in youth.	5-18	N/A	Guide included
Goal Review	Rating sheets for client to track progress. Different rating sheets for older and younger clients	5-18	I F	Goal Charts included
About Me	Assists with transferring information from one provider to another during a case transfer or premature termination.	5-18	I F	Worksheet included. Pen, pencil or maker
Bag of Skills	Art activity. End result produces a "bag" of concrete skills for client.	5-18	I F G	2 sheets of paper, pens, pencils, markers. Paper bag
Basketball	Kinetic activity using Step 3 themes. Can be used for all 4 termination steps. Engaging and non-threatening. Great for all, especially kids with language or cognitive challenges.	5-18	I F G	Scissors, small container for basketball hoop and ball for shooting. Includes basketball court and cards
Road to my Success	Creative activity. Uses theme of 'road to success' to identify coping skills and plan for future challenges. Engaging, interactive	5-18	I F G	Worksheet included. Colorful pens, crayons, markers
My Survival Kit	Concrete, cognitive activity. Client can develop written strategies to manage various topics.	7-18	I F	Scissors. Pen, pencil. Survival kit cards included
Clay Activity: For My Future	Clay activity. Expressive arts. Uses symbols to identify items needed to maintain success.	5-18	I F G	Clay. Pen, pencil or marker. Activity Sheet Included.
It Will Pass Calendar	Calendar to list anniversaries and develop pre-emptive coping strategies.	5-18	I F G	Pen or pencil. Calendar included
Look for the Rainbow	Creative Activity. Uses the theme of the rainbow to prepare for life after treatment.	5-18	I F G	Colorful pens, pencils and markers. Worksheet included
Step-by-Step	A kinetic game using Step 3 themes. Spans all 4 termination steps. Engaging and non-threatening. Great for kids with language or cognitive challenges.	5-18	I F G	Pen, pencil, marker. Scissors. Stepping Stone template included.
Color My Time in Counseling	A continuation from step 2. Creative, art activity to address Step 3 themes. Encourages processing. Can be used to complement *Color My Future*.	5-18	I F G	Paper. Colorful pens, pencils and markers.

Color My Future	Art activity to prepare for future challenges. Can be used alone or to complement "Color My Time in Treatment". Expressive, interactive	7-18	I F G	Paper. Colorful pens, pencils and markers.
Coping Word Search	Problem solving game play. Uses a word search made of coping words to prepare for the future.	7-18	I F	Pen, pencil or marker. Word search included
My Story: Chapter 3	Narrative activity. Creative, expressive.	5-18	I F	Pen, pencil, crayons or markers. Book included

Step Four	**Honor the relationship with rituals, keepsakes, namesakes and other items that can be used as transitional objects when treatment ends. Encourage client to make meaning out of the therapeutic experience by giving back, altruism and corrective activities.**			
Intervention	**Goal**	**Age**	**M**	**Materials Needed**
Hand Prints	Art activity. Uses symbolism of the hand to make a keepsake. Theme: how hands can heal. Engaging	5-18	I F G	Paper, colored pens, pencils, pencils, paint or large ink pad
Positive Affirmation Activities	Several activities that incorporate positive affirmations into projects. Process how positive words can help others. Creative, interactive	5-18	I F G	Paper. Colorful markers, pens, pencils. Optional craft items. See instructions
Strength Word Activities	Several activities that incorporate strength words into projects. Process how the client's strengths can help others. Interactive, creative	5-18	I F G	Paper, markers, pens, colored pencils. Optional craft items. See instructions
Fortune Teller	Uses the fortune teller for commemoration and finding meaning. Playful, engaging.	5-18	I F G	Paper. Pen, pencil or marker
The Power of Positive Words Crossword Puzzle	Uses a crossword puzzle to encourage discussion of strengths, successes, support system and helping others. Problem solving fun, engaging	7-18	I F	Pen, pencil or marker. Crossword puzzle included.
Blow It Into the Future	Uses bubble blowing to honor and find meaning. Expressive, creative, engaging, playful	5-18	I F G	Bubbles. Index cards. Binder rings or container for cards
Clay Activity: Hand Me the Future	Memorialize hand and finger prints. Encourages theme of using hands to help others. Interactive, engaging, creative and playful	5-18	I F G	Clay. Writing tool for clay.
Planting a Seed	Plant a fast-growing seed. Use plant theme as a metaphor for future growth	5-18	I F G	16 oz. plastic cup. Soil. 3-4 sunflower seeds. Water
Step-by-Step	A kinetic game using Step 4 themes. Engaging and non-threatening. Great for kids with language or cognitive challenges.	5-18	I F G	Pen, pencil, marker. Scissors. Stepping Stone template included.
Basketball	A kinetic game using Step 4 themes. Engaging and non-threatening. Great for all, especially language or cognitive challenges.	5-18	I F G	Scissors, small container for basketball hoop and ball. Basketball court and cards included.
Message Book	Narrative Activity. Creative, expressive	5-18	I F G	Paper. Binder. Colorful writing utensils
When I Look Into My Future: Guided Imagery	Relaxation and visualization. Culminates in an art activity. May also be used with the *Letter to My Future Self* activity	7-18	I F G	Paper. Pen, pencil or marker. Optional magazine pictures. All scripts included
Letter to My Future Self	Client writes a letter to be mailed to client @ 6 weeks after termination. Narrative, creative, expressive	5-18	I F G	Paper. Pen, pencil or marker. Optional magazine pictures
My Story: Chapter 4	Narrative Activity. Creative, expressive	5-18	I F	Pen, pencil, crayons or markers. Book included

Activities for the Last Session	**Creative ideas and instructions for what to do on the last session. Includes ethical and legal considerations regarding celebrations.**			
Intervention	**Goal**	**Age**	**M**	**Materials Needed**
Celebrations	To Say Good-bye and End Treatment	5-18	I F G	Various, see instructions
Hand Prints	To Say Good-bye and End Treatment	5-18	I F G	Paper, colored pens, pencils, pencils, paint or large ink pad
Gift Bags	To Say Good-bye and End Treatment	5-18	I F G	Gift bag. Various items.
Certificates	To Say Good-bye and End Treatment	5-18	I F G	Certificates or paper. Template
Bookmarks	To Say Good-bye and End Treatment	5-18	I F G	Paper. Bookmark Template
Letter from the Treatment Provider	To Say Good-bye and End Treatment	5-18	I F G	Paper
Speeches	To Say Good-bye and End Treatment	5-18	I F G	As needed to facilitate speech
Graduation Picture	To Say Good-bye and End Treatment	5-18	I F G	Camera. Film. Printing ability

Guidelines for Practitioners

4-Easy Steps to Termination: This manual has four sections that explain each of the 4-termination steps. Each section begins with "What to do" and "How to do it" instructions that are followed by a chapter summary and interventions for each step. Because the skills progressively build on one another, users should begin at Step 1 and end at Step 4. Following these four steps will give you the confidence that the termination process is being thoroughly addressed and that your clients are leaving treatment with enough protective assets to manage future challenges and the hope to remain open to future relationships.

A Good Fit for Any Setting: This manual applies to work with children and adolescents across many settings including: community-based mental health; foster care, group homes, and residential treatment centers; elementary, middle, and high schools; juvenile correctional programs; inpatient care centers, and hospitals; child welfare agencies, and private practice. The worksheets refer to the treatment provider as a "counselor" as an all-inclusive term. Feel free to change the worksheets to reflect your work as a counselor, case manager, social worker, psychologist, play therapist, etc.

Works With Challenging Populations: Contains insights for working with youth having histories of maltreatment, juvenile delinquency and externalizing behaviors. Interventions are culturally sensitive, research-based, and harness the power of resilience-building developmental assets, which are proven to positively impact the lives of young people, including at-risk youth.

Age Range:

Each activity has an age range assigned to it. Many activities apply to more than one age group and are identified as such.

1. Young (ages 5-6)   Enjoy symbolic activities
2. Middle (ages 7-11)   Enjoy concrete games and activities with rules
3. Adolescents (ages 12- up)   Enjoy both concrete games and activities that encourage abstract thinking.

Legend:

➢ "Counselor" is an all-inclusive term for mental health provider. Mental health professionals fulfill many different roles including clinical case manager, social worker, psychologist, play therapist, academic counselor, psychologist, clinical counselor, wraparound provider, school psychologist, nurse, behavior coach and the list goes on. For ease of use, the worksheets refer to the treatment provider as a "counselor". Feel free to change the worksheets to reflect your work as a therapist, counselor, case manager, social worker, psychologist, play therapist, etc.

➢ "Parent" means any adult who is a primary caretaker of a client.

➢ "Kidz" is synonymous with any child or adolescent client.

➢ "S/He" is an abbreviation that means "she or he".

➢  Identifies items meriting close attention

Play Therapy: The term, Play Therapy is used as defined by the Association for Play Therapy as "The systematic use of a theoretical model to establish an interpersonal process, wherein trained play therapists use the therapeutic powers of play to help clients prevent or resolve psychosocial difficulties and achieve optimal growth and development."

> **Stop and reflect:** Have you experienced an ending to a relationship where the person did not properly say good-bye to you or have an opportunity to say good-bye?
>
> • How did this experience make you feel? How did it impact your feelings about good-byes? Did it impact how you felt about beginning a relationship with a new person?
>
> • How might your client's experiences be similar or different from your own? How might your clients feel about endings and saying good-bye?

INTRODUCTION

21st Century Seminars

where professionals grow

Termination With At-Risk Youth

Termination describes the act of closing a case and ending treatment with a client. It is a process that honors the client and the therapeutic relationship. Through termination, mental health practitioners support clients to:

1. Embrace their strengths, so they can successfully manage residual emotions and future challenges in a more adaptive way.

2. Actualize their coping skills so they can move through life without being overwhelmed by it.

3. Experience a positive therapeutic ending so they will remain open to future relationships without (or with less) fear.

At-Risk Youth

When clients face having to say goodbye to a trusted treatment provider during the termination process, sensitive loss and abandonment issues may be triggered (Cohen, Mannarino and Deblinger, 2006). Practitioners must be sensitive to their client's loss histories, especially when working with clients with complex trauma histories (Worden, 2009). These clients may have an uneasy sense that they have little or no power to make things different in their environment

> **Traumatized clients may routinely experience relationships that end traumatically, or suddenly, or are out of their control.** (Cohen, Mannarino and Deblinger, 2006).

and may also overgeneralize the mistakes of one relationship to all future relationships (Blaustein and Kinniburgh, 2010). Unlike adults, who form alliances more easily in the early stages of treatment, the therapeutic alliance for youth tends to grow stronger in the middle to later stages of treatment (Shirk and Karver, 2003). This pattern of extended alliance building is especially true for youth with histories of maltreatment, juvenile delinquency and externalizing behaviors. For this at-risk population, the quality of the therapeutic alliance rates low in the beginning but strengthens during the middle to latter stages of treatment and is highly predictive of positive treatment outcomes (Eltz, Shirk & Sarlin, 1995; Florsheim et al., 2000; Rauktis et al., 2005; Hogue et al., 2006).

The implications of these studies are important for termination. Consider these points:

- This may explain why some children and adolescents can be challenging to engage in the early stages of the treatment process.

- Your therapeutic relationship with a child or adolescent client may be still forming as you move into termination, highlighting the importance of ending treatment in a planned, sensitive manner.

- The way a treatment provider ends a relationship with a traumatized client may impact treatment outcomes and how that client views future relationships with other providers.

More long-term damage is done to the client by an unhealthy termination than by the client not meeting all of his or her treatment goals. Logically speaking, even if a client did not accomplish all of the desired goals, as long as the client remains open to returning to treatment, the work may continue at any point in the future. However, if that same client ended treatment in a way that caused him or her to feel closed to future relationships with other treatment providers, then the likelihood of engaging in future treatment is compromised.

> **For at-risk youth the quality of the therapeutic alliance strengthens during the middle to latter stages of treatment and is highly predictive of positive treatment outcomes.**

With so much at risk, it is imperative that the therapeutic relationship ends in a planned, sensitive manner.

Most mental health practitioners agree that termination is an important part of the treatment process, but it can be difficult to know what to do to make termination successful.

3

A Successful End Starts At The Beginning

To prepare for a successful termination, you must begin your therapeutic relationship with termination in mind. The best terminations start at the very beginning of treatment, not at the end of treatment.

Discuss Termination at the Onset of Treatment

Ideally, your first conversation about termination should be at the beginning of treatment as a part of informed consent. From the onset of treatment, the client should be informed of the limitations of treatment, the timelines, and the means by which progress will be evaluated. Role expectations should be addressed in terms of what the client can expect of you and what you expect of the client. If your model has a prescribed range of sessions, the length of treatment is determined by insurance guidelines, or the end of treatment is due to a maturational event (the school year ending, an internship/practicum ending, or a maternity leave) this should be discussed at the onset of services.

> **Clarifying role expectations can decrease early termination**

Some studies suggest that addressing client role expectations prior to treatment can also decrease the rate of dropout (Reis & Brown, 2006; Scamardo, Bobele, & Biever, 2004; Walitzer, Dermen, & Conners, 1999; Zwick & Attkisson, 1985). It is thought that psychoeducation about the services may help develop client expectations that are more congruent with what actually happens in treatment and more similar to the expectations treatment providers have for their clients (Reis & Brown, 2006; Swift & Callahan, 2008). This is particularly important for children and adolescents since drop out rates for child mental health treatment in outpatient community-based settings can fall between 40% and 60% (Armbruster & Kazdin, 1994; Gould, Shaffer, & Kaplan, 1985; Barrett, Chua, Crits-Christoph, Gibbons, & Thompson, 2008; Swift, Callahan, & Levine, 2009; Wierzbicki & Pekarik, 1993).

The Therapeutic Relationship is Temporary

The therapeutic relationship is temporary by design; similar to when a student enters a grade, learns certain skills, and then moves on. In her book, *Treating Traumatized Children - New Insights and Creative Interventions* (1989), Beverly James states the mental health provider's purpose is to work with the client to achieve certain goals and once those goals are achieved, the relationship ends.

> **Unless there are extenuating circumstances, you must be clear from the beginning that treatment is to help your client function without you** (Kramer, 1990).

- As treatment progresses, conduct periodic mini-reviews to assess for progress.
- As goals are achieved, termination ensues as a natural progression.

Since problems with client and provider agreement on what treatment is and what happens during the treatment process are associated with premature termination, accurately framing the relationship from the beginning may help inoculate it against early termination (Tracey, 1986; Reis & Brown, 2006; Swift & Callahan, 2008).

Follow The 4 Termination Steps

This training manual separates termination into 4 easy-to-follow steps. Ideally, you should begin at Step 1 and end at Step 4. While there is some ordering to the steps, you should allow for flexibility. As you move through the steps, you may find it helpful to briefly revisit themes from earlier stages.

The 4 termination steps are designed to prepare children and adolescents to end mental health treatment feeling hopeful about the future and having enough protective assets to support them to thrive in future challenges. The interventions were designed utilizing research from resiliency, brain development and evidence-based practice areas and take into account clients with language barriers, physical disabilities, and developmental or cognitive delays.

4-Steps to A Successful Termination

1) **Educate Client About Termination**

   - Make the Termination Announcement.
   - Focus on client's strengths and progress as reason for termination.
   - Provide psychoeducation on possible reactions to termination.
   - Do not allow new stressors to distract you from processing termination; theme new events to termination.

2) **Process the Range of Feelings About Termination**

   - Support client to express a range of feelings, including ambivalence.
   - Educate the client on how termination may trigger feelings of previous losses.
   - Monitor your own counter-transference feelings and reactions.

3) **Prepare Client to Manage Life After Termination**

   - Review treatment goals, discuss progress made and remaining work to be fine-tuned.
   - Build Resilience: Prepare client to maintain skills and manage future challenges, anniversaries and trauma reminders.
   - Build Resilience: Encourage client to connect with caregivers and community supports.

4) **Honor the Therapeutic Relationship and Terminate Treatment**

   - Support client to make an enduring connection to the mental health provider and the therapeutic relationship.
   - Build Resilience: Encourage making meaning out of the therapeutic experience through altruism and corrective activities.
   - Have a final celebration session and end treatment
   - Client leaves treatment with skills that promote resiliency and remains open to future relationships.

Termination Checklist

Step 1: Educate Client About Termination

☐ **Make the Termination Announcement.** Use *Termination Scripts* to guide you through the announcement. Give client a concrete ending date. Clearly explain what termination is and why treatment is ending. Clarify what will take place over the weeks leading to termination. Most Step 1 interventions will support this process. Case transfers include and explanation of why and when the case will be transferred, and when and how the client will meet the new treatment provider. Each week after the termination announcement, count down the remaining weeks/sessions. *My Goodbye Calendar* or *Countdown Tokens* are helpful interventions for this step.

☐ **Focus on client's strengths and progress as reason for termination.** Focus on the gains made during treatment. If appropriate, taper/lessen the number of sessions. Support client to have a role in planning the termination. Select Step 1 interventions to support this process.

☐ **Provide psychoeducation on possible reactions to termination.** Review and give client/parent a copy of the handout *Common Reactions as Treatment Ends*. Give parent a copy of *Letter to Parent as Treatment Ends*. Clarify how and why client may return to treatment in the future and if there can be a relationship after treatment ends. Clarify policy on ongoing contact (cell phone, social media, email...) after termination.

☐ **Do not allow new stressors to distract you from processing termination; theme new events to termination.** See *Termination Scripts* on page 28 to help you with theming new stressors to termination.

Step 2: Process the Range of Feelings About Termination

☐ **Support client to express a range of feelings, including ambivalence.** Normalize client's reactions and feelings- allow for set-backs. Do not rush the process, help the client identify and express his/her feelings. Accept the client's feelings unconditionally. Select Step 2 interventions to support this process.

☐ **Educate the client on how termination may trigger feelings of previous losses.** Normalize how good-byes are a normal part of life, share everyday life examples. Process what previous good-byes were like for the client. Educate how saying good-bye to treatment provider may cause feelings about previous good-byes to surface. Select Step 2 interventions to support this process.

☐ **Monitor your own counter-transference feelings and reactions.** Be aware of your own reactions such as strong feelings before, during or after client sessions; avoiding the termination countdown; not talking about termination each week; or, not following your usual policies with clients (Refer to Appendix C for more helpful details).

Step 3: Prepare Client to Manage Life After Termination

☐ **Review treatment goals; discuss progress made and remaining work to be fine-tuned.** Use *Goal Review* worksheet. After identifying needs, theme the remaining work to termination. Use the *About Me* worksheet for premature terminations and case transfers.

☐ **Build Resilience: Prepare client to maintain skills and manage future challenges, anniversaries and trauma reminders.** Use before, during and after treatment themes and what I need for the future themes to build resilience. Select Step 3 interventions to support this process.

☐ **Build Resilience: Encourage client to connect with caregivers and community supports.** Select Step 3 interventions to support this process.

Step 4: Honor the Therapeutic Relationship and End Treatment

☐ **Support client to make an enduring connection to the mental health provider and the therapeutic relationship.** Honor the relationship with rituals, keepsakes, namesakes and other items that can be used as transitional objects when treatment ends. Select Step 4 interventions to support this process.

☐ **Build Resilience: Encourage making meaning out of the therapeutic experience through altruism and corrective activities.** Select Step 4 interventions to support this process.

☐ **Have a final celebration session and terminate treatment.**

Building Resilience During Termination

Resiliency is the ability "to recover from adversity and resume functioning even when suffering serious trouble, confusion or hardship" (Zastrow, C & Kirst-Ashman, K., 2010, pg. 15). Resiliency emphasizes the use of protective factors that help one thrive in the face stressful life events or adverse environmental conditions (Gutheil & Congress, 2000; Norman, 2000). After studying several million youth, the Search Institute identified a list of positive factors in youth, families, communities, and schools that help children and adolescents thrive (Sesma, A., Jr., & Roehlkepartain, E. C., 2003; Benson, P. L., et. al., 2006). These positive factors, called *The 40 Developmental Assets*, were found to have a positive influence on young people regardless of their gender, socio-economic status, race, or ethnicity. This means, at-risk youth can do more than just survive, but will thrive with the proper supports.

Developmental assets not only protect youth from high-risk behaviors such as engaging in violence, using tobacco, gambling, early sexual activity and illicit drug use, but also reduce the likelihood of youth experiencing depression, suicide attempts, antisocial behavior, school problems, and drinking and driving (Benson, P. L., et. al., 2006). Assets provide more than protection from at-risk behaviors, but also promote healthy behavior in youth such as valuing diversity, maintaining good health and succeeding in school (Sesma, A., Jr., & Roehlkepartain, E. C., 2003; Benson, P. L., et. al., 2006). In fact, studies indicate the more positive assets a young person has, the greater the likelihood of thriving and not engaging in high-risk behaviors. The number of assets is a stronger determinant of success or failure than poverty or being from a single-parent household. Studies indicate youth having 31 to 40 assets are the most resilient (Sesma, A., Jr., & Roehlkepartain, E. C., 2003; Benson, P. L., et. al., 2006).

Assets That Help Youth Thrive

*Adapted from The Search Institute's 40 Developmental Assets (The Search Institute, 2006)

Family/Home Assets:

• Family climate is loving and supportive

- Positive communication with family. Youth is willing to seek advice and council from parents/caregivers
- Involved in and helps youth succeed in school
- Sets consistent clear rules and consequences and supervises youth's whereabouts
- Youth feels safe at home
- Parents/Caregivers model positive, responsible behavior
- Parents/Caregivers encourage youth to do well
- Supports youth to read for pleasure three or more hours per week
- Supports youth to complete one hour of homework per school day
- Supports youth to spend three or more hours per week in sports, clubs or organizations at school or in the community
- Supports youth to spend three or more hours per week in lessons or practice in music, theatre or other arts
- Supports youth to spend one or more hours per week in activities in a religious institution

School Assets:

- School is a caring and encouraging place
- Youth feels safe at school
- Establishes clear rules and consequences
- Teachers encourage youth to do well
- School culture engages youth in learning
- Gives one hour of homework per school day
- Supports youth to read for pleasure three or more hours per week
- Teachers model positive, responsible behavior
- Youth receives support from three or more nonparent adults
- Youth spends three or more hours per week in sports, clubs or organizations in the school (or community)
- Youth spends three or more hours per week in lessons or practice in music, theatre or other arts in school (or community)

Community Assets:

- Youth receive support from three or more nonparent adults
- Youth has caring neighbors
- Youth experiences that adults in his/her community value youth
- Youth are given useful and valued roles in the community
- Youth serves his/her community one hour or more per week
- Youth feels safe in his/her community

- Neighbors assist in monitoring youth's behavior
- Youth spends three or more hours per week in sports, clubs or organizations in the community (or school)
- Youth spends one or more hours per week in activities in a religious institution
- Spends three or more hours per week in lessons or practice in music, theatre or other arts in the community (or school)

The Youth's Own Personal and Interpersonal Assets:

- Is willing to seek advice and council from parents/caregivers
- Feels safe at home, school and in the community
- Best friends model responsible behavior
- Spends three or more hours per week in lessons or practice in music, theatre or other arts
- Spends one or more hours per week in activities in a religious institution
- Spends three or more hours per week in sports, clubs or organizations in the community
- Engages in unstructured "hanging out" time with friends two or fewer nights per week
- Motivated to do well in school
- Actively engaged in learning
- Cares about his/her school
- Reads for pleasure three or more hours per week
- Highly values helping others
- Highly values promoting equality and reducing hunger and poverty
- Acts on convictions and stands up for his or her beliefs
- Is truthful even when it is not easy
- Believes it is important to not be sexually active or to use alcohol or drugs
- Knows how to plan ahead and make choices
- Has empathy, is sensitive and friendship skills
- Has knowledge of and is comfortable with people of different cultural, racial and ethnic backgrounds
- Is able to resist negative peer pressure and dangerous situations
- Resolves conflicts nonviolently

Preschool Age Children

Resilient preschool children have a sense of self and age-appropriate structure (Mendez, Fantuzzo & Cicchetti, 2002). They are able to manage emotions, particularly frustration tolerance. Additionally, resilient preschoolers are able to seek and elicit support from others (Mischel, Shoda, & Rodriguez, 1989; Shoda, Mischel, & Peake, 1990).

During Termination with Preschool Children:

• Ensure the client leaves treatment with well-developed coping skills and a written coping plan. The coping plan should include a variety of skills that can be applied to various scenarios. Pay particular attention to reinforcing emotional regulation, anger management, and impulse control skills. It is important to involve the parent(s), who can coach, encourage and monitor the child's progress at home.

• Support the preschooler to embrace a sense of self. Incorporate Play Therapy activities to help the client identify his/her strengths, enhance self-esteem, and build self-confidence.

• Assess the number of assets the preschooler has within his/her home, preschool, and community. Strengthen as many assets as possible prior to closing the case.

• Coach and prepare the preschooler on how to seek out and elicit support from those in his/her support system such as; parent(s), family, community members, and preschool staff.

School Age Children

Having positive self-esteem and personal competency is highly predictive of a positive outcome at this stage of development (Bolger, Patterson, & Kupersmidy, 1998; Kim & Cicchetti, 2003). Resilient school aged children are skilled at being able to take time to think rather than behaving impulsively (Cicchette, Rogosch, Lynch & Holt, 1993; Shoda et al., 1990; Zelazo, 2001). They have a developing internal locus of control and believe they can influence the world (Wyman, Cowen, Work, & Parker, 1991). Resilient school aged children also have a variety of coping strategies and skills, including a sense of humor, which they can apply to a variety of life scenarios. They also have more positive relationships with peers and adults than their less than resilient age mates.

During Termination with School Age Children:

• Develop concrete coping skills designed to enhance emotional regulation, impulse, and self-control. Build skills that support the client's internal locus of control; teach a variety of coping strategies (including having a sense of humor) and support self-care skills such as engaging in fun, constructive activities. Engage the client in Play Therapy activities that both teach and model the importance of enjoyment.

• Engage client in activities that enhance self-esteem and build a sense of personal competency such as, identifying strengths, personal assets, and goals achieved during treatment. Enhance self-efficacy and develop an internal locus of control by creating strategies to manage anniversaries, trauma reminders, and future challenges.

• Encourage the client to engage in an age-appropriate activity to give back to others. This can vary from something simple like writing a positive message to help future clients, to more involved activities such as volunteering at a non-profit or philanthropic organization like a homeless shelter, local church, library, or school. Giving back can help clients feel connected to their community, encourage making meaning out of their therapeutic experience and reinforce that they are capable of influencing the world around them.

• Assess the number of assets the client has within his/her home, school, and community. Strengthen as many assets as possible prior to closing the case.

• Connect the client to his/her family, school, peer, religious and community supports. Strategize how s/he can enjoy and maintain more positive relationships with others.

Adolescents

Resilient adolescents have a sense of personal responsibility and social maturity. They believe in their ability to exert some control over their own fate and have a desire to do so (Campbell-Sills, Cohan & Stein, 2006). They are somewhat achievement oriented and can exercise age-appropriate independence. They have an established, internalized set of values, and are able to use these values to make moral, ethical, and life decisions. Finally, they are able to interact positively with others and are socially perceptive and capable of building and maintaining relationships (Resnick et al., 1997).

During Termination with Adolescents:

• Review strengths and goals achieved to reinforce the adolescent's belief tha s/he has the skill and ability to exert some control over his or her own fate.

• Ensure client has strong, flexible coping skills. Role play problem solving scenarios, rehearse coping skills, create survival kits and coping plans as appropriate to the client's presenting problems. Pay particular attention to emotional regulation, cognitive coping and behavior management skill development. Coping plans also support the adolescent to take responsibility for his/her actions and challenge him or her to achieve future goals.

• Put a plan in place to address anniversaries, trauma reminders, and set-backs. This will support the adolescent's desire to have control over his/her own fate and promote belief in a positive personal future.

• Encourage the adolescent to engage in an altruistic activity. This can vary from something simple, like writing a positive message to help future clients, to volunteering at a homeless shelter, local church, library or school. Giving back can help the client to make meaning out of his or her emotional trauma while making a contribution to the larger community.

• Assess the number of assets the adolescent has within his/her home, school, and community. Strengthen as many assets as possible prior to closing the case.

• Support the client to connect to his or her external supports such as family and extended family; school and religious community; peer and community groups and strategize how s/he can enjoy and maintain more positive relationships with others.

The Brain And Termination

This section reviews the functions of the left and right hemispheres of the brain, self-regulation, and how each contributes to a successful termination. While overly simplified, this discussion is adequate enough to give treatment providers a basic understanding of neurobiology. For more elaborate discussions about the human brain and emotions, see the recommended readings list at the end of this section.

The Left and Right Hemispheres

The human brain is divided into two hemispheres, the left and the right. We will call the left hemisphere, the left brain and the right hemisphere, the right brain. A fibrous band of tissue called the corpus callosum facilitates communication between the two sides and connects the two hemispheres. Each hemisphere is responsible for different functions (Carter, 2012; Gainotti, 2012; Hellige, 1993; MacNeilage, 1990; MacNeilage, Rogers, & Vallortigara, 2009; McGilchrist, 2009; Schore, 2003b, pp. xiv-xvii; Semrud-Clikeman, Fine & Zhu, 2011).

Left Brain Functions

Generally speaking, the left side of the brain:

- Is primarily responsible for speech and language.
- Facilitates reasoning and analysis.
- Stores conscious memories.
- Is the side of the brain we think of as controlling the conscious, cognitive, rational, and verbal mental states...the verbal, analytical side.

The client's thoughts about why their case is terminating; judgments about his/her strengths and progress in treatment; and beliefs about whether s/he can be successful in managing life after treatment ends are left brain functions.

Right Brain Functions

Generally speaking, the right side of the brain:
- Manages sensory information.
- Controls auditory and visual processing.
- Stores unconscious memories.
- Is responsible for spacial-temporal awareness (our awareness of what is happening in the environment around us).
- Processes emotional experiences and affect, facial recognition, tone of voice and psychobiological states.
- Senses emotional or physical danger and initiates the fight, flight or freeze protective response.
- Facilitates creative abilities. We think of the right brain as creative, emotional and non-verbal (although some language is stored in the right brain).

How a client feels about termination for example, loss, abandoned, confused, relieved, joyous, ambivalent, satisfied, proud, etc., are right brain functions.

The Amygdala and Self-regulation

The brain contains a small almond shaped structure called the amygdala (pronounced a-mig-dah-lah). The amygdala is located beneath the temporal lobes on each side of the brain. The left amygdala responds more to verbalizations and the right amygdala processes fear responses, facial recognition, attachment and arousal (Whalen & Phelps, 2009; Schore, 2003 a, 2003 b). From birth, the amygdala scans for threats in the environment. When emotional or physical dangers are sensed, the amygdala tells other neurobiological systems to initiate the fight, flight and/or freeze protective responses. As vulnerable infants and young children, we need the amygdala's quick fight, flight or freeze response system to help insure our survival. However, as we mature, continued reliance on the amygdala as our primary means to respond to stress:

1) Makes it difficult for one to accurately discriminate among levels of threat (small threats are responded to with the same intensity as larger threats)

2) Creates a dysregulated arousal system that responds to stress in an erratic combination of over-reactive, underactive, or an unpredictable combination of both responses.

The amygdala "errs on the side of caution; it 'behaves first and thinks later'" (Montgomery, 2013. Pg 66). What begins as an advantage at birth becomes problematic when age-appropriate self-control skills and the ability to modulate emotional responses are needed to successfully interact with others. To resolve this developmental dilemma the brain has other structures, such as the limbic system or higher cortical functions, which manage stress with less reactivity and intensity than the amygdala. However, these systems develop later than the amygdala. As they mature, these structures will eventually take over the responsibility of threat and stress management from the amygdala; reserving the amygdala for those rare moments when we need its fast response system to protect ourselves from serious threat.

Chronic stress caused by early childhood trauma, cumulative traumatic experiences, poor attachment history, brain injury, substance use, developmental delays, etc., may impact the healthy development of our threat response systems (Sapolsky, 2005; Schore, 2003 a; 2003 b). Chronic stress and trauma:

1. Create an overdependence on the amygdala to respond to threat instead of allowing the higher right brain structures to do so.
2. Cause our higher right brain structures to develop poorly or to not develop at all.

When clients are able to manage their thoughts, behaviors and emotions adaptively, we call this being emotionally regulated. During moments of arousal, the higher upper right-brain functions are able to manage stress at a deliberate pace. When clients are not able to manage their thoughts, behaviors and emotions in an adaptive way, we call this being dysregulated. Meaning, the more thoughtful upper right-brain structures are constantly over-ridden by the overactive amygdalar responses. Termination implies that clients have made enough progress in treatment that they are able to tolerate moments of distress and remain emotionally regulated. When moments of dysregulation occur, they are short-lived and minimally disruptive.

A Case Example: Jenny

Neurobiology informs us that *talking* to the client about termination has limitations. Language is a left brain function whereas nonverbal feelings are processed through the right brain. For example, a high school aged client named, Jenny, completed the Termination Questionnaire below (See page 46 for complete *Termination Questionnaire* instructions and worksheet). Jenny's treatment provider hesitated giving her the questionnaire stating, "I told Jenny about termination already and she told me she understands...giving her this questionnaire feels redundant."

After reluctantly agreeing to administer the termination questionnaire, the provider was shocked when Jenny responded: YES, *she was surprised that counseling was ending; YES, she was unsure why counseling was ending; She sometimes wondered if she had done something wrong to cause counseling to end; YES, she was curious about what would happen to her counselor when services ended; and, YES, now that she knows counseling is ending she may not want to come anymore.*

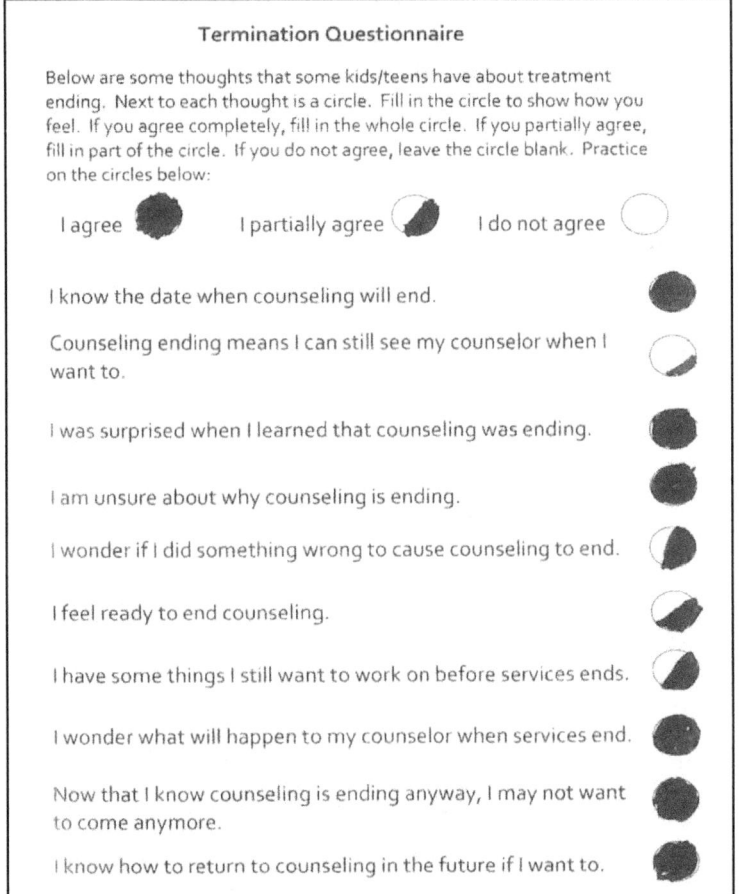

Termination Questionnaire

Below are some thoughts that some kids/teens have about treatment ending. Next to each thought is a circle. Fill in the circle to show how you feel. If you agree completely, fill in the whole circle. If you partially agree, fill in part of the circle. If you do not agree, leave the circle blank. Practice on the circles below:

I agree ●   I partially agree ◕   I do not agree ○

I know the date when counseling will end. ●

Counseling ending means I can still see my counselor when I want to. ○

I was surprised when I learned that counseling was ending. ●

I am unsure about why counseling is ending. ●

I wonder if I did something wrong to cause counseling to end. ◕

I feel ready to end counseling. ◕

I have some things I still want to work on before services ends. ◕

I wonder what will happen to my counselor when services end. ●

Now that I know counseling is ending anyway, I may not want to come anymore. ●

I know how to return to counseling in the future if I want to. ●

As this case example demonstrates, the client may have *said* she understood termination but her answers indicated she had unresolved *feelings* about the process. Language is primarily a left brain function. To access the feelings, you must access the right brain.

Accessing the Left and Right Brains

The cognitive triangle of thoughts, feelings and behavior provides a helpful model of how the left and the right brains interact. Using the above case as an example, Jenny's thoughts about the termination process (*I was surprised when I learned counseling was ending; I am unsure why counseling is ending; I sometimes wonder if I did something wrong to cause counseling to end; Now that I know counseling is ending anyway, I may not want to come anymore.*) may trigger potentially distressful emotions (anger, rejection, anxiety, discouragement etc.) about the termination process. If Jenny has adequate coping skills to manage these thoughts (for example, self-talk, self-soothing techniques, processing her feelings, challenging distorted cognitions, etc.), she may remain regulated and will probably move through the termination process fairly smoothly. However, if she has fragile or less adaptive coping skills, she may become dysregulated. The right brain, sensing the client's vulnerability and distress over the termination process, may activate a fight (acting out angry feelings about termination), flight (avoiding appointments, early termination) or freeze (shutting down, withdrawing during sessions) response in reaction to the client's emotional distress.

> **To process termination successfully, treatment providers must access both sides of the brain.**

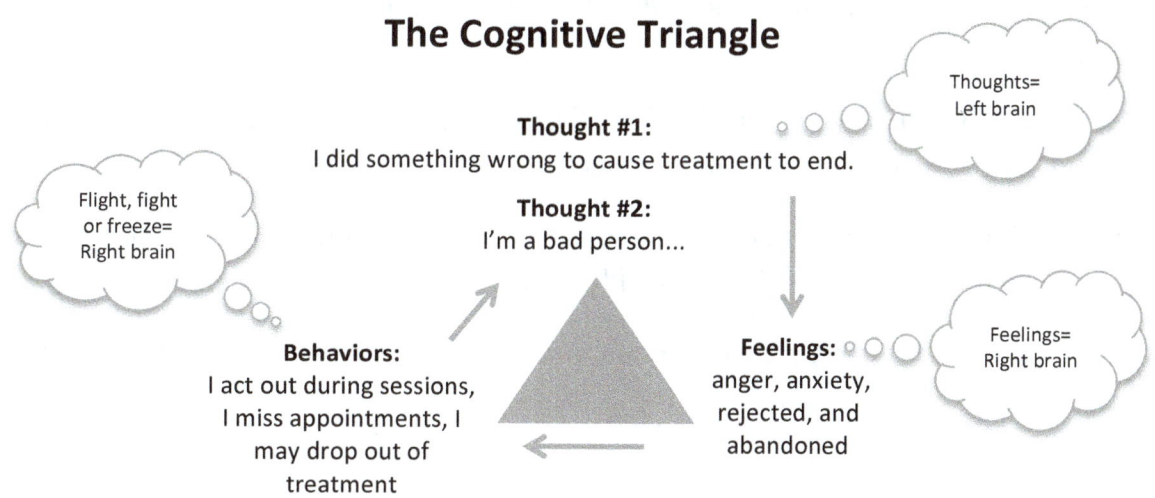

The Cognitive Triangle

Thoughts= Left brain

Thought #1:
I did something wrong to cause treatment to end.

Thought #2:
I'm a bad person...

Flight, fight or freeze= Right brain

Behaviors:
I act out during sessions, I miss appointments, I may drop out of treatment

Feelings: anger, anxiety, rejected, and abandoned

Feelings= Right brain

The thoughts generated in the left brain, trigger emotions in the right brain, which in turn activates a behavioral response that could either support or disrupt the termination process; in Jenny's case, there was a potential for disruption.

The *Termination Questionnaire* is an intervention for Step 1 of the termination process. However, all of the interventions in this training manual, from Step 1 to Step 4, are designed to engage both sides of the brain in a complementary process. Using these brain-informed interventions, the treatment provider can successfully help the client process the emotional-affective content (right brain function) while simultaneously supporting the client to develop healthy cognitions, cognitive coping skills and adaptive strategies (left brain function) to embrace the termination process and more importantly, to effectively manage life after termination.

Recommended Readings

To learn more about interpersonal neurobiology see:

Applegate, J. S., & Shapiro, J. R. (2005) *Neurobiology for clinical social work: Theory and practice.* New York, NY: Norton.

Carter, R. (2009). *The human brain.* New York, NY: DK Publishing.

Montgomery, A. (2013). Neurobiology Essentials for Clinicians. New York, NY: Norton.

Porges. S. W. (2011). *The polyvagal theory: Neurophysiological foundations of emotions, attachment, communication and self-regulation.* New York, NY: Norton.

Ratey, J. J. (2001). *A user's guide to the brain: Perception, attention, and the four theatres of the brain.* New York: Random House.

Schore, A.N. (2003a). *Affect dysregulation and disorders of the self.* New York, NY: Norton.

Schore, A.N. (2003b). *Affect regulation and the repair of the self.* New York, NY: Norton.

Chapter Summary: Introduction

- **Developmental assets promote resiliency** in all young people regardless of their gender, socioeconomic status, race, or ethnicity and are stronger predictors of success or failure than poverty or being from a single-parent household.

- **Developmental assets protect youth** from engaging in high risk and problem behaviors like illicit drug use, suicide attempts and anti-social behavior and they promote thriving behavior such as valuing diversity, maintaining good health and succeeding in school.

- The **quality of the therapeutic relationship** remains the best predictor of treatment outcome, regardless of treatment model, child developmental level, age, gender, ethnicity, and symptom severity.

- For children and adolescents, the therapeutic alliance grows stronger in the **middle to later stages of treatment** when compared to adults, who form alliances more readily in the beginning of treatment.

- The therapeutic alliance is **especially predictive** for children and adolescents with a history of maltreatment, juvenile delinquency, and externalizing behaviors.

- **The way a mental health professional terminates the therapeutic relationship** can impact the client's progress made during treatment and have a significant influence on the way a client views all future relationships.

- Because the therapeutic relationship is so impactful, mental health professionals must terminate this relationship in a **planned, sensitive manner.**

- Termination is **most effective** when: 1) discussed at the onset of treatment; 2) framed as a natural part of the treatment process; and, 3) follows the 4-steps to a successful termination outlined in this manual.

- Language is a **left brain** function whereas feelings are processed through the **right brain**.

- If a practitioner only engages the left brain through **talk therapy**, the client will be able to talk about termination without adequately processing the feelings about it.

- Simply engaging the right brain through **non-verbal creative activities** accesses the client's feelings without developing sufficient cognitive coping skills to understand the process of termination or to adequately cope with future challenges.

- This manual offers an easy-to-follow, 4-step guide to termination that incorporates resiliency-enhancing activities into the termination process and supports treatment providers to end treatment in a planned, sensitive manner.

STEP ONE

Educate Client About Termination

STEP ONE

Educate Client About Termination

Providing psychoeducation is typically the first step in most evidence-based practice models. Psychoeducation helps normalize the client's response to an event, allows for exploration of distorted thinking, and encourages accurate, healthier cognitions (Cohen, Mannarino, Deblinger, 2006). Likewise, with termination, the first step is to educate the client on what termination is and what the client can expect from the process. By providing psychoeducation first, you are helping the client accept that termination is real and is happening. Rhetorically speaking, how can the client fully embrace the termination process, unless s/he first accepts the reality that treatment will, in fact, end?

What to do:

- Make the termination announcement.
- Focus on client's strengths and progress as reason for termination.
- Provide psychoeducation on possible reactions to termination.
- Do not allow new stressors to distract you from the termination process; theme new events to termination.

How to do it:

1. **Make the Termination Announcement.**

   - Inform the client that treatment is ending.
   - Give a concrete ending date, then each week count down the remaining weeks/sessions left.
   - Explain what termination is and why treatment is ending.
   - Clarify what will take place over the next weeks leading to the last session.

Case Transfers should include an explanation of why and when the case is being transferred, when the client will meet the new treatment provider and if there will be conjoint sessions between the departing treatment provider, new provider, and the client.

Use clear, honest language without euphemisms

Just as grief counselors recommend not using euphemisms for the word death, such as gone, lost, or asleep, it is important for mental health providers to use clear, concrete, honest language to describe termination. When announcing termination, avoid statements like; "Our time is coming to a close"; "We will be done soon"; "We will be stopping shortly". These explanations are unclear and subject to misinterpretation and may leave room for the client to deny or minimize the reality of the loss. See *Termination Scripts* for examples of the termination announcement.

Each week, count down the remaining number of sessions.

After the termination announcement is made, you should count down the remaining weeks/sessions at the beginning of each session or meeting. This will help keep termination present in the treatment process. Typically, the younger the client, the more concrete the reminders should be. Using reminders such as a calendar with the final date circled on it, numbered tokens, dice, or chains made of links of construction paper (with each link representing weeks or sessions remaining) for example. With older children and adolescents, calendaring or verbal reminders are usually sufficient.

 **Counter-transference Alert!** If you find yourself avoiding the countdown and not talking about termination at the beginning of each session or meeting, this is a clue that you may be experiencing counter-transference.

2. Focus on client's strengths and progress as the reason for termination.

Focusing on the gains made reinforces the concept that the client is leaving you rather than on you leaving the client. Conducting regular goal reviews throughout treatment helps the client to be aware of progress made and reinforces the expectation of graduating from treatment once goals are achieved.

Sometimes sessions/meetings are tapered from weekly to biweekly or monthly until the last session or meeting. Lessening the frequency of sessions reinforces that treatment is ending due to the client's progress, as evidenced by a decrease in

24

sessions. It also communicates that the client can manage without the treatment provider.

Case Transfers should focus on the strengths or progress the client has achieved while working with the provider and how these strengths will assist with the transfer process.

Support client's role in planning termination

Encouraging a client to have a role in planning a termination celebration helps to empower a client that s/he is an active, important part of termination; reinforces the reality that treatment is ending; and, may also pre-empt early termination by keeping the client invested in treatment. You must be sensitive to your client's loss history, especially when working with clients with complex trauma histories. These clients may have an uneasy sense that they have little or no power to make things different in their environment. One of the your goals must be to make termination a different kind of loss and one that the client is an important and active participant in rather than a helpless bystander of.

Engaging a client around the termination celebration need not be a long and involved process. You can simply inform the client that a part of termination is to celebrate the progress made, much like one does at the end of each school year or at a graduation. (See Appendix A: Ideas for the last session).

3. Provide psychoeducation on possible reactions to termination.

After making the termination announcement, you should provide psychoeducation on normal reactions to termination. Give the client a copy of the handout, *Common Reactions as Treatment Ends*, and review it together. The handout assists clients to better understand what to expect from termination and lays the groundwork for treatment providers to process common feelings, questions, and reactions about termination. The handout is not exhaustive, but is intended to provide a helpful guide. The psychoeducation about termination will also help inoculate the client against distorted thinking, negative feelings and negative behavior that may follow the termination announcement. It is important to discuss the possibility of premature termination and to put supports in place (contracts, verbal agreements, check-ins, or parent or treatment team support) to reduce the risk. (See Appendix D for a more thorough discussion on transference issues).

Clarify how and why the client may return to treatment in the future.

Treatment is a process and it is not uncommon for clients to return to services for various reasons. You should educate your client that a return to treatment is quite normal and healthy. Explain that some life circumstances may include:

Cognitive Maturation: Sometimes clients return to treatment due to cognitive maturation (James, 1989). Issues may arise as a client matures cognitively and gains the ability to process the traumatic event differently.

Sensitive Life Events: Other times, clients return to treatment for tune-ups or check-ins to support them through sensitive life events. Sometimes appointments are scheduled around an event the client may be concerned about; such as the start of a new school year, the anniversary of a trauma, a perpetrator's release from prison, or other life event. In these instances, you may choose to see a client temporarily to support him/her through the event.

Other Considerations: Insurance restrictions or long waiting lists may preclude a return to treatment. If this is the case, the client should be told honestly and directly if the enrollment process is prohibitive or difficult. It is ethical to provide referrals for obtaining treatment elsewhere.

Clarify if there can be a relationship after treatment ends.

An important part of helping a client to accept the reality of termination is to clarify whether or not there can be a relationship after treatment ends or after the case is transferred. Some clients retain a fantasy that they will continue to see you even after services end. Other clients may have questions about what you will be doing, or what agency you may be going to, and if they can continue the relationship at your new site or in your new role. You should be prepared to answer these questions directly and honestly or raise the issue on your own if the client does not bring it up (clients are usually thinking about it even if they do not talk about it).

School-based services may have the confounding variable of treatment ending with a planned school break. Innocently, the client may believe services will continue or that at least they will be able to visit you when school resumes (like they can visit their favorite office staff or teacher). It is important for mental health providers in school-based settings to raise this issue with the client and to clarify the facts, to avoid any misunderstandings. By doing this pre-emptive work, you avoid the tragedy of your client returning from break, only to be disappointed that you have not returned. If one of the goals of termination is to end the therapeutic relationship in a way that leaves clients open to future relationships, you do not want your client's last experience of your relationship to feel like a betrayal.

May I have your cell phone number? May I email you? Can we text? Will you come to my graduation or honors ceremony? These are all common requests mental health practitioners receive from school-aged clients. It is important to not pathologize these requests because this type of contact with school staff may be a normal part of the school culture. The client may not fully understand how your therapeutic relationship may be different from their relationship with school staff. However, due to their own training and views about treatment, some school-based providers attend celebratory events and others do not. As long as you are clear about why you are attending (or not) and what your role is in the event, there is no right or wrong answer. Clarifying your policy about cell phone, text, email contact and/or socializing, from the onset of treatment may pre-empt

> **You do not want your client's last experience of your relationship to feel like a betrayal.**

potential awkward exchanges about this issue. However, if this was not clarified early on, or the client raises the issue again, find a sensitive way to educate your client about your policy. You want to avoid your client ending treatment feeling rejected or embarrassed because of a seemingly innocent request. If you have conflicted feelings about this issue, it is important to consult with an objective licensed supervisor or a licensed colleague for support.

Involuntary, inpatient, and residential clients may feel conflicted about termination. As cited in the introduction, the therapeutic relationship is particularly predicative of treatment outcomes for clients with a history of maltreatment and externalizing behaviors. So on the one hand, termination implies regaining some sense of freedom and autonomy from an involuntary setting or a court order. On the other, clients may be faced with saying good-bye to a trusted, helpful member of their treatment team. Ending this alliance in a planned, sensitive manner is crucial. Clients may certainly not want to return to an involuntary setting, but they may be interested in whether or not they can continue a relationship with their trusted treatment provider.

Social media, text and video messaging, email and cell phone capabilities make termination more challenging than in a pre-internet world. Clients may be able to locate their treatment providers via social media sites and request ongoing contact. It is important to clarify your policy on social media exchanges with clients at the beginning of treatment so role expectations are clearly defined from the onset. In our culture of growing technology, it is more common for human beings to sustain contact through social media. So, this may be a very normal and innocent request from clients who are unfamiliar with the staunch traditions of the mental health profession.

Other clients may request ongoing contact with you because they are grappling with the end of the therapeutic relationship. It is important to address this issue with care and sensitivity. You want to avoid your client ending treatment feeling rejected or embarrassed by his/her seemingly innocent request. If you have conflicted feelings about this issue, it is important to consult with a licensed supervisor or an objective licensed colleague for support.

4. **Do not allow new stressors to distract you from discussing termination; theme new events to termination.**

It is not uncommon for new stressors or unexpected events to arise after you make the termination announcement. Do not allow this to deter you from your weekly countdown, simply theme your discussion about the crisis or urgent situation, to termination. Suggestions include:

- You have come so far since the beginning of treatment. I remember when this issue would have been very overwhelming for you. We know that treatment will be ending for us in _____ weeks. But, let's say if treatment had already ended, how would you deal with this issue?

- Since your last session will be on _____, and we will be closing your case, let's see how we can address this situation in the next _____ weeks.

- Given that treatment is about to end in _____ weeks, what skills have you learned during our time that will help you cope with this problem?

- Since treatment will be ending in _____ weeks, this is perfect timing for this issue to come up. Let's pretend you have already left our program and this issue came up. How would you deal with it?

- (For case transfers) If this situation happened and you were with your new (therapist, case manager, social worker...) how would you handle it?

If the new stressor is severe enough to overwhelm your client's developing coping skills and/or the client's support system is fragile, use your judgment to determine whether termination remains appropriate.

How Some Clients React to Termination

As with grief and loss, reactions to termination vary widely and depend on your client's natural disposition, ability to adjust to change, and their previous loss history. Some clients make a smooth transition out of treatment and others do not. While important to review these reactions with your client, it is helpful for you, as the treatment provider, to also be aware of emotional and behavioral reactions to look out for, so you can process these reactions with your client. The following chart, *Client Reactions To Termination*, is for the treatment provider. It gives some short descriptions of how some clients react to the termination process and interventions to help the clients. These behaviors may surface at any point during the termination process. Use this guide to help you identify potential issues that may need to be addressed.

Client Reactions To Termination
©21st Century Seminars

Client	Client Reactions	Helpful Interventions
The **Model** Client	This client moves through termination easily, like a model client. While they seem well adjusted on the surface, they may deny or avoid unpleasant or difficult feelings about termination to please you.	Review worksheet *Common Reactions to Termination* with the client to provide psychoeducation about termination.
The **I Don't Like Good-bye's** Client	This client avoids the feelings about termination by missing sessions, terminating early, "forgetting" session times or being too "busy" with other things (i.e., having to study for a math test or parents may suddenly have conflicting appointments).	Engage the client with activities like the *Termination Questionnaire* or *Penny for My Thoughts Game.* This will help you process their underlying thoughts and feelings openly and honestly. Encourage working through the feelings.
The **Where are You Going?** Client	This client reacts to termination by wanting to remain connected to you after treatment ends. S/he may ask questions about whether treatment has to end, what you will be doing after treatment finishes and if s/he may continue a relationship with you. This client may ask you for your contact information so s/he can remain in touch with you.	Be supportive and normalize the reactions (including the feeling of not wanting to attend treatment anymore, feeling ambivalent about or less motivated to attend treatment).
The **Shut-Down** Client	This client continues to come to treatment but shows resistance or less motivation to engage when in session. These clients may show up late for or seem less talkative and involved when meeting with you.	Address any distorted thoughts, misunderstandings or unhelpful thoughts about the reasons for termination.
The **I Had an Epiphany** Client	This is the client who has not made the best use of treatment, but has a turn around upon learning about termination. To your surprise, these clients may suddenly make better use of their treatment sessions, begin to disclose sensitive material not discussed before, or show greater comfort with the treatment process than in the past. For some clients, having a concrete ending date makes the treatment process less threatening and inspires them to make better use of the remaining time.	Put supports and a concrete plan in place to prevent early termination. It may be helpful to use statements like: "Many clients feel…." Or "Some clients think…" Or "It is very common for clients to tell me….". to normalize and process the client' feelings.
The **I Did Something Wrong** Client	This client thinks services are ending because s/he did something inappropriate or upsetting to you to cause treatment to end (especially with clients whose attendance or participation was not ideal).	As the weeks progress, do periodic check-ins with the client and/or parent to monitor emotional/behavioral reactions with the goal of pre-empting early termination.
The **Regressed or Angry** Client	This client experiences an emotional set-back or behavior regression after learning about termination. They may also feel angry with the you for terminating the relationship.	

Chapter Summary: Step One

- **Psychoeducation** helps normalize the client's response to an event, allow for exploration of distorted thinking, and encourage accurate, healthier cognitions.

- In most circumstances, **educating the client about treatment ending** is the first step to a successful termination.

- When making the **termination announcement** it is important to explain what termination is and why treatment is ending; to give a concrete date and count down the remaining weeks/sessions left, and to clarify what will take place over the weeks leading up to termination.

- Focus on the client's **strengths and progress** as the reason for termination.

- Provide **psychoeducation** on possible reactions to termination, including premature termination. Some clients have stronger reactions than others, depending on their own loss history.

- Educate the client about a possible return for future treatment. Possible reasons are, **cognitive maturation or sensitive life events.** If a return to treatment will be difficult, due to insurance restrictions, agency policy, or a long wait list, you should provide an appropriate referral.

- Clarify if there can be a therapeutic relationship after treatment ends. Particular sensitivities occur in **school-based settings or with involuntary, inpatient, and residential clients.** Be clear about your policy regarding social media, text and video messaging, email, cell phone contact, and socializing with clients.

- Supporting client's role in **planning termination** helps to empower the client that s/he is an active, important part of termination, reinforces the reality that treatment is ending, and may also pre-empt early termination by keeping the client invested in services.

- Do not allow **new stressors** to distract you from discussing termination each week. Theme the new events to termination by saying something like; *"Since treatment will be ending for us on _____, this is a perfect time for this issue to come up. What skills have you learned during our time together that will help you figure out how to address this issue?"*

STEP ONE

Educate Client About Treatment Ending

Interventions:

1. Termination Scripts
2. Common Reactions As Treatment Ends Handout (English and Spanish)
3. Letter to Parents About Treatment Ending (English and Spanish)
4. My Goodbye Calendar
5. Countdown Tokens
6. Termination Questionnaire
7. A Penny for My Thoughts Game
8. Termination Puzzle
9. Tic - Tac - Toss
10. Chips Away
11. The Matching Game
12. Step-by-Step
13. Basketball
14. Tip the Scales
15. My Story: Chapter 1

*The worksheets refer to the treatment provider as a "counselor". Feel free to change the worksheets to reflect your work as a counselor, case manager, social worker, psychologist, etc.

What To Do:

1. Make the termination announcement.
2. Focus on client's strengths and progress as reasons for termination.
3. Provide psychoeducation on possible reactions to termination.
4. Do not allow new stressors to distract you from processing termination; theme new events to termination.

STEP ONE

Educate Client About Treatment Ending

#	Intervention	Goal	Age	M	Materials Needed
1	Termination Scripts	Scripts to assist counselor with finding sensitive phrases for the termination announcement	5-18	N/A	Script included
2	Common Reactions as Treatment Ends	Psychoeducation handout for clients and parents. English/Spanish	5-18	I F G	English/Spanish handouts included
3	Letter to Parents	Sample letter to parents explaining termination. English/Spanish	5-18	I F	English/Spanish letters included
4	My Good-bye Calendar	Tracks sessions/weeks to termination. For middle-age to adolescents.	11-18	I F G	Calendar included
5	Countdown Tokens	Uses tokens to track sessions/weeks to termination. Tokens are concrete for younger clients.	5-11	I F G	Template for tokens included
6	Termination Questionnaire	Client shades how much s/he agrees/disagrees with statements kids make about termination. Non-threatening. Allows for a range of thoughts/feelings. Encourages engagement.	5-18	I F G	Questionnaire included. Pen, pencil, or marker
7	Penny For My Thoughts Game	Flip a coin to play a board game. Fun and engaging.	5-11	I F G	Scissors, a penny coin. Template and worksheet included.
8	Termination Puzzle	Puzzle activity. Non-threatening, creative, fun.	5-18	I F G	Puzzle included. Scissors. Pen or pencil.
9	Tic-Tac-Toss	Uses movement. Good for kinetic learners, language or cognitive difficulties.	5-11	I F G	3 sheets of paper. Pen or marker. Optional bean bag
10	Chips Away	Game using poker chips. Good for younger clients, language issues, emotional restrictiveness.	5-18	I F G	1 sheet of paper. At least 20 poker/plastic/wooden chips
11	The Matching Game	Card Game. Counselor tries to match client's answers, then processes how answers are the same or different.	5-18	I F G	Game cards included. Scissors.
12	Step-by-Step	Uses movement. Focuses on Step 1 themes. Good for kinetic learners. Activity can be used for all 4 termination steps. Engaging and non-threatening. Great for kids with language or cognitive challenges.	5-18	I F G	Pen, pencil, marker. Scissors. Stepping Stone template included.
13	Basketball	Good for kinetic learners. Focuses on Step 1 themes. Activity can be used for all 4-termination steps. Engaging and non-threatening. Great for all, especially kids with language or cognitive challenges.	5-18	I F G	Scissors, small container for basketball hoop and ball for shooting. Includes basketball court and cards
14	Tip the Scales	Uses scaling technique to engage client. Processing a range of thoughts and feelings. Encourages engagement.	7-18	I F	Pen, pencil or marker. 6 small tokens (any small, flat object like a coin or paperclip)
15	My Story: Chapter 1	Narrative activity. Creative, expressive.	5-18	I F	Pen, pencil, crayons or markers. Book included

Termination Scripts

Ages: Young (5-6), Middle (7-11), and Adolescents (12- up)

Materials:

- Termination Scripts

Rationale:

Scripts give helpful guidance with finding words in delicate situations. The following *Termination Scripts* support the treatment provider to begin a discussion about termination. These scripts do not represent a complete termination announcement but provide ideas to help guide the discussion. In time, you will find your own style to make the termination announcement.

Directions: (See the chapter introduction for more details.)

1. Make your termination announcement including:
    - An explanation of what termination is.
    - Why treatment is ending.
    - The date treatment will end.
    - What will take place over the next weeks leading to the last session.

2. Use clear, honest language without euphemisms.
3. Focus on client's strengths and progress as reasons for termination.
4. Provide psychoeducation on possible reactions to termination. Use handouts, *Common Reactions as Treatment Ends* and *Letter to Parents* to aid the discussion.
5. Clarify if there can be a therapeutic relationship after treatment ends.
6. Support client's role in planning termination.

Termination Scripts

****

We regularly talk about your progress and when you will be ready to end counseling. From our discussions and through tracking your goals, it's clear you are doing so well and have so much to be proud of. I'd like to talk with you about working on ending counseling in the next ____ weeks. Our last session will be on____.

You have made so much progress, it is time to talk about working towards ending counseling. You are doing so well, you have reached your goals and have so much to be proud of. Let's look at this calendar and schedule a date for your last session. This will be a day when we will celebrate your progress so I want you to give some thought to how you want to celebrate your graduation (feel free to replace graduation with progress).

Today we are going to talk about counseling ending. When we began, we talked about how our work together was a lot like your relationship with your teacher in school. We work together to reach the goals we made together, then you graduate and move on with stronger skills. You have reached your goals and are ready to graduate from our program...

...over the next ____ weeks we will work together on preparing you to end counseling. We will review your goals and work on a few things to make sure you are ready and on the last day, we will end with a celebration to honor you for all of your hard work...

We have ___ sessions remaining until we end and say good-bye to one another. This means you will move on with stronger skills. We will not be meeting any more. So over the next few weeks, we will be focusing on what has gone well and will work on the few things left to address. On our last day, we will...

Psychoeducation Handout
Common Reactions as Treatment Ends

Ages: Young (5-6), Middle (7-11), and Adolescents (12- up)

Materials:

- Common Reactions as Treatment Ends (English and Spanish)

Rationale:

40% to 60% of child and adolescent mental health treatment cases end prematurely. Some studies suggest premature termination is related to the client having different expectations of treatment than the treatment provider. However, studies also support that psychoeducation about role expectations and the treatment process can mitigate early termination. The handout *Common Reactions as Treatment Ends* assists clients to better understand what to expect from termination and lays the groundwork for the treatment provider to process common feelings, questions, and reactions about termination. The handout is not exhaustive, but is intended to provide a helpful guide. It is important to discuss and put supports in place (contracts, verbal agreements, check-ins, parent or treatment team support) to reduce the risk of early termination.

Directions: (See the chapter introduction for more details.)

1. Use the following handout to assist both your client and his/her parent(s) to better understand the termination process. Review the handout with the client first, in their individual session, then with the parent. This way, you allow your client an opportunity to process his/her thoughts and feelings with you before involving the parent.

2. The handout is a tool to help guide your discussion with the client and parent. You may want to avoid distributing the handout by mail as this minimizes opportunity to process the content, or address cognitive distortions or misunderstandings about treatment ending.

36

Common Reactions as Treatment Ends

(You may have some, none, or all of these reactions.)

Normal Feelings:

- Taken by surprise, shocked, or confused to learn treatment is ending.
- Relieved in some ways...happy in other ways and a little sad too.
- Hurt, rejected, or abandoned by my counselor.
- Proud to have accomplished my goals.
- Worried about what will happen to me after services ends.
- Unsure whom I will be able to trust with my feelings after counseling ends.

Common Questions:

- How many sessions or weeks do we have left?
- What if I still have some things to work on?
- What if I do not want to end?
- Can I end now and not wait a few more weeks?
- Will I be able to come back if I want to?

Typical Reactions:

- I may feel more easily upset or stressed inside and don't know why.
- I may have thoughts about leaving early and not completing the program.
- I may start to have trouble again with things I already worked out in counseling.
- I may find it hard to say good-bye, especially if good-byes in the past were upsetting for me.

Helpful Ways to Cope:

- Realize most of the feelings I have are normal and will pass in time.
- Share the thoughts and feelings I have with my counselor. I may also talk with my parent or a trusted person who can help.
- Don't give up and keep coming to treatment to finish the good work I have started.

Reacciones Típicas Cuando Termina El Tratamiento

(Ud. podría experimentar algunas, ningunas, o todas estas reacciones.)

Sentimientos Normales:

- Sorpresa, shock, o confusión cuando averiguó que el tratamiento está por terminarse.
- Alivio en ciertos aspectos... felicidad en otros y un poco de tristeza también.
- Sentir agravio, rechazo o abandono causados por el/la consejero.
- Orgullo por haber logrado sus metas.
- Sentirse con preocupación respecto a lo que sucederá después de que termine el tratamiento.
- No sabe en quien podrá confiar expresando sus sentimientos ya que termine el tratamiento.

Preguntas Frecuentes:

- ¿Cuántas sesiones o semanas nos quedan?
- ¿Qué sucedería si todavía me quedaran cuestiones que resolver?
- ¿Qué pasa si yo no quiero terminar?
- ¿Puedo terminar ahora mismo sin tener que esperar varias semanas más?
- ¿Podré regresar si quiero hacerlo?

Reacciones Comunes:

- Se perturba o siente estrés con más frecuencia sin saber por qué.
- Podría sentir como que ya no quiere asistir al consejero.
- De nuevo surgen problemas con ciertas cuestiones que ya habían sido resueltas gracias al tratamiento.
- Dificultad en despedirse, particularmente si en el pasado le dolió decir "adiós".

Métodos Efectivos de Adaptarse:

- Tomar en cuenta que la mayoría de los sentimientos que esté experimentando son normales y que pasarán con el tiempo.
- Expresar los pensamientos y sentimientos que esté experimentando con su Terapista...también padre, madre u otra persona quien le podría ayudar.
- No se rinda y siga asistiendo a la terapia con el fin de completar el buen trabajo que ya ha emprendido.

Psychoeducation Handout
Letter to Parents about Treatment Ending

Ages: Young (5-6), Middle (7-11), and Adolescents (12- up)

Materials:

- Letter to Parents about Treatment Ending (English and Spanish)

Rationale:

Parent involvement is an important component of evidence based practice treatment with children and adolescents. To what extent the parent is involved in treatment will vary on a case-by-case basis. Some states allow minors to consent to their own mental health treatment, provided certain provisions of the law are met. If this is the case, we hope the issues preventing parent involvement are resolved by the end of treatment because parents can be important assets during the termination process.

The *Letter to Parent as Treatment Ends* educates parents to better understand what to expect from the termination process and invites them to be a part of it. This letter is a sample and is not intended to address every unique situation. Feel free to alter this letter in any way you see fit to address the needs of your families.

Directions: (See the chapter introduction for more details on making the termination announcement.)

- Once you have made your termination announcement, use the following letter to help parents better understand the termination process. Feel free to alter the letter to meet your program needs.

- The letter is a tool to help guide your discussion with the parent. Avoid sending the letter by mail as this minimizes opportunity to process the content, or to address cognitive distortions or misunderstandings about treatment ending.

Letter to Parents About Treatment Ending (English)

Dear Parent:

Thank you for your support with _____ involvement in counseling. Your child has made much progress and it is now time for services to come to an end. Our last session/meeting is scheduled for _____. Until that time, _____ and I will be preparing for treatment to end by reviewing goals and planning ways for him/her to continue success even after services end.

Ending counseling is a process that impacts everyone differently. Sometimes people find saying "good-bye" difficult so I am giving you a copy of the handout; "Common Reactions As Treatment Ends". You or your child may experience some, none, or all of the reactions listed.   Please review the handout with your child and let me know if either of you feels, or seems, more emotional, or stressed over the next weeks or, is thinking about ending services early. Please know these reactions may be normal after learning counseling is ending; it is important for us to talk about how you and your child are feeling.

Please let me know what questions you have about this process and I will be happy to share what the next steps will be in ending services with your child.

Sincerely,

_____

Letter to Parents About Treatment Ending (Spanish)

Estimados Padres:

Gracias por apoyar a _____ participando del tratamiento. Su hijo/a ha realizado mucho progreso así que llegó el momento de terminar los servicios. Se programó la última sesión de tratamiento para el _____/_____/_____.

mes / día / año

Hasta que llegue el momento, _____ y yo prepararemos la conclusión del tratamiento revisando las metas del tratamiento y planificando los medios que aplicar para mantener el éxito realizado aunque el tratamiento haya terminado.

La terminación del tratamiento impacta cada participante de modo diferente. A veces, le dificulta despedirse. Por eso le entrego una copia del folleto "*Reacciones Típicas Cuando Termina El Tratamiento*". Tanto Ud. como su hijo/a podrían experimentar algunas de, ningunas de o todas las reacciones identificadas. Por favor estudie el folleto junto con su hijo/a. Déjeme saber si cualquiera de los dos (o las dos) se siente o parece más emocionable o con más estrés durante las semanas próximas. También déjeme saber en caso de que estén pensando en terminar con los servicios antes de que se cumpla el plazo que se programó. Por favor tome en consideración que estas reacciones suceden frecuentemente tras averiguar que los servicios está por terminarse. Así que es importante examinar lo que tanto Ud. como su hijo/a esté sintiendo.

Por favor no dude en expresar cualquier pregunta que se le ocurriera respecto a cualquier aspecto del proceso. Me será un placer indicarle lo que sucederá, paso a paso, con su hijo/a ya que termine su tratamiento.

Atentamente,

_____

My Goodbye Calendar

Ages: Middle (7-11) and Adolescents (12- up)

Materials:

- My Goodbye Calendar

Rationale:

The *My Goodbye Calendar* is a tool to help reinforce the reality that treatment is ending. Once you have set a date for termination, it is helpful to place the date of the last session or meeting on the calendar. You should refer to the calendar at the beginning of each session or meeting to keep the theme of termination alive.

The younger the developmental level, the more concrete the reminder should be. For younger to middle-age clients who are more concrete, use the *Countdown Tokens*.

Family or group application: The treatment provider makes a family or group calendar with the ending date circled. Use your judgment to determine if giving each member a personal calendar is feasible.

Directions:

Keep a Good-bye Calendar for the client with the date of the last session circled. Review the calendar at the beginning of each session or meeting and cross off the days or sessions as time moves on. If appropriate, the client should also keep a copy at home.

My Goodbye Calendar

Month: _____   Year: _____

Monday	Tuesday	Wednesday	Thursday	Friday	Saturday	Sunday

My last session will be on: _____

43

Countdown Tokens

Ages: Young (5-6) and Middle (7-11)

Materials:

- Photocopy sample tokens.
  Tokens may be laminated or glued onto poster or cardboard for durability.

- Countdown Tokens

Rationale:

Once you have set a date for termination it is helpful to use *Countdown Token* reminders to reinforce the reality that treatment is ending. The lower the child's developmental level, the more concrete the cues should be. Use the *My Goodbye Calendar* for middle-age children and adolescents.

Family or group application: To each member of the group, the treatment provider gives a token that is labeled with the appropriate number that represents the remaining weeks or sessions before treatment ends.

Directions:

At the beginning of each session, give a token reminder that is labeled with the number of weeks/sessions remaining, to your client(s). For example, with 5 weeks/sessions remaining, give a client a token with the number 5 on it. With 4 weeks/sessions remaining, give a token with the number 4 on it and so forth. You can mix and match different tokens for creativity. Tokens can be made from stickers, wooden coins, poker chips, or pieces of paper.

Countdown Tokens: Copy tokens and cut them out (laminate if desired)

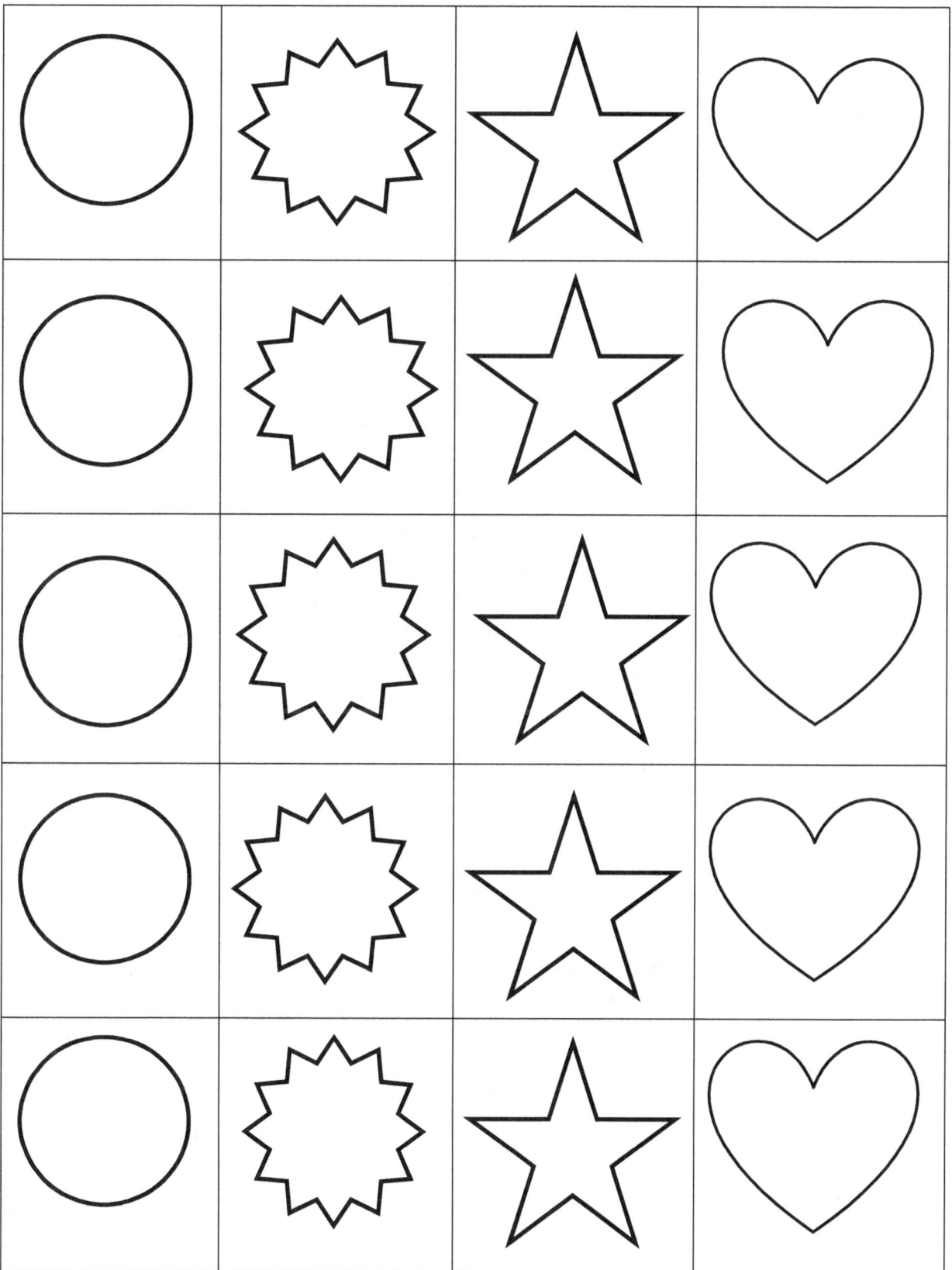

Termination Questionnaire

Ages: Middle (7-11) and Adolescents (12- up)

Materials:

- A copy of the Termination Questionnaire Worksheet
- Colored Pens, Pencils or Markers

Rationale:

The *Termination Questionnaire* supports middle-adolescent aged clients to process the termination announcement and provides education about treatment ending. The activity directs the client to read thoughts or feelings kids sometimes have about treatment ending. The client then shades in a circle next to the statement to show how much they agree with the statement. Shading in circles lends the client opportunity to reflect gradations of thoughts and feelings and engages the nonverbal, emotional, creative right brain. For students with learning disabilities, language barriers or challenges with reading, the provider may read to or read with the client. Since this activity requires some ability to think abstractly, younger or more concrete thinkers should be given the *A Penny for My Thoughts Game.*

Family or group application: Each person completes their own questionnaire while the treatment provider processes which answers are the same and different, and points out the emerging themes.

Directions:

1. **Treatment Provider Says:** *Now that we know counseling is ending, there is a questionnaire I want you to take. It lists thoughts that (kids/teens) may have after learning about counseling ending. It will help us talk about what it really means for services to end. Let's review the directions together.* Client practices coloring in the sample circles next to "I agree"; "I partially agree" and "I do not agree". Provider supports as needed to ensure client understands directions.

2. Provider processes the client's answers. If you believe the client's answers warrant further exploration, use the technique of; *"I know you left the circle blank...tell me about that...sometimes kids color it in a bit more because they may feel..."*

Termination Questionnaire

Below are some thoughts that some kids/teens have about treatment ending. Next to each thought is a circle. Fill in the circle to show how you feel. If you agree completely, fill in the whole circle. If you partially agree, fill in part of the circle. If you do not agree, leave the circle blank. Practice on the circles below:

I agree ◯   I partially agree ◯   I do not agree ◯

I know the date when counseling will end. ◯

Counseling ending means I can still see my counselor when I want to. ◯

I was surprised when I learned that counseling was ending. ◯

I am unsure about why counseling is ending. ◯

I wonder if I did something wrong to cause counseling to end. ◯

I feel ready to end counseling. ◯

I have some things I still want to work on before services ends. ◯

I wonder what will happen to my counselor when services end. ◯

Now that I know counseling is ending anyway, I may not want to come anymore. ◯

I know how to return to counseling in the future if I want to. ◯

I have an idea how I want to celebrate counseling ending. ◯

47

A Penny for My Thoughts Game

Ages: Young (5-6) and Middle (7-11)

Materials:

- A copy of the Penny for My Thoughts Game sheet
- Scissors and a penny coin

Rationale:

A *Penny for My Thoughts* game can be played individually, with a family or a group. It is designed for the more concrete young to middle-age client who is either still in or emerging out of the concrete operations phase of cognitive development. The game is themed to help the client process the termination announcement, reinforce the reality that services are ending, and pre-empt early termination from treatment. After you set up the game sheet, each square will have a paper penny covering it. You and your client take turns flipping a coin penny. A "tails" means you pass your turn. A "heads" means you take a turn and remove a paper penny. Some squares contain fun things to do. Other squares contain questions about termination. The treatment provider may participate as desired. For students with learning disabilities, language barriers, or challenges with reading, the treatment provider may read to, or read with, the client.

Family or group application: Family or group members alternate answering questions while the provider facilitates the group discussion and processes the emerging themes.

Directions:

1. **Treatment Provider says:** *Now that we know counseling is ending, there is a game I want us to play that will help us talk about what it really means for services to end. Let's review the directions together.*

2. Provider supports as needed to ensure client understands directions and is engaged in the game.

3. Provider facilitates the game and processes the client's answers. If needed, provider can use the technique of; *"Mmmm, I know you said ...tell me about that because sometimes kids may feel this way or that way..."*

48

A Penny for My Thoughts Game

Each square has a penny covering it. Flip a penny coin. For each "heads" remove any penny of your choice and see what is underneath. Pass your turn on "tails". Some pennies are hiding fun things, others are hiding some things kids think, feel, or do after learning that treatment will end. Some of your thoughts may be the same or different. Share your thoughts and feelings honestly with your counselor and have fun.

I was surprised when I learned that counseling was ending	Name 2 things that make you really proud of yourself	I wonder if I did something wrong to make counseling end
What is the date when counseling will end for you?	Now that I know counseling is ending, I may want to stop now and not wait until the last session	Give someone a "high 5"
It is ok to come back to counseling in the future	Stand on one foot for 10 seconds or hold your breath for 10 seconds - you choose	Graduating from counseling is a good thing. How do you usually celebrate good things?
Sometimes I wonder if I will I see my counselor again	I feel ready to end counseling	Can you wiggle Your ears Without using your hands?

A Penny for My Thoughts Worksheet

Directions: Cut out the pennies and place over the questions on the "A Penny for My Thoughts" Game sheet.

The Termination Puzzle

Ages: Young (5-6), Middle (7-11), and Adolescents (12- up)

Materials:

- Copy of the Termination Puzzle
- Safety Scissors
- Colored Pens, Pencils, Markers
  Options: Laminate the puzzle for durability or, glue it onto a piece of poster or cardboard.

Rationale:

Puzzles are a good way to engage the client around a sensitive topic. *The Termination Puzzle* can be used individually, with a family or a group. It is themed to help the client process the termination announcement. It reinforces that treatment is ending and addresses early termination.

Family or group application: 1) Family members alternate turns answering questions from the same puzzle; they assemble it at the end of the game. The family keeps the puzzle as a keepsake. Or, 2) Group members complete their own individual puzzles and take turns answering questions as the treatment provider processes the group's experience and reflects common themes. Group members keep their own puzzles.

Directions:

1. Cut out the puzzle pieces, place in a container and draw out the pieces, one by one. Or, keep the puzzle in one unit and work through the questions

2. **Treatment Provider Says:** *Now that we have talked about counseling ending, I have a puzzle I want us to do together. It will help us talk about what it means to end services.*

3. Provider facilitates the client completing the puzzle pieces. Depending on the age or ability level, the client or treatment provider can write the answers on each piece.

4. Glue the puzzle together if desired.

Termination Puzzle

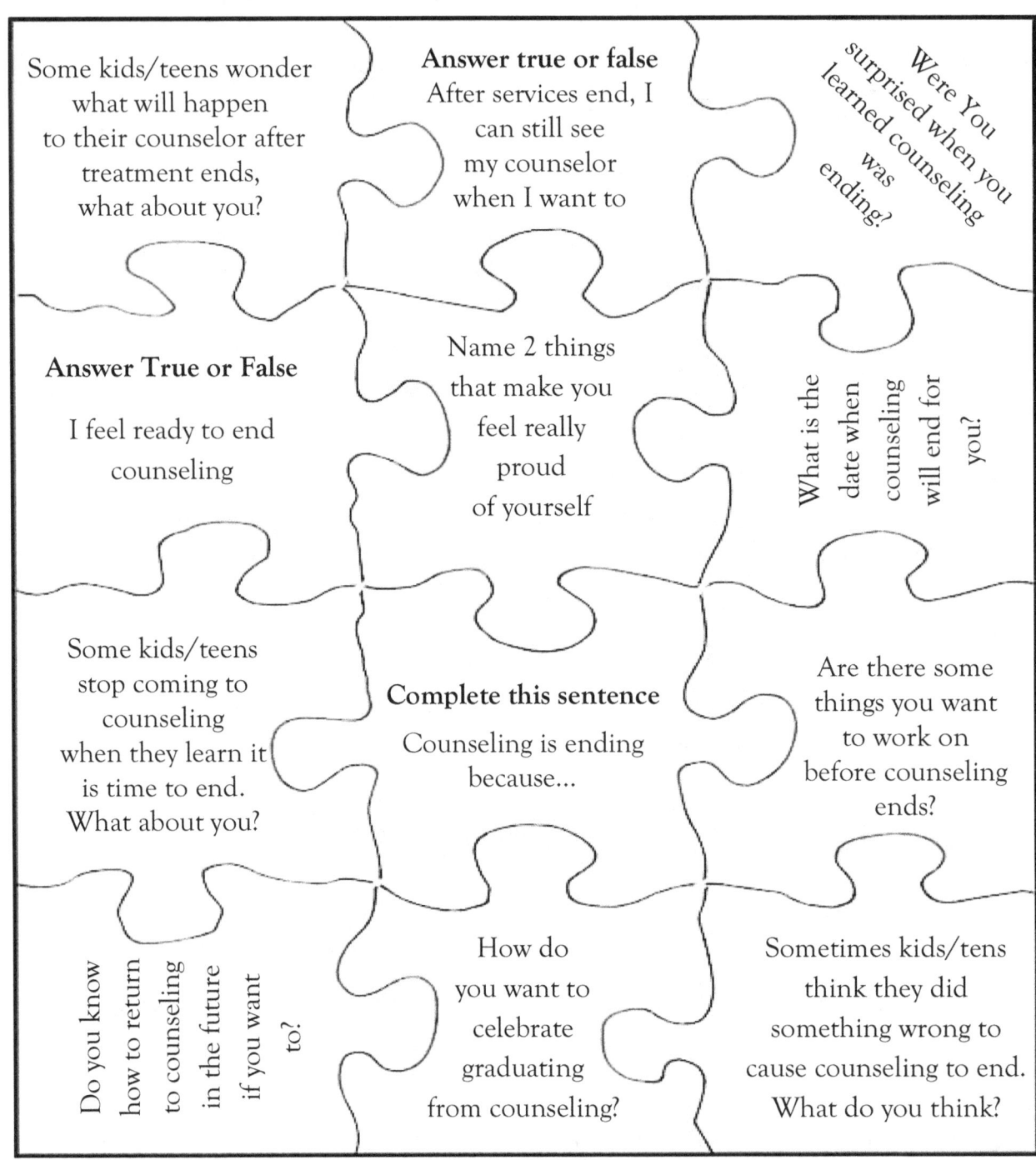

Some kids/teens wonder what will happen to their counselor after treatment ends, what about you?

Answer true or false
After services end, I can still see my counselor when I want to

Were You surprised when you learned counseling was ending?

Answer True or False

I feel ready to end counseling

Name 2 things that make you feel really proud of yourself

What is the date when counseling will end for you?

Some kids/teens stop coming to counseling when they learn it is time to end. What about you?

Complete this sentence

Counseling is ending because...

Are there some things you want to work on before counseling ends?

Do you know how to return to counseling in the future if you want to?

How do you want to celebrate graduating from counseling?

Sometimes kids/tens think they did something wrong to cause counseling to end. What do you think?

Tic-Tac-Toss

Ages: Young (5-6) and Middle (7-11)

Materials:

- 3 sheets of paper
- Pen, Pencil or Marker
- Optional bean bag, music

Rationale:

Tic-Tac-Toss is a kinetic play therapy game. The treatment provider reads termination related questions to the client. To answer the questions, the client moves toward and steps onto one of three answer sheets on the floor labeled "yes," "no," or "maybe". This game can be played individually, with a family or a group. Kinetic activities involving movement are fun and engaging for young – middle-age clients (and some adolescents, even if they will not admit it.) Many children (and adolescents) are able to sustain their attention more effectively when movement is included in a learning activity. If mobility is an issue due to physical disability or limitation, you can use a beanbag that the client can toss onto the answer sheets. Background music can be added for fun. Have fun with various moves like: Do the chicken walk to your next answer...; walk like a monkey; move like a snake; hop like a rabbit; do your coolest walk, etc.

Family or Group Application: Directions are given collectively and the family or group members are asked to go stand on or near their answer. The treatment provider facilitates a discussion on how many people answered "yes," "no," or "maybe" and processes the emerging themes. For larger groups, spread the answer sheets far enough a part to accommodate the group size.

Directions:

1. Treatment provider writes "Yes," "No," and "Maybe" on three separate sheets of paper. Paper can be laminated for durability. The three pieces of paper are placed in three separate places on the floor.

2. **Treatment Provider Says:** *We are going to play a game together; it is called tic-tac-toss. I will read you a question and you will decide the answer by moving towards and stepping on one of the pieces of paper marked "yes," "no," or "maybe." We may change how you walk between answers so you'll have to listen closely to my directions.*

3. Optional: Facilitate a practice round with the client to ensure client understands the directions.

4. Treatment provider processes the client's answers as the activity progresses. Remember to use praise and encouragement.

Discussion Statements:

I know the date when counseling will end.

Ending means I can still see my counselor when I want to.

I was surprised when I heard counseling was ending.

I am unsure about why counseling is ending now.

I wonder if I did something wrong to cause counseling to end.

I feel ready to end counseling.

I have some things I still want to work on before counseling ends.

I wonder what will happen to my counselor when services end.

Now that I know counseling is ending anyway, I may not feel like coming anymore.

Graduating from counseling is a good thing that should be celebrated.

I will return to counseling again if I needed to.

Fun questions to mix in at treatment provider's discretion:

I like eating lemons

I like sour candy

I like taking math tests

Chocolate ice cream is my favorite flavor

I can wiggle my ears without touching them with my hand

Chips Away

Ages: Young (5-6), Middle (7-11), and Adolescents (12- up)

Materials:

- Chips Away Question Sheet
- One sheet of paper
- Playing Chips (at least 20 chips)

Rationale:

The *Chips Away* game can be used individually, with a family, or a group. This activity directs the client to listen to statements about termination and give their answers by using playing chips. Because this intervention requires less verbalization, it is a good intervention for clients that have under-developed reading skills, are emotionally restricted, have cognitive delays, or are challenged by a language barrier. Feel free to add your own questions to meet your client's unique needs.

Family or group application: Each person receives a sheet of paper to answer questions simultaneously. The treatment provider processes how the group's answers were the same or different and facilitates a discussion per the emerging themes.

Directions:

1. **Treatment provider says:** *Now that we have talked about ending counseling, there is an activity I'd like us to do. It has statements about thoughts or feelings (kids/teens) sometimes have after they learn counseling is ending. I will read the statements to you. If you agree, make a big pile of chips on the paper in front of you. If you disagree don't put any chips on the paper. If you agree a little, put just a couple of chips on the page. We will practice on the first question.*

2. The treatment provider reads a question and waits for the client to give the answer with chips. The provider should process each question with the client before moving on to the next one. Very young children may need a higher level of involvement/input from the provider.

Chips Away Questions

Practice question: Chocolate is my favorite ice cream flavor.

Questions to ask the client:

I know when my last counseling session/meeting will be.

Ending means I can still see my counselor when I want to.

I was surprised when I heard counseling services were ending.

I am unsure about why counseling is ending now.

I wonder if I did something wrong to cause counseling to end.

I feel ready to end counseling.

I have some things I still want to work on before counseling ends.

I wonder what will happen to my counselor when services end.

Now that I know counseling is ending, I may not feel like coming anymore.

Graduating from counseling is a good thing that should be celebrated.

The Matching Game

Ages: Young (5-6), Middle (7-11), and Adolescents (12- up)

Materials:

- Question Cards and Answer Cards
- Optional: Fun Cards
- Scissors

Rationale:

Card games are fun, engaging and can be adapted for individual, family and group treatment. In *The Matching Game,* the client and treatment provider take turns reading termination related questions out loud. They each select a *true, false or maybe* card to answer the question and compare their answers. For example, if a question is: "I am ready to end counseling" and the treatment provider suspects that the client may have mixed feelings, the provider may answer "maybe". Process the answers by saying: *"You said yes you are ready to end treatment but, I said 'maybe', why do you think I said maybe? "* Make the process dramatic and fun. For students with learning disabilities, language barriers or challenges with reading, the treatment provider may read the questions aloud to facilitate the activity.

Family or Group Application: Family members try to match the client's answers. In a group, the group members answer the questions at the same time. The treatment provider facilitates a discussion on how the answers matched or did not match and processes the emerging themes.

Directions:

1. Cut out the question cards and the answer cards.

2. Client and treatment provider each have a set of answer cards.

3. Place the question cards face down on a playing surface.

4. **Treatment provider says:** *Now that we have talked about ending counseling, we are going to play a game that will help us talk about our thoughts about services ending. The game is called "The Matching Game" because I will try to match your answers. The Question cards will ask us different questions. The 3 cards you have and the 3 cards I have are Answer cards. As you can see, the only choices are "true", "false" or "maybe". You can look at your cards now but keep them private when we are playing. (For younger children, review what true, false, or maybe means). After we read a question, you silently decide if the answer is true, false, or maybe for you. Take your card and put it face down. At the same time, I will select a card and try to match your answer. We will then turn our cards over at the same time and see if our cards match.*

5. Provider reviews and processes the client's answers and processes if and how the answers were the same or different.

6. Optional: Facilitate a practice round with younger children, those with learning disabilities or language barriers to ensure the client understands the directions.

7. Sample practice question:

Broccoli is my favorite vegetable.

The Matching Game Question Cards:

True-False-Maybe I know the date when counseling will end	True-False-Maybe When services end, I can still see my counselor when I want to
True-False-Maybe Counseling is ending because I did something wrong	True-False-Maybe I am ending counseling because things are better
True-False-Maybe I have reached my counseling goals	True-False-Maybe If I needed to, I would come back to counseling in the future
True-False-Maybe Some kids wonder what will happen to his/her counselor when treatment ends, is this something you wonder about?	True-False-Maybe Now that I know counseling is ending, sometimes I may not feel like coming anymore
True-False-Maybe Graduating from counseling is a good thing that should be celebrated.	True-False-Maybe I felt surprised when I heard counseling was ending

The Matching Game Fun Cards:

True-False-Maybe **I can wiggle my ears without using my hands**	True-False-Maybe **I can stand on one foot for 5 seconds**
True-False-Maybe **I can make myself burp when I want to**	True-False-Maybe **Broccoli is my favorite vegetable**
True-False-Maybe **I like the color pink**	True-False-Maybe **Basketball is my favorite sport**
True-False-Maybe **I like pepperoni pizza**	True-False-Maybe **Christmas is my favorite holiday**
True-False-Maybe **I can cross my eyes and wiggle my ears**	True-False-Maybe **I can whistle**

60

The Matching Game Answer Cards:

(Client's Set)   (Treatment provider's Set)

True

True

False

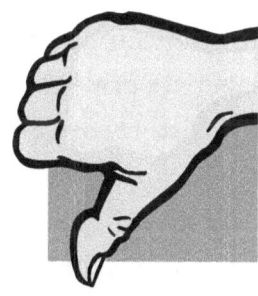

False

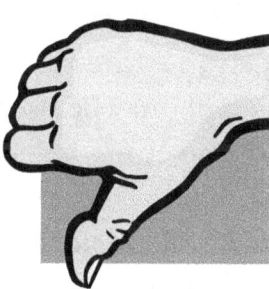

Maybe

Maybe

Step-by-Step

Ages: Young (5-6), Middle (7-11), and Adolescents (12- up)

Materials:

- Make several copies of the "stones" that accompany this activity.
- Pen, Pencil, or Marker. Scissors.
- The "stones" can be laminated for durability.

Rationale:

Step-by-Step is a kinetic play therapy game. Games involving physical challenges are fun and engaging for most people and are a good way to engage the client around a sensitive topic. In this game, the client moves from one "stone" to another to answer questions about termination. After stepping on a stone, the client (or treatment provider) picks up the stone, reads the question written on it, and answers the question. There are Step-by-Step activities for Steps 1, 2, 3 and 4. This section addresses Step 1 issues to educate the client about treatment ending. This activity may be used independently or used over several sessions to work through the entire termination process. If used the latter way, alter the script to include: *Imagine this path is like your life and each step will take us closer to ending counseling and to you reaching your life goals. Each week we will lay out more stones to help us set goals, practice the things we have learned together and prepare for your graduation from counseling.* On the last session, the stones can be placed in a notebook, bound together or placed in an envelope and given to the client as a transitional object.

Family or Group Application: Members take turns stepping on the stones and answering questions. Treatment provider facilitates a discussion per the emerging themes.

Background music can be added for fun. Have fun with various moves like: Do the chicken walk to your next answer...; walk like a monkey; move like a snake; hop like a rabbit; do your coolest walk, etc. If office space is an issue, vary placement of the stones among the floor, walls, and furniture...be creative. If mobility is an issue due to physical disability or limitation, you can use a beanbag that the client can toss onto the stones.

Directions:

1. Treatment provider writes one discussion question onto each stone. Place each stone on a different place on the floor. If floor space is limited, alternate stones among the floor, walls and furniture. Make a path or pattern. Be creative.

2. **Treatment provider Says**: *Now that we have talked about ending counseling, we are going to do an exercise that will help us learn a bit more about ending. The exercise is called "step-by-step." There is a question written on each stone. As you step on each stone, read and answer the question written on it.*

3. As appropriate, the provider incorporates the theme of taking "one step at a time" and how it relates to the termination process and a larger life-lesson for the client.

4. Treatment provider facilitates discussion and processes feelings as the client moves through the questions. For example, with the discussion question; "I was surprised when I learned counseling was ending," the provider might say, "Hmmm that's a good question, because sometimes kids feel surprised when..."

5. **Discussion Questions:**

   1. I know when my last counseling session/meeting will be.
   2. Ending means I can still see my counselor when I want to.
   3. I was surprised when I heard counseling services were ending.
   4. I am unsure about why counseling is ending.
   5. I wonder if I did something wrong to cause counseling to end.
   6. I feel ready to end counseling.
   7. I have some things I still want to work on before counseling ends.
   8. I wonder what will happen to my counselor after services end.
   9. Now that I know counseling ending, I may not feel like coming anymore.
   10. Ending counseling is a good thing that should be celebrated.

6. **Fun questions can be mixed in at the treatment provider's discretion:**

   - Riding a roller coaster feels like?
   - If I could visit anywhere in the world, I would visit?
   - My favorite song is?

"Stone" for Step-by-Step Activity:

Basketball

Ages: Young (5-6), Middle (7-11), and Adolescents (12- up)

Materials:

- Over-the-door Basketball Hoop or;
- Any container that can be substituted for a basketball hoop.
- Small ball, or make a basketball out of a crumpled piece of paper or aluminum foil.
- Basketball Cards and Board Game. Scissors.

Rationale:

Basketball can be played individually, with a family, or a group. It directs the client to shoot a ball into to a "hoop" and to draw termination-themed cards. There are basketball games for Steps 1, 2, 3 and 4. The cards in this activity were specifically designed to help the client work through the issues outlined in Task 1. The basketball game can be used over several sessions to process the different tasks (just add on the appropriate cards each week) or the games can be played independently depending on the needs of the client. You can mix in the "fun" cards at your discretion.

Family or group application: Family or group members alternate answering questions while the treatment provider facilitates the group discussion and points out common themes.

Directions:

1. **Treatment provider says**: *Now that we have talked about ending counseling services, there is a game I would like us to play together. It will help us learn a bit more about ending. We are going to shoot baskets. If you make it, take a 'hoop card' and if you miss a shot, take a 'brick card.'*

2. Treatment provider draws and answers cards as well. Provider processes the client's answers or facilitates ideas as appropriate.

3. If one deck of cards becomes depleted before the other, the provider can say something like, *"Let's see what the other cards say, just for the fun of it..."*

Step 1 Basketball Cards:

Hoop:	Brick:
Agree or Disagree: Ending counseling is a good thing that should be celebrated.	On a scale of 1 to 5 (1=not ready; 5= very ready. How ready do you feel to end counseling?
Hoop: When will your last counseling session or meeting be?	**Brick:** What should you do if you want to return to counseling after it ends?
Hoop: Complete this sentence: I am graduating from counseling because…	**Brick:** Do you think you did something wrong to cause counseling to end?
Hoop: Were you surprised when you heard counseling was ending?	**Brick:** If I needed to, I would come back to counseling in the future?
Hoop: Some kids wonder what will happen to his/her counselor when services end. Is this something you wonder about?	**Brick:** After learning counseling is ending, sometimes kids: (choose one) a. Stop coming b. Miss more sessions than usual c. Don't miss any sessions

Fun Cards for Basketball:

Hoop: Take another card	**Brick:** Make a shot with your eyes closed
Hoop: Make a trick shot	**Brick:** Say something positive about yourself and take a shot
Hoop: Miss a turn	**Brick:** Make a shot on one foot
Hoop: Turn around 3 times then take a shot	**Brick:** Take another card
Hoop: Make an over-the-shoulder shot	**Brick:** Either jump up and down 5 times or turn around 2 times and take a shot

Basketball Board Game

Hoop Cards

Hoop Cards

Brick Cards

Brick Cards

Basketball Game Board

Tip The Scales

Ages: Middle (7-11) and Adolescents (12- up)

Materials:

- Copy of Tip The Scales Activity Sheet
- Pen, Pencil, or Marker
- 6 Tokens: Any small, flat object that can be used (Poker chips, coins, paperclips, stones, popcorn)

Rationale:

Scaling is often used in evidence-based practice techniques because it allows the client to examine their thoughts and feelings by looking at a range of possibilities. *Tip The Scales* exercise is another tool to help clients process their thoughts and feelings about treatment ending. It is a concrete reminder that services are ending and addresses early termination from treatment. This intervention may be used individually, with a family, or group.

Family application: Family or group members alternate answering questions while the treatment provider facilitates the group discussion and points out common themes.

Directions:

1. **Treatment provider Says:** *Now that we have talked about ending counseling services, there is an activity I'd like you to do. It will help us figure out how to plan for counseling to end in the time we have left. Let's review the directions together.*

2. Depending on the reading level, you may choose to read to or read with the client. You should do the first question with the client to ensure understanding of how to use scaling.

3. Client completes the activity. Provider reviews and processes the client's answers. If the client's answers warrant further exploration, the provider can use the technique of; *"I noticed you answered...tell me about that...that's interesting, sometimes kids say...because they may feel..."* to deepen the processing.

Tip The Scales

Directions: Each scale below shows thoughts and feelings some kids/teens have about counseling ending. Circle or put a token on the thought or feeling closest to your own. You may also have thoughts or feelings that fall on the lines in-between the statements.

1. **Counseling ending means...**

   I will no longer meet with my counselor ———— I'll get to see my counselor sometimes ———— I am unsure what ending means

2. **Now that counseling is ending...**

   I feel ready to end ———— I am unsure if I am ready to end ———— I am not ready to end

3. **About why counseling is ending...**

   I understand why counseling is ending ———— I am confused or wonder if I did something wrong ———— I do not understand why counseling is ending

4. **About my goals...**

   I met all my goals ———— I have some things left to work on ———— I have a lot of things left to work on

5. **Now that I know counseling is ending...**

   I may stop coming ———— I may find it harder to come to sessions ———— I will keep coming until the final session/meeting

6. **If I want to return to counseling in the future...**

   Sometimes kids/teens return to counseling and I would too ———— I am unsure if I would return to counseling ———— I do not want to return to counseling again

70

My Story: Chapter 1

Ages: Young (5-6), Middle (7-11), and Adolescents (12- up)

Materials:

- My Story - Chapter 1
- Pen, Pencil, Crayons, Markers, Colored Pencils, Pastel Colors
- Include any activity from Step 1: Processing the Range of Feelings About Treatment Ending. Insert into Chapter 1 after the introduction.

Rationale:

The complete *My Story* has four chapters that you can use to process all 4-Termination Steps. It is best used with an individual to process the therapeutic experience (some treatment providers have used it successfully with families). Storytelling is a powerful clinical tool that is often used in evidenced-based practice models. Constructing a creative narrative about the treatment experience gives the client the opportunity to process his/her thoughts and feelings in a concrete way with the support of a trusted treatment provider. If desired, combine the chapters into one book and give it to the client during the last session or meeting.

> **Though this is a narrative activity, engage the right brain with colors, symbols, pictures and other creative elements.**

Chapter 1 processes the termination announcement. Optional: Include any Step 1 activity in the workbook, such as the *Common Reactions as Treatment Ends* handout or the *Good-bye Calendar*. Young clients or those with language or cognitive challenges may require more involvement from the treatment provider to complete the workbook.

Directions:

1. Read each section and follow the directions to complete the activity.
2. The cover can be decorated as appropriate. Adding a picture of the client is a nice touch, but is optional.
3. The treatment provider supports the client to complete the activity with as much or as little involvement as is clinically appropriate.
4. Once the activity is completed, the provider processes the activity with the client.

Below is a description of what each section contains:

Chapter One: Educates the client about treatment ending and puts supports in place to pre-empt early termination.

Chapter Two: Processes the client's range of feelings about treatment ending, including that addressing feelings may trigger previous losses.

Chapter Three: Prepares the client to manage life after treatment ends.

Chapter Four: Honors the relationship and brings treatment to an end.

My Story

By...

My Story

Chapter 1

Introduction to Counseling

My name is _____ and this
story is about my time in counseling.

These are my thoughts, feelings or pictures about why I began counseling...

These are some thoughts, feelings, or pictures about helpful things
I learned in counseling...

I learned in counseling how important healthy thoughts, healthy feelings, and healthy behaviors are. I have worked on my goals and it is time to end services. Below are the true, helpful thoughts about counseling ending:

My last session will be _____

Counseling is ending because _____

_____

I did not do anything wrong to cause counseling to end.... True or False

I am a good person and my counselor cares about me... True or False

Some kids/teens feel more upset or stressed inside after learning counseling services are ending and this feeling is normal... True or False

I can return to counseling in the future if I want to... True or False

I will keep coming to counseling until the last session to finish the good work I have started... True or False

We will celebrate the ending of counseling by doing something fun to honor my work... True or False

STEP TWO

Process the Range of Feelings About Treatment Ending

21st Century Seminars

where professionals grow

78

STEP TWO

Process the Range of Feelings About Treatment Ending

Feelings identification and expression is a typical part of the treatment process. Treatment providers using Trauma-Focused Cognitive Behavior Therapy (TF-CBT) or Dialectical Behavior Therapy (DBT) may call these activities affective expression and modulation, self-regulation, or emotion exposure and management. Moreover, having strong emotional and cognitive regulation and self-control skills are building blocks for resiliency. Before your client moves on to Step 3: Preparing for life after treatment ends, it is important to first process the range of feelings about treatment ending. If the client has not made sense of the range of feelings about treatment ending, his/her ability to emotionally invest in preparing for a life after treatment ends may be compromised.

If you have a client who is not able to identify and talk about his/her feelings in general, you may want to re-assess the client's readiness to end treatment. If termination is inevitable, you may consider making a referral for continued services.

What to do:

1. Support the client to express a range of feelings about treatment, including ambivalence.
2. Educate the client on how termination may trigger feelings of previous losses.
3. Monitor your counter-transference feelings and reactions.

How to do it:

1. Support client to express a range of feelings about treatment, including ambivalence

Whether positive, negative, or indifferent, your client must be encouraged to express the range of feelings about his/her treatment experience. Mental health

79

treatment is a process that may feel exciting, overwhelming, intimidating, comforting, helpful, or even boring at times. Depending on the reason for entering services, your client may have very mixed or conflicted feelings about his/her therapeutic journey. Involuntary clients, or those in inpatient or residential settings, may feel relieved to be ending treatment but may feel very different about ending a relationship with a trusted member of their treatment team. It is important to not rush the process. You must be prepared to accept the client's feelings unconditionally, help the client acknowledge and talk about his/her feelings, and allow for understanding and putting feelings in perspective.

Normalize client's reactions and feelings and allow for set-backs.

You should encourage the client to continue to talk about his/her feelings while you listen, support, and normalize his/her feelings. Provide education to your client on how termination may impact his/her emotions and trigger previous losses. The client may find himself or herself temporarily feeling more sad, keyed-up, or agitated. Feelings not felt since the earlier weeks in treatment could resurface. It is important to educate the client that some set-backs are a normal part of termination. This may not indicate that the client needs to remain in treatment longer. You can use set-backs as an opportunity to review and strengthen skills the client will need for future challenges. Keep in mind that individual's responses will vary.

2. **Educate the client on how termination may trigger feelings of previous losses.**

Normalize the experience of saying good-bye to significant relationships. Share examples in the client's life, in which saying good-bye is a part of the relationship (teachers, at the end of the school year; neighbors, when we move; friends, when we change schools; the sun at the end of each day; the moon at the end of each night or waves in the ocean; bubbles when they pop, etc.). Goodbyes happen each day and each night. Process with the client what previous good-byes were like (with family, friends, or community) and how this one may feel the same and how it will be different. Educate the client on how the good-bye between the two of you may

80

cause feelings from the past to resurface. Saying good-bye is a normal part of life and this good-bye does not have to be as difficult as others have been in the past.

3. Monitor your counter-transference feelings and reactions.

Termination may bring up a range of feelings for the treatment provider, just as it can for the client. These feelings may range from guilt, to ambivalence, or even, relief. Some treatment providers may dread saying good-bye to their favorite client, while others may feel relief that treatment is coming to a close. It is also very common for treatment providers, particularly newer providers, to feel guilt or insecurity about their own skill or competence level and whether this had an impact on treatment (did I help my client enough?). The reasons for termination may also impact how a treatment provider feels. Termination due to a client fully completing treatment goals tends to feel more satisfying than an unexpected, premature termination.

It is important for you to be aware of your own counter-transference feelings during this step and of how insidious these feelings can be. If not monitoring counter-transference feelings, you may be vulnerable to avoiding talking about the feelings related to termination, not counting down sessions, allowing sessions to run long, cutting sessions short, increasing the frequency of sessions to address emotional set-backs, or seeing clients on unscheduled days or at unscheduled times.

If any of the above occurs, feel free to refer to Appendix C in this manual for helpful suggestions on how to manage counter-transference issues. You may also seek supervision with a licensed supervisor, or consult with an objective, licensed colleague for support and guidance.

Chapter Summary: Step Two

- Having **strong emotional and cognitive regulation and self-control skills** are building blocks for resiliency.

- **Before** beginning work on the concrete skills to prepare the client for life after treatment, it is important to first process the range of feelings about receiving services. Not processing the client's feelings first, may compromise his/her ability to emotionally invest in preparing for a life after treatment ends.

- It is important to explore the **range of feelings** about treatment, including ambivalence.

- Some **set-backs are normal** during termination and may not indicate the client needs to remain in treatment longer.

- It is important to **normalize** the experience of saying good-bye. Process with the client what previous good-byes were like and how termination may be the same or different. It is important to educate the client on how termination may trigger feelings of **previous losses.**

- Termination may bring up a range of **counter-transference** feelings for the treatment provider, just as it can for the client. These feelings may range from guilt, to ambivalence, or even relief.

- It is very common for **treatment providers, especially newer providers**, to feel guilt or insecurity about his/her own skill or competence and whether this had an impact on treatment (did I help my client enough?).

- It is important to be aware of your own **counter-transference** feelings and monitor them closely. Signs to look for are: Not counting down sessions, allowing sessions to run long, cutting sessions short, or seeing clients on unscheduled days or at unscheduled times.

- **Appendix C** has tips on how to identify and manage counter-transference feelings. You can also seek supervision with a licensed supervisor, or consult with an objective, licensed colleague for support and guidance.

STEP TWO

Process the Range of Feelings About Treatment Ending

Interventions:

1. Feeling Faces Puppets
2. A-Mazing Feelings
3. In Living Color
4. Feelings Dice
5. Basketball
6. Color The Feelings In
7. Step-by-Step
8. The Feelings Puzzle
9. My Feelings About Goodbyes
10. Good and Not So Good
11. Feelings Target
12. My Collage - Reloaded
13. Color My Time in Counseling
14. My Story: Chapter 2

*The worksheets refer to the treatment provider as a "counselor". Feel free to change the worksheets to reflect your work as a counselor, case manager, social worker, psychologist, etc.

What To Do:

1. Support the client to express a range of feelings about treatment ending, including ambivalence.

2. Educate the client on how termination may trigger feelings of previous losses.

3. Monitor your counter-transference feelings and reactions.

STEP TWO

Process the Range of Feelings About Treatment Ending*

#	Intervention	Goal	Age	M	Materials Needed
1	Feeling Faces Puppets	Stick puppets made of feeling faces. Fun and engaging, symbolic. Great for kids with limited vocabulary, language or cognitive challenges.	5-11	I F G	Scissors, 8 popsicle sticks, crayons or markers, glue stick or tape.
2	A-Mazing Feelings	Client explores feelings via a maze. Different mazes for older and younger clients. Encourages processing	5-18	I F	Pen, pencil, or marker
3	In Living Color	Creative art activity. Client uses colors to express feelings	12-18	I F G	Colorful pens, pencils, crayons, or markers.
4	Feelings Dice	Client rolls dice to match feelings. Creative, interactive, engaging	5-18	I F G	Scissors. Dice templates included or use real dice
5	Basketball	Kinetic activity using Step 2 themes. Can be used for all 4 termination steps. Engaging and non-threatening. Great for all, especially kids with language or cognitive challenges.	5-18	I F G	Scissors, small container for basketball hoop, and ball for shooting. Includes basketball court and cards
6	Color The Feelings In	Projective. Client colors feelings that a child his/her age might feel. Safe, non-threatening.	5-11	I F G	Colorful pens, pencils or markers.
7	Step-by-Step	Kinetic activity using Step 2 themes. Can be used for all 4 termination steps. Engaging and non-threatening. Great for kids with language or cognitive challenges.	5-18		Pen, pencil, marker. Scissors. Stepping Stone template included.
8	The Feelings Puzzle	Problem solving game play. Non-threatening, fun.	5-18	I F G	Puzzle included. Scissors. Pen or pencil. Optional glue or poster board
9	My Feelings About Goodbyes	Explores how past good-byes impact current feelings about termination	5-18	I F G	Colorful pens, pencils or markers
10	Good and Not So Good	Uses the time tested "line down the middle of the page" activity to safely explore range of feelings about treatment	7-18	I F G	Colorful pens, pencils or markers. Optional magazine pictures
11	Feelings Target	Client throws clay bombs at a target to identify feelings. Kinetic, fun, engaging, interactive, playful	5-18	I F G	Targets included. Make darts out of wet clay, toilet tissue, cotton, or putty
12	My Collage-Reloaded	Takes a new spin on collaging. Creative, thoughtful, engaging, playful	7-18	I F G	Scissors. Glue stick, collaging materials
13	Color My Time in Counseling	Art activity. Uses colors to express a range of feelings. Encourages processing.	5-18	I F G	Paper. Colorful pencils, pens, crayons or markers
14	My Story: Chapter Two	Narrative Activity. Creative, expressive	5-18	I F	Pen, pencil, crayons or markers. Book included

*The worksheets refer to the treatment provider as a "counselor". Feel free to change the worksheets to reflect your work as a counselor, case manager, social worker, psychologist, etc.

Feeling Faces Puppets

Ages: Young (5-6) and Middle (7-11)

Materials:

- Feelings Faces Puppets Cut-outs
- 8 - Wooden Craft Sticks (straw, pipe cleaners, or strips of cardboard can also be used)
- Crayons, Markers - Glue Stick or Tape

Rationale:

The *Feeling Faces Puppets* use stick puppets to support young to middle-aged children to explore their feelings about treatment ending. This intervention may be used individually, or with a family or a group. Young children are concrete learners and their vocabulary is limited so this activity focuses on 8 feeling faces to avoid overwhelming them. The treatment provider can reduce the number of faces for very young clients.

Family or group application: Each family or group member receives his/her own set of feeling faces puppets. The treatment provider reads questions to the group and facilitates a discussion about how the answers are the same or different and helps the group to process the emerging themes.

Directions:

1. Cut out the 8 feeling faces.

2. Glue or tape feeling faces onto craft sticks (straw, pipe cleaners, or strips of cardboard can also be used) to make stick puppets.

3. Review the meaning of each feeling faces for clarity.

4. **Treatment provider Says:** *Now that we have talked about ending counseling services, we are going to talk a little about what it has been like to be in treatment. I'm going to ask you some questions about how you feel. You answer using one of the feelings shown*

on your stick puppets. After you show your stick puppet, then you say why you feel that way. If the feeling you want to use in your answer is not on one of the feeling faces puppets, that's okay, just say the feeling you would have answered with. (Provider should have client practice first.)

5. You may use the discussion prompts as a guide. Feel free to modify or add questions as appropriate. "Fun" questions can be mixed in to increase the client's tolerance for the process.

6. Remember to use praise and positive body language (smiling, "high 5's") to encourage and give positive feedback to the client.

 An alternative to the craft intervention is to have the client color the faces (the treatment provider can assign colors to the feelings or allow the client to choose). The client can point to the faces, or, place a poker chip, bean, sandtray miniature, or other object on the face to answer the questions.

Feeling Faces Puppets

Discussion Prompts:

(Practice question): What feeling do you have when you eat ice cream?

- When I first met _____ (counselor's name) I felt...
- Doing well on my goals feels like...
- Show me the sad face and share a time when you felt sad during counseling...
- What feeling have you had when saying good-bye to someone special in the past?
- Which feeling tells me how you feel about counseling ending?
- Show me the scared face and tell me what makes you scared about counseling ending?
- Show me the happy face and tell me what makes you happy about counseling ending?
- Show me a shy face and tell me a time when you felt shy during counseling.
- Show me the confused face and tell me a time when you felt confused during counseling.
- Show me the proud face and tell me about a time when you felt proud of yourself during counseling.

Fun questions to mix in at treatment provider's discretion:

- What feeling might you have during an earthquake?
- Show me the feeling you might have if you could fly like a bird?
- Show me the feeling you might have when you watch your favorite movie?

Happy – Sad – Mad – Scared Feelings Faces

HAPPY FACE

SAD FACE

SCARED FACE

MAD FACE

Embarrassed – Confused – Proud –Shy Feelings Faces

Embarrassed Face

Confused Face

Proud Face

Shy Face

A-Mazing Feelings

Ages: Young (5-6), Middle (7-11), and Adolescents (12- up)

Materials:

- A-Mazing Feelings Worksheet for (young and middle)
- A Mazing Feelings Worksheet for (middle - adolescents)
- Colored Pen, pencil, marker

Rationale:

The *A-Mazing Feelings* activity uses a maze theme to explore the range of feelings about treatment. It can be used individually or with a family but is contraindicated for group use. Introducing a maze into a treatment group may evoke the element of competition and take the focus off of termination. All ages enjoy mazes. The younger child should enjoy the simple maze to match the appropriate cognitive level. Middle to adolescent-age clients can enjoy the more complex maze. Their expanded cognitive growth allows them to enjoy multi-tasking and using creativity to solve problems. Because maze solutions are not fully dependent on language proficiency, clients with language delays or barriers may also find the activity enjoyable. If the treatment provider believes it helpful, s/he may assist with the reading involved in this activity.

Family application: Each family member takes a turn and finds his/her way to a different word in the maze. The treatment provider facilitates a family discussion and observes themes as they emerge.

Directions:

1. Younger clients should use the simple maze. The words help to guide the client through the maze. Middle to adolescent age clients can use the more

complex maze. Feel free to use one of the mazes provided or you can use the blank maze to customize the feelings and questions to your client's unique experience.

2. Avoid making the maze too complicated. Pattern the words to guide your client through the maze. The goal is to use the maze to process your client's feelings. You do not want to take the enjoyment out of the activity by making the task too difficult.

3. Review the directions with the client.

4. Support client to move through the maze at his/her own pace.

5. Process the termination-related feeling words as the client passes through the maze.

Additional Discussion Prompts:

1. What feeling best describes how you felt at the beginning of counseling?
2. How has counseling helped you feel better?
3. What were times when counseling made you feel worse?
4. What feeling describes how it felt to say good-bye to others in the past?
5. What feeling describes how you feel about counseling ending?
6. What makes you worried about counseling ending?
7. What makes you feel sad about counseling ending?
8. What makes you feel happy about counseling ending?

A-Mazing Feelings

Counseling services help us work through a maze of thoughts and feelings. Begin at the start line and find your way through the maze of thoughts and feelings. As you move through a word in the maze, talk about a time during counseling when you experienced that feeling.

Start

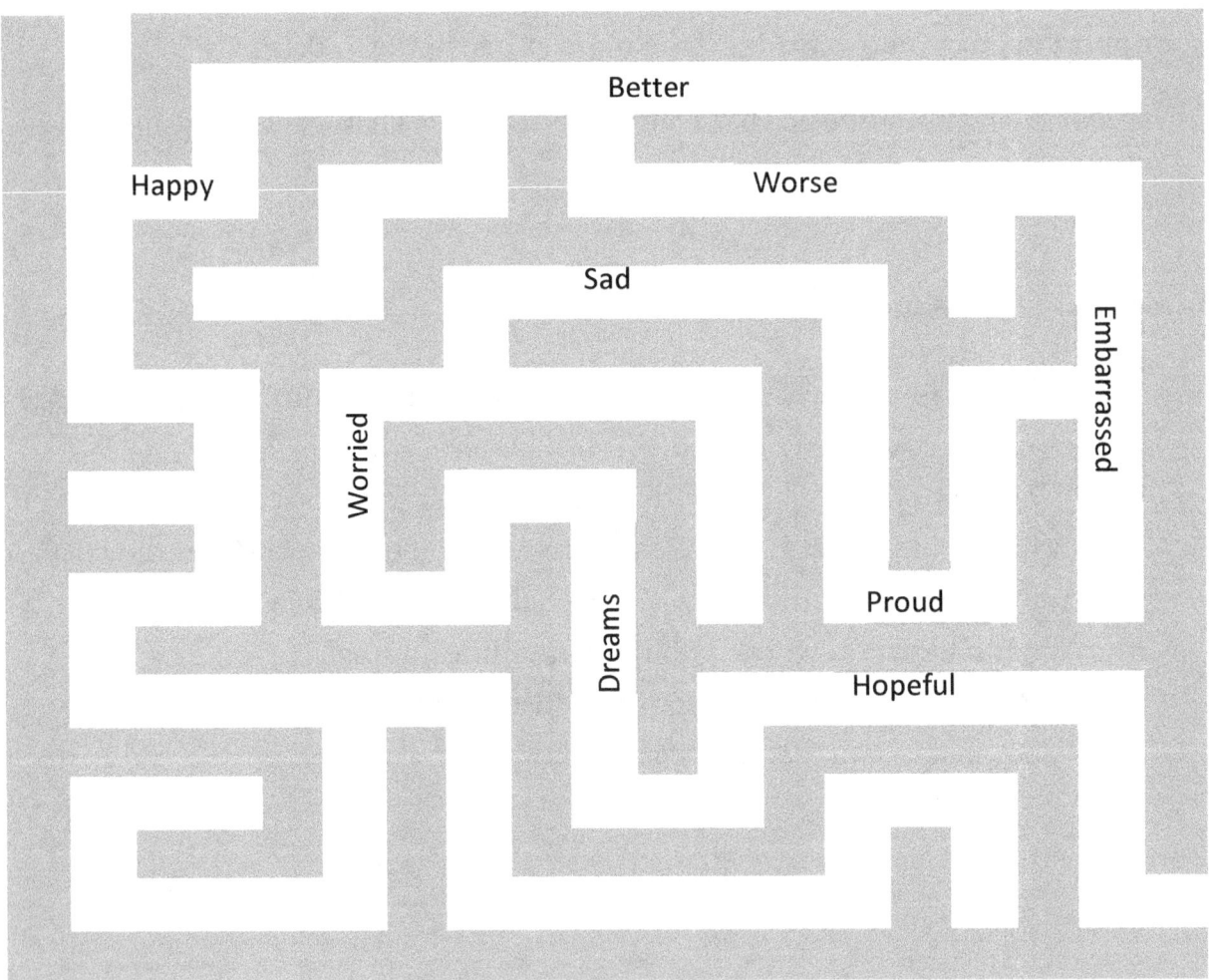

End

A-Mazing Feelings

Counseling services help us work through a maze of thoughts and feelings. Begin at the start line and find your way through the maze of thoughts and feelings. As you move through a word in the maze, talk about a time during counseling when you experienced that feeling.

Start

End

A-Mazing Feelings

Directions: Counseling services help us work through a maze of thoughts and feelings. Begin at the start line and follow the arrows to find your way through the maze of thoughts and feelings. As you move through a word in the maze, talk about a time during counseling when you experienced that feeling.

Start Here

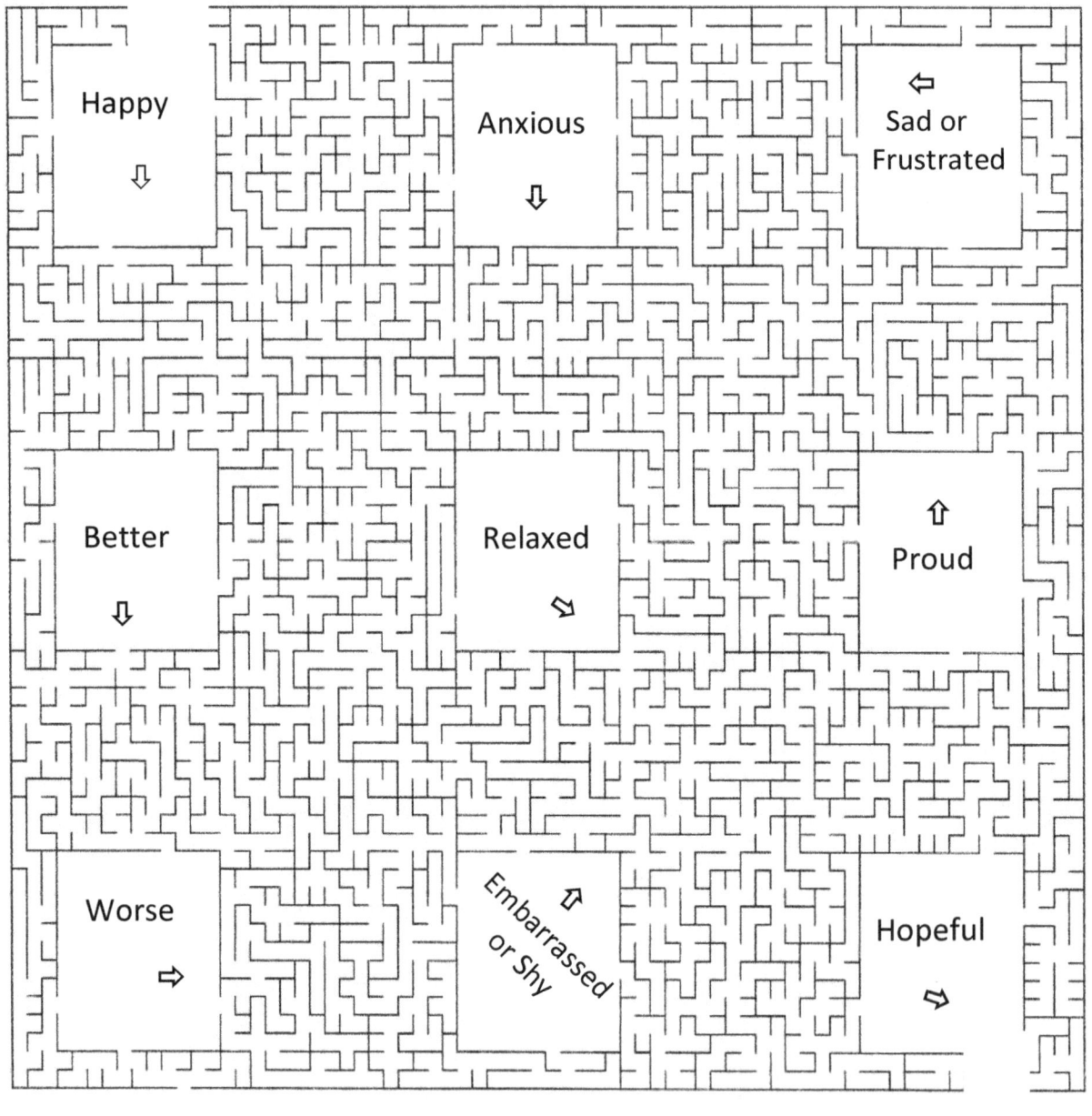

End Here

A-Mazing Feelings

Directions: Counseling services help us work through a maze of thoughts and feelings. Begin at the start line and follow the arrows to find your way through the maze of thoughts and feelings. As you move through a word in the maze, talk about a time during counseling when you experienced that feeling.

Start Here

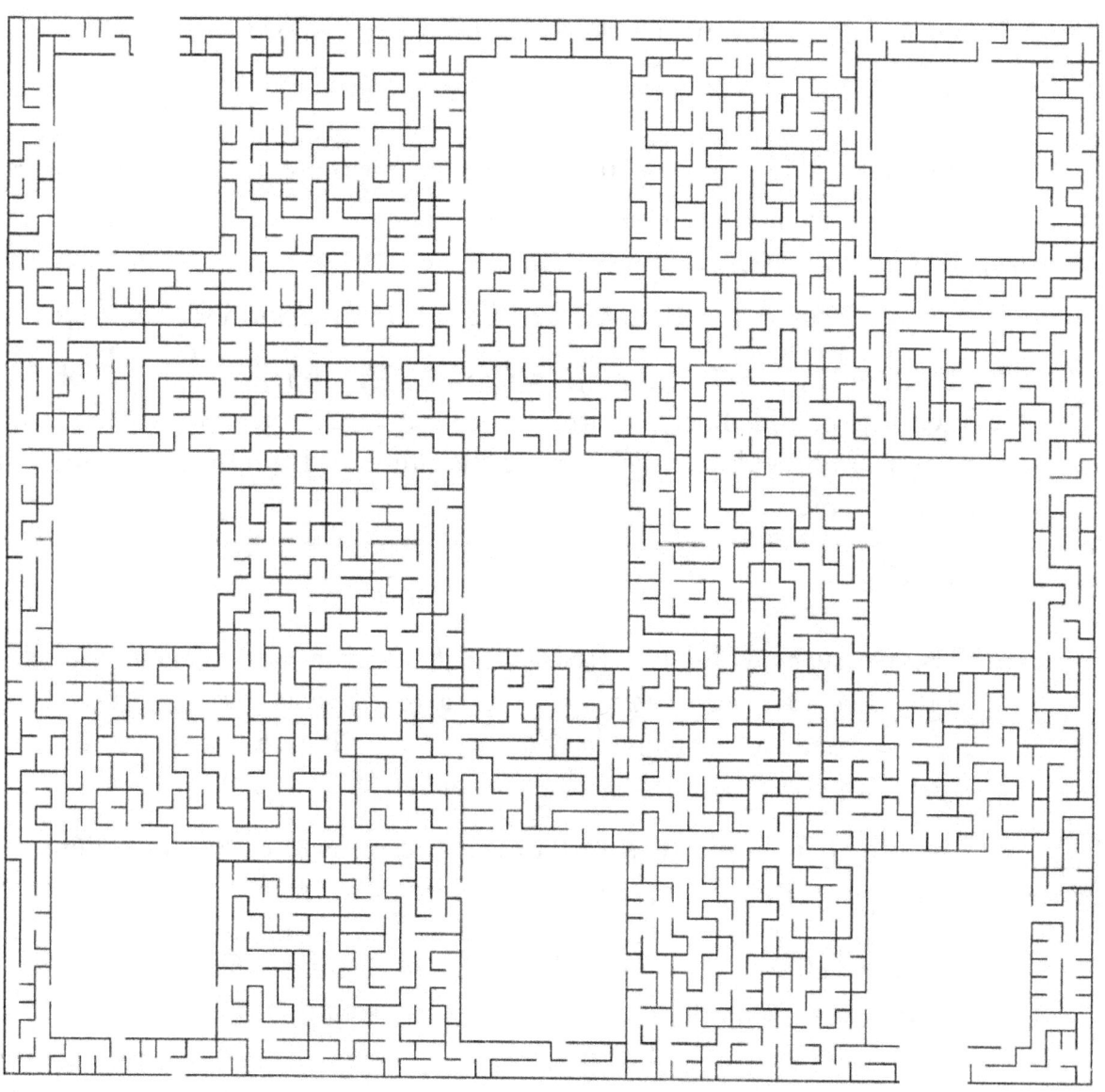

End Here

In Living Color

Ages: Adolescents (12- up)

Materials:

- The In Living Color Activity Sheet
- Crayons, Markers, Colored Pencils, or Pastels

Rationale:

The *In Living Color* is a powerful exercise that uses colors to process the range of emotions about treatment ending. Because it requires the use of abstract thinking, this intervention is most appropriate for adolescents. However, you know your client best so use your judgment if using this intervention with younger ages.

Family or group application: Each family or group member completes his or her own worksheet and shares it with the group. The treatment provider facilitates a discussion on how the worksheets are the same or different and points out emerging themes.

Directions:

1. **Treatment provider says:** *Today we will continue our talk about counseling ending. In this exercise we are going to use colors to describe how counseling has been for you. After you read the questions, select a color(s) and fill in the circle to describe the feelings. After you finish we will talk about your project.*

2. The provider should review all of the questions to ensure the client understands them.

3. Allow the client to complete the entire worksheet before processing. This will avoid interrupting the client's creativity and spontaneity.

4. A client can use one color, more than one color at a time, or a mix of colors- encourage creativity. The colors are not as important as allowing the client the opportunity to process his/her journey in treatment.

In Living Color

Directions: The following questions ask you to fill in the circles below with a color or colors that describe your feelings about certain topics. You may use a color as many times as you wish or use several colors at the same time. Be creative.

For example: Eating my favorite food feels like the color... ◯

....

When I started counseling, I felt like the color... ◯ As I came to counseling more and more, I learned services can have ups and downs. The best part of counseling felt like the color... ◯ . And, the tough times felt like the color... ◯ . . Now, reaching my goals feels like... ◯ . Because of my progress, it is time to end counseling and say good-bye to my counselor. In the past, saying good-bye to people has felt like the color... ◯ . I imagine saying good-bye to my counselor may feel like the color... ◯ . The part of counseling I will not miss feels like the color... ◯ . The part of counseling that I will miss or remember the most feels like the color... ◯ My favorite feeling or memory of being in counseling feels like the color... ◯

Feelings Dice

Ages: Young (5-6), Middle (7-11), and Adolescents (12- up)

Materials:

- Safety scissors
- Dice Templates
    - Young - middle: make 2 dice
    - Middle - adolescent: make 4 dice

Rationale:

Feelings Dice supports the client to discuss his/her feelings about mental health treatment using a set of dice. It can be used individually, with a family, or a group. Rolling dice is a fun way to support clients to explore the range of feelings they have about services ending. The treatment provider uses 2 dice with young to middle-age clients and 4 dice with middle-adolescent clients.

Some cultures or religions are opposed to the use of dice. If this is the case for your client, out of sensitivity to your client's and/or family's beliefs, either: 1) Select another intervention from this section; 2) Replace the dice with colored cubes and assign feelings to the colors on the cubes; or 3) Replace the dice with feeling cubes and write feeling words on the cubes.

Family or group application: 1) Each family or group member alternates turns, throwing the dice and answering a question. Or, 2) Each family or group member has his/her own set of dice. Members throw the dice at the same time as the other members. Then, all members compare their feelings. The treatment provider facilitates a discussion on how the answers are the same or different and points out emerging themes.

Directions:

1. Use the dice templates accompanying this activity to make dice for your game. Use two dice (numbered 1-6) for young to middle-age clients and four dice (two numbered 1-6, and two numbered 7-12) for middle to adolescent age clients. You can also use traditional dice or make dice out of small wood blocks.

2. Assign feelings to the numbers. The treatment provider can "stack" the exercise with feelings important to processing the range of feelings the client may have about treatment. (Feel free to use your own, but, for example: 1=Happy, 2=Sad, 3= Angry, 4=Scared, 5=Proud, 6=Confused, 7= hopeful; 8= Embarrassed; 9= Alone; 10= Encouraged; 11= Supported; 12= Relieved).

3. Write the numbers and their corresponding feelings on a piece of construction paper, chalkboard or whiteboard and post it for the client to see.

4. **Treatment provider Says:** *Now that we have talked about counseling ending, there is an activity I'd like to do that will help us talk about the different feelings you have had from the beginning of services until now.*

5. **Treatment provider Says:** *I will read a question then you will roll the dice. We will pick from the feelings you rolled on the dice to answer the questions. If the feeling you want to use in your answer was not rolled it's okay, just say the feeling you would have answered with.*

   Remember: Flexibility is key; the activity is less about what the dice says and more about the opportunity to discuss the client's feelings.

6. Younger children may require help matching the numbers to the corresponding feelings.

7. The provider can make-up "fun" questions for variety to increase the client's tolerance for the process.

Feelings Dice

Feel free to use the following discussion prompts as a guide:

Practice Question(s):

Eating my favorite ice cream feels like...(*roll the dice*)
Riding a rollercoaster feels like...(*roll the dice*)
I imagine winning a million dollars feels like...(*roll the dice*)

Discussion Questions:

1.   Before I started counseling I had a lot of this feeling...
2.   When I first met my counselor, I felt...
3.   During the best part of counseling, I felt...
4.   During the toughest part of counseling I felt...
5.   Reaching my goals feels like...
6.   In the past, saying good-bye to people felt like...
7.   I imagine saying good-bye to my counselor will feel like...
8.   The part of counseling I will not miss feels like...
9.   The part of counseling I will miss most feels like...

Sample fun questions:

Watching my favorite movie/cartoon feels like...
Getting lost feels like...
Taking a math test feels like...
Eating vegetables feels like...
Winning a million dollars would feel like...
The best day of my life would feel like...
Meeting my favorite rap artist/singer would feel like...

Feelings Dice Templates:

Directions: Cut out the di. Fold in the shape of a cube and paste the gray sections to the inside of the di.

Young – Middle: Make 2 dice

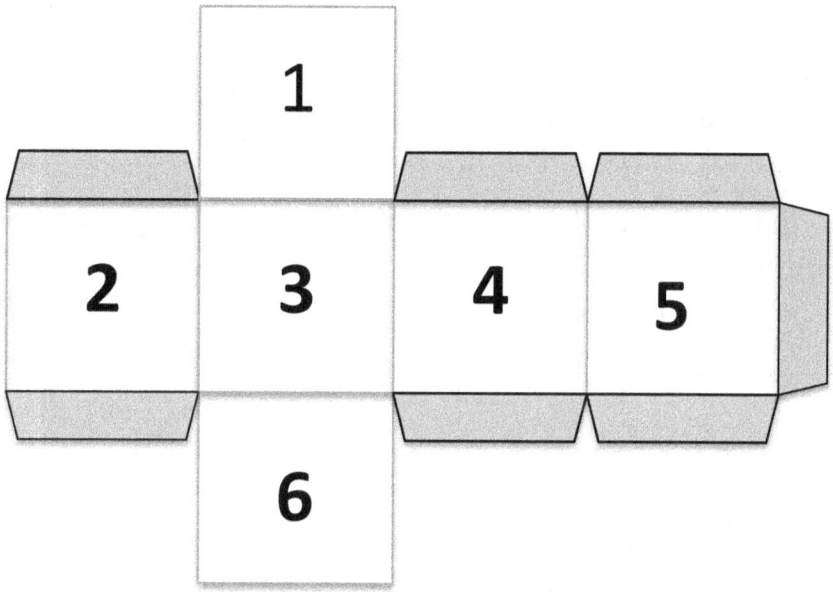

Middle – Adolescents: Make 4 dice (2 numbered 1-6 and 2 numbered 7-12)

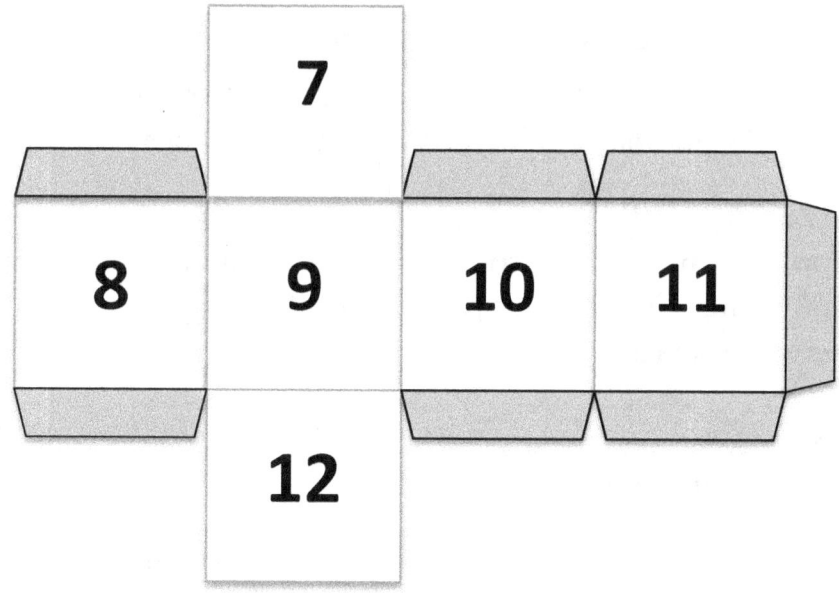

Basketball

Ages: Young (5-6), Middle (7-11), and Adolescents (12- up)

Materials:

> **How This Activity Builds Resilience:**
> Having strong emotional and cognitive regulation and self-control skills create building blocks for resilience. Reinforces sense of humor, self-efficacy, goal attainment and personal competence.

- Over-the-door Basketball hoop Or, any container that can be substituted for a basketball hoop.

- Small ball or make a basketball out of a crumpled piece of paper or aluminum foil.

- Basketball Cards and Game Board

- Treatment provider mixes in some, none or all of the "fun" cards

Rationale:

Some clients are kinetic learners and make good use of activities that are combined with physical activity. *Basketball* directs the client to shoot a ball into to a "hoop" and to draw cards that ask the client termination-themed questions. It may be used for individual, family and group sessions. There are basketball games for Steps 1, 2, 3 and 4. The cards in this activity were specifically designed to help the client work through the issues outlined in Step 2 (processing the range of feelings about treatment ending). The game directions are the same but the cards change according to the task. The basketball game can be used over several sessions to process the different tasks (just add on the appropriate cards) or the games can be played independently depending on the needs of the client.

Family or group application: Each person takes a turn shooting a basket and answering a question while the treatment provider facilitates a group discussion and points out emerging themes.

Part One: Educates the client about treatment ending and puts supports in place to pre-empt early termination.

Part Two: Processes the client's range of feelings about treatment ending, including that addressing feelings may trigger previous losses.

Part Three: Prepares client to manage life after treatment ends.

Part Four: Commemorates the relationship and brings treatment to an end.

Directions:

1. **Treatment provider Says:** *Now that we have talked about ending counseling, there is a game I would like us to play together. It will help us talk about the different feelings you have had from the beginning of counseling until now. We are going to shoot baskets. If you make it, take a 'hoop card' and if you miss a shot, take a 'brick card'.* **Optional:** Write the client's answers on the back of each card. For the last session, bind the cards together with a binder ring(s) to make a booklet or place the cards in a decorated container. Give the cards to the client on the last session as a transitional object.

2. Treatment provider draws and answers cards as well. Provider processes the client's answers or facilitates ideas as appropriate.

3. If one deck of cards becomes depleted before the other, the provider can say something like, *"Let's see what the other cards say, just for the fun of it..."*

4. The cards can be photocopied and laminated for durability.

Step 2...Basketball Cards:

Hoop: What is the best thing about being in counseling?	**Brick:** What is the worst thing about being in counseling?
Hoop: What does it feel like to reach your goals?	**Brick:** Talk about why you came to counseling
Hoop: What will you miss most about counseling?	**Brick:** What will you miss the least about counseling?
Hoop: Name 3 things you learned from counseling	**Brick:** What has saying "good-bye" to others been like for you in the past?
Hoop: When I think about saying good-bye to my counselor on the last day, I feel…	**Brick:** What did you think or feel when you first met your counselor?

Fun Cards for Basketball:

Hoop: Take another card	**Brick:** Make a shot with your eyes closed
Hoop: Make a trick shot	**Brick:** Say something positive about yourself and take a shot
Hoop: Say something nice about your counselor and allow him/her to take your turn	**Brick:** Make a shot on one foot
Hoop: Turn around 3 times then take a shot	**Brick:** Take another card
Hoop: Make an over-the-shoulder shot	**Brick:** Make a shot with your opposite hand

Basketball Game Board

Hoop Cards

Hoop Cards

Brick Cards

Brick Cards

Basketball Game Board

Color The Feelings In

Ages: Young (5-6) and Middle (7-11)

Materials:

> **How This Activity Builds Resilience:** Having strong emotional and cognitive regulation and self-control skills create building blocks for resilience. Reinforces self-efficacy, goal attainment and personal competence.

- Color My Feelings Worksheet
- Colored Pens, Pencils, or Markers

Rationale:

The *Color The Feelings In* activity directs the client to use a template of a person to color in the feelings someone his/her same age may have about treatment ending. It is appropriate for individual, family, and group sessions. Because the client is not being asked to express his/her feelings directly, this activity allows for a safe, non-threatening way to express the range of feelings about treatment ending.

Family or group application: Each family or group member completes his or her own worksheet and shares it with the group. The provider facilitates a discussion on how the worksheets are the same or different and processes emerging themes.

Directions:

1. **Treatment provider says:** *Now that we have talked about counseling ending, let's talk a bit about how someone your age may feel about services coming to an end. Here is an outline of someone your age, let's pretend s/he was just told that they will have to end counseling. I'd like you to fill up the figure with the feelings you think s/he has. You can use as many feelings as you wish.*

2. The client uses colors, symbols, and different types of lines or symbols to express his/her feelings. Treatment provider supports client and honors the process as the client colors in the outline. When complete, the provider processes the experience with the client.

3. This activity is process oriented so the provider should keep the processing focused on termination. See the following discussion prompts:

- Identify what the feelings are.
- Explore the range of feelings.
- Normalize the feelings.
- Discuss past "good-byes" and impact on current feelings/reactions.

4. Relatedness to Termination:

- The best thing about counseling
- The most difficult thing about counseling
- What will be missed most about counseling
- What will be missed the least about counseling
- What will it be like to say goodbye to the counseling

Color The Feelings In

Step-by-Step

Ages: Young (5-6), Middle (7-11), and Adolescents (12- up)

Materials:

- Pen, Pencil or Marker. Scissors
- Copy "stones" as needed
- Optional: Laminate "stone"

> **How This Activity Builds Resilience:**
> Having strong emotional and cognitive regulation and self-control skills create building blocks for resilience. Reinforces sense of humor, self-efficacy, goal attainment and personal competence.

Rationale:

Step-by-Step is a kinetic play therapy game. Games involving physical challenges are fun and engaging for most people and are a good way to engage the client around a sensitive topic. In this game, the client moves from one "stone" to another to answer questions about termination. After stepping on a stone, the client (or provider) picks up the stone, reads the question written on it, and answers the question. There are Step-by-Step activities for Steps 1, 2, 3 and 4. This section addresses Step 2 issues to process the range of feelings about treatment ending. This activity may be used independently or used over several sessions to work through the entire termination process. If used the latter way, alter the script to include: *Imagine this path is like your life and each step will take us closer to ending counseling and to you reaching your life goals. Each week we will lay out more stones to help us set goals, practice the things we have learned together and prepare for your graduation from counseling.* On the last session, the stones can be placed in a notebook, bound together or placed in an envelope and given to the client as a transitional object.

Family or Group Application: Members take turns stepping on the "stones" and answering questions. Treatment provider facilitates a discussion per the emerging themes.

Add background music for fun. Play with various moves like: Do the chicken walk to your next answer; walk like a monkey; move like a snake; hop like a rabbit; do your coolest walk, etc. If office space is an issue, vary placement of the stones among the floor, walls and furniture...be creative. If mobility is an issue due to physical disability or limitation, you can use a beanbag that the client can toss onto the answer sheets.

Directions:

1. Treatment provider writes one discussion question onto each "stone" and places "stones" on the floor. (For example: if using 5 questions, there should be 5 stones)

2. **Treatment provider says:** *Now that we have talked about ending counseling, we are going to do an exercise that will help us talk about what being in services has felt like. The exercise is called "step-by-step". There is a question written on each stone. As you step on each stone, read and answer the question written on it.*

3. As appropriate, the provider incorporates the theme of taking "one step at a time" and how it relates to the termination process and a larger life lesson for the client.

4. Treatment provider facilitates discussion and processes feelings as the client moves through the questions. For example, with the discussion question, "What has saying good-bye been like for you in the past?" the provider may respond, "hmmm that's a good question, because sometimes saying goodbye in the present can remind us of difficult good-byes we have had in the past."

5. Remember to use praise, encouragement and highlight the client's strengths and progress.

6. **Discussion Questions:**
   - Talk about why you came to counseling?
   - When I first met my counselor, I felt...
   - Name 3 positive things you learned from counseling.
   - Talk about how you feel about your goals...
   - What did you enjoy the most about counseling?
   - What was the worst part about counseling?
   - What has "saying good-bye" to people been like for you in the past?
   - What do you think saying good-bye to your counselor will be like?
   - What will you miss the most about counseling?
   - What will you miss the least about counseling?

7. **Fun questions to mix in at the treatment provider's discretion:**
   - Riding a roller coaster feels like?
   - If I could visit anywhere in the world, I would visit?
   - My favorite song is?
   - Can you say "See the silly sea shells on the shiny sea shore" 3 times?

111

"Stone" for Step-by-Step Activity:

The Feelings Puzzle

Ages: Young (5-6), Middle (7-11), and Adolescents (12- up)

Materials:

- Copy of the Feelings Puzzle
- Safety Scissors
- Pen, Pencil, or Marker; glue and poster board
   Optional: Laminate the puzzle for durability. Or, glue it onto a piece of poster or cardboard.

Rationale:

Puzzles are fun and engaging for most people and are a good way to engage the client around a sensitive topic. *The Feelings Puzzle* is themed to assist the client to process his/her feelings about termination. It can be used individually, with a family or a group.

Family or group application: 1) Family members alternate turns answering questions from the same puzzle, and collectively assemble the puzzle at the end of the game. The family keeps their puzzle as a keepsake. Or, 2) Group members complete their own individual puzzles and take turns answering questions as the treatment provider processes the group's experience and reflects common theme. Group members keep their own puzzles.

Directions:

1. Options for the Feelings Puzzle:
    a. Cut out the puzzle pieces and work through each piece
    b. Keep the puzzle in one unit and work through the questions

2. **Treatment provider Says:** *Now that we have talked about counseling ending, I have a puzzle I want us to work on. It will help us understand more about our feelings about services ending.*

3. Treatment provider facilitates the client completing the puzzle pieces. If needed, provider can write the answers on each piece. **Optional:** Glue completed puzzle pieces together.

Feelings Puzzle

When I think about saying good-bye to my counselor on the last day, I feel...

The best thing about counseling is...

What is the worst thing about being in counseling?

What does it feel like to reach your goals?

Talk about why you came to counseling

What will you miss most about counseling?

What will you miss the least about counseling?

Name 3 things you learned from counseling

Say something positive about yourself

What did you think or feel when you first met your counselor?

In the past, what has saying "good-bye" to others been like for you?

If you could choose your own nickname, what would it be?

My Feelings About Goodbyes

Ages: Middle (7-11) and Adolescents (12- up)

Materials:

> **How This Activity Builds Resilience:** Having strong emotional and cognitive regulation and self-control skills create building blocks for resilience. Reinforces personal values and using these values to make decisions.

- Pen, pencil, or marker
- My Feelings About Ending Worksheet

Rationale:

The *My Feelings About Goodbyes* helps middle to adolescent-age clients better understand how sometimes what they feel about treatment ending is related to how they have said good-bye to others in the past. This is a powerful individual, family or group intervention. However, it is not the best activity for younger clients or for middle-age clients who are very concrete. This activity requires reversibility, which develops during the concrete operations stage of cognitive development (7 to 11 or 12 years of age). Very concrete middle-age clients may struggle with the concept of applying past feelings to the present.

Family or group application: Each family or group member completes his/her own worksheet and shares it with the group. The treatment provider facilitates a discussion on how the worksheets are the same or different and processes emerging themes.

Directions:

1. Review the directions with the client.

2. Support client to complete the worksheet.

3. Educate the client on the connection between previous experiences and the current experience of saying good-bye during termination. Discuss the possibility of early termination and put a plan in place to pre-empt it (ie., *Sometimes when it's hard to say goodbye some people avoid saying goodbye by not coming...*).

4. Remember to make the activity fun and enjoyable.

115

My Feelings About Goodbyes

Understanding our own feelings is a big part of what we learn in counseling. Sometimes what we feel about services ending has to do with how we have said good-bye to others in the past. Write some of the feelings you have had about saying good-bye to others in the past in the balloons below. Remember some feelings may be bigger than others. You may add extra balloons and feelings if needed.

Great! Some of these feelings may also be the same about saying goodbye to your counselor. Draw a string from the balloons above to the star to connect the feelings that are the same. Then talk about how saying good-bye to your counselor may be the same and how it may be different than past goodbyes.

116

Good and Not So Good

Ages: Middle (7-11) and Adolescents (12- up)

Materials:

- Pen or Pencil
- (Optional) collaging pictures, glue stick
- *Good and Not So Good* Worksheet

> **How This Activity Builds Resilience:** Having strong emotional and cognitive regulation and self-control skills create building blocks for resilience. Reinforces personal values and using these values to make decisions.

Rationale:

The *Good and Not So Good* activity directs clients to make a list of what is "good" and "not so good" about treatment ending. It can be used individually, with a family or a group. Message to your clients that their expertise on the subject will help future clients better understand treatment. This may help the client express his/her feelings about ending treatment in a non-threatening way. The treatment provider should help facilitate the discussion and writing process.

Family or group application: 1) Family or group members complete his or her own individual activity sheet and shares it with the group. Or, 2) A family completes one activity sheet collaboratively. The treatment provider processes the group's experience and highlights emerging themes.

Directions:

1. **Treatment provider says:** *Now that we have talked about counseling ending, I want to get your input on how to better work with other young people in the future. Let's talk a bit about how someone your age may feel about services coming to an end. Here is a worksheet that can help. On the side called, "Good", you can write words, or draw, or paste pictures of the things that are good about counseling and what will be helpful to other young people. On the side of the page called "Not so Good", you can write words,*

draw or paste pictures of what was difficult about counseling and what other young people may not like so much about it. It is important to be completely honest.

2. Treatment provider supports client and honors the process as the client completes the worksheet. When complete, the provider processes the experience with the client. Identify what the feelings are and what point during services the feelings emerged. Explore the range of feelings the client has and accept them fully.

3. **Discussion Questions:**

- What helps young people the most about participating in counseling?
- What helps young people the least about participating in counseling?
- What should we change about our counseling program?
- What should we keep the same about our counseling program?
- What will you miss most about participating in counseling?
- What will you miss the least about participating in counseling?
- What has saying good-bye been like in the past?
- What will it be like to end and say goodbye to your counselor.

Good and Not so Good

Directions: On the side called, "Good", you can write words, draw, or paste pictures of the things that are good about counseling and what will be helpful to other young people. On the side of the page called "Not so Good", you can write words, draw or paste pictures of what was difficult about counseling and what other young people may not like so much about it. It is important to be completely honest.

Good	Not So Good

Feelings Target

Ages: Young (5-6), Middle (7-11), and Adolescents (12- up)

> **How This Activity Builds Resilience:** Having strong emotional and cognitive regulation and self-control skills create building blocks for resilience. Reinforces sense of humor, self-efficacy, goal attainment and personal competence.

Materials:

- Feelings Target
- Darts can be made out of silly putty, wet clay, wet toilet paper or wet cotton balls.

Rationale:

Feelings Target is a kinetic play therapy activity. Clients are directed to throw darts at a target and answer termination-related questions based on the feelings written on the target. The game can be played with individuals, a family or a group. This game is especially good for kinetic learners who enjoy physical activity.

Family or group application: Each person takes a turn throwing a dart and answering a question while the treatment provider facilitates a group discussion and points out emerging themes.

Directions:

1. Select a target for the client's age and developmental level. The target with 6 slots is for younger-middle aged clients. The target with 12 slots is for middle-adolescent aged clients. Target can be laminated for durability.

2. Treatment provider writes one feeling per slot on the target. Target should be placed on the wall at client's eye-level.

3. **Game #1** (young to middle) **Treatment provider says:** *Today we are going to play a game that will allow us to talk about what being in counseling has been like. We are going to throw soft darts at the target on the wall. When the dart lands on the target, we will select the feeling closest to the dart and talk about a time during counseling when we had that feeling. A bullseye allows client to choose any feeling. If a dart lands between two feelings the client chooses between the two feelings.*

120

4. **Game #2** (middle to adolescents) **Treatment provider says:** *Today we are going to play a game that will allow us to talk about what being in counseling has been like. I will read you a question and you pick the feeling on the target that best answers the question for you. Then, we will try to hit that feeling.*

5. Middle-Adolescents in particular like the challenge of trying to hit a desired target. If the targeted feeling is missed, that's fine...just talk about the feeling the client was trying to hit or why the feeling the target landed on would not apply (ie., "I was trying to hit confident because I feel I can face anything...the tdart landed on afraid. I felt that way in the beginning of counseling but not now.")

6. Because this activity is less structured than some of the others, the provider must be mindful to keep the theme centered on termination.

7. **Darts:** Should be the size of a nickel. Your clay, toilet paper or cotton ball darts will stick with the right amount of water added (you may have to practice).

Discussion Prompts:

1. I felt....about beginning counseling.
2. When I first met my counselor, I felt...
3. During the best part of counseling, I felt...
4. What is the feeling that describes the toughest part of counseling...
5. Reaching my goals feels like...
6. In the past, saying good-bye to people felt like...
7. I imagine saying good-bye to my counselor will feel like...
8. The part of counseling I will not miss feels like...
9. The part of counseling I will miss most feels like...

Fun Questions:

Watching my favorite movie/cartoon feels like...

Taking a math test feels like...

Eating vegetables feels like...

Winning a million dollars would feel like...

The best day of my life would feel like...

Meeting my favorite singer/rap artist would feel like...

121

Feelings Target

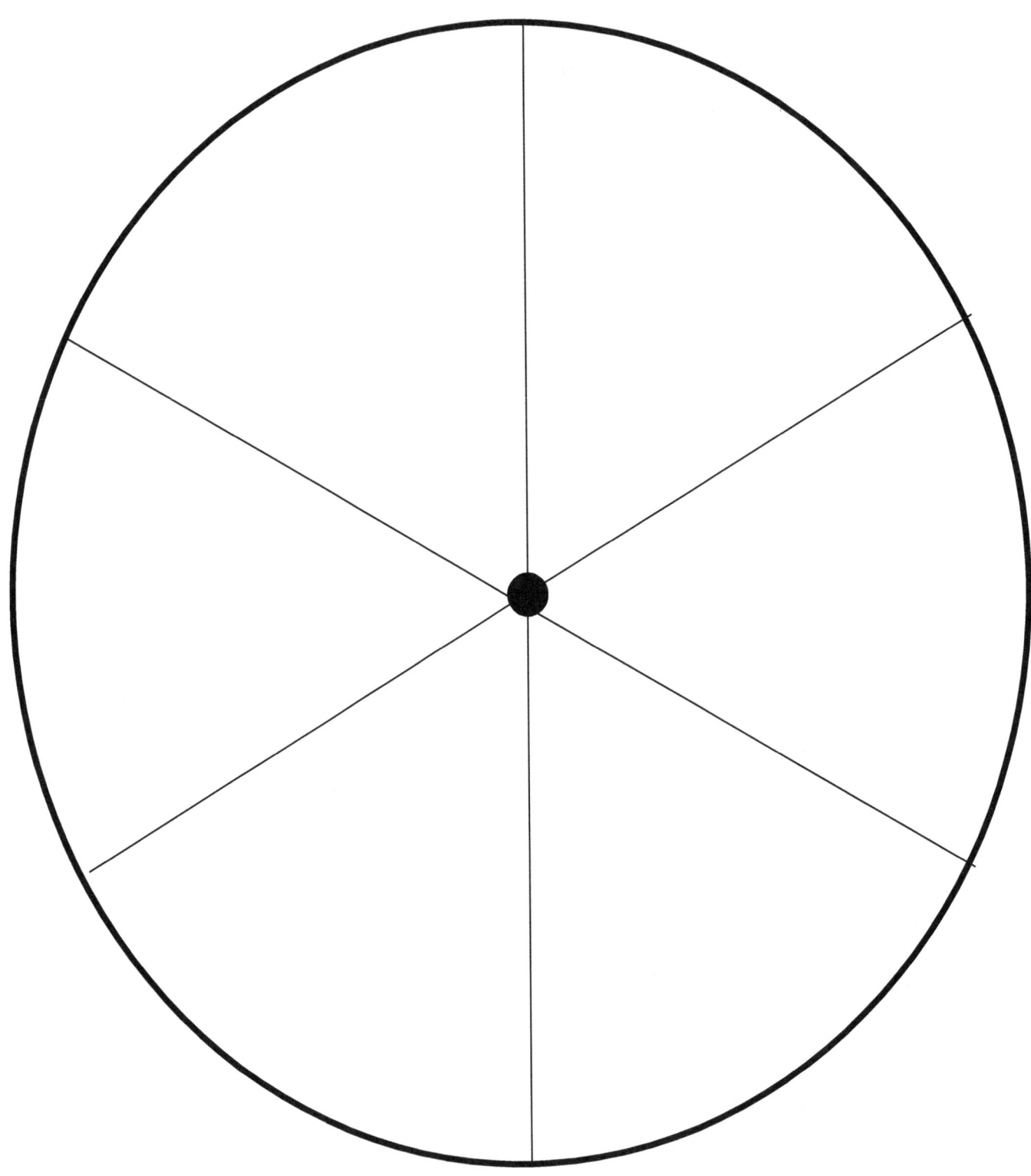

Feelings Target

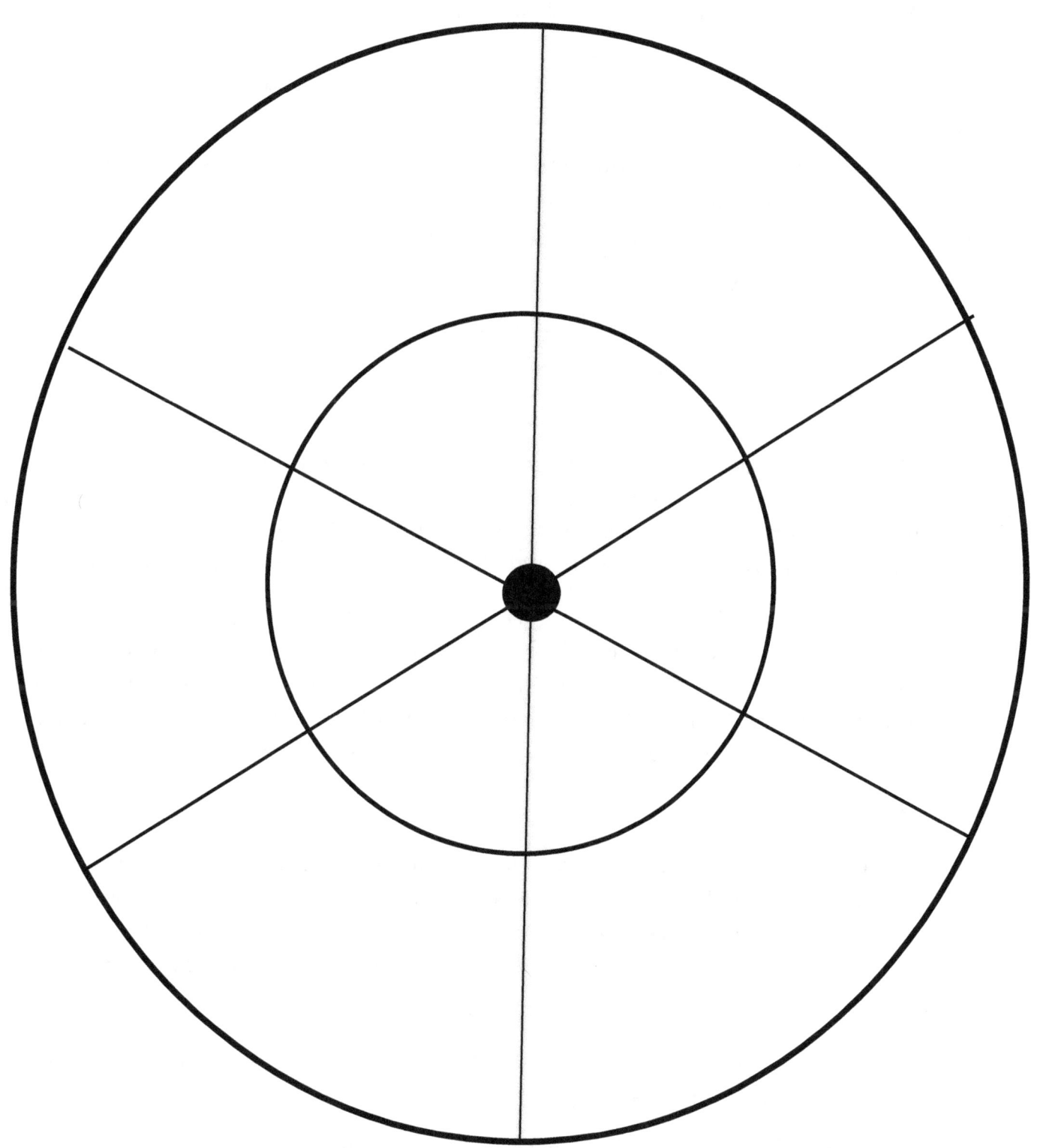

My Collage - Reloaded

Ages: Middle (7-11) and Adolescents (12- up)

Materials:

- Construction paper
- Safety scissors, non-toxic glue
- Copy of the My Collage-Feelings Chart
- Magazines or box of several pre-cut pictures
- Optional: Stickers, markers, crayons, color pencils

Rationale:

My Collage- Reloaded takes a different spin on collaging. While not a new concept, collages are a time-tested, fun, and non-threatening tool that is still an effective and relevant intervention to use with clients. As such, collaging is included in this manual. This is a meaningful individual activity and is very powerful when used with a family or a group.

Family or group application: 1) The family or group members complete collages individually and share their individual projects with the group. Or, 2) Family or group members collaborate on one community collage. The treatment provider processes the group experience and points out emerging themes.

Directions:

1. **Treatment provider Says:** *Now that we have talked about counseling ending, Let's make a collage that describes what services have been like for you from the beginning to now. Since this collage focuses on feelings, let's first choose some feelings from the chart that describe your journey in counseling. What feelings about counseling will you include?*

2. Treatment provider may use the following questions to help client select and cut out feelings from the chart.

   - What feelings did you have about beginning counseling?

- What feelings do you have about goals you had?
- What feelings describe making progress in counseling?
- What feelings describe saying good-bye?
- What feelings describe what you will miss the most about counseling?
- What feelings describe what you will you miss the least about counseling?

3. Client cuts out feeling words and glues them to the construction paper (theme the feelings together...I had these feelings in the beginning...I felt this about my goals...I felt these feelings about my progress...).

4. Client searches for collaging pictures that express the feelings glued to the construction paper, then glues the picture(s) over the feeling word(s).

5. In the finished product, all the words are covered and the page is filled with pictures.

6. **Treatment provider processes the collage:**

- Tell me about your collage...
- What part speaks to the beginning of counseling?
- What part speaks to the goals you had?
- What part speaks to the best part of counseling?
- What part speaks to what it is like to say good-bye?
- What part of counseling will you miss the most?
- What part of counseling will you miss the least?

My Collage - Feelings Chart

Able to dream	Alive	Forgiving
Mistrustful	Angry	Hurt
Understood	Bored	Embarrassed
Brave	Comforted	Touched
Rejected	Crushed	Tormented
Open	Happy	Alive
Upset	Hateful	Lost
Relieved	Healed	Positive
Calm	In Control	Determined
Lucky	Joyful	Glad
Free	Pleased	Comforted
Hopeful	Rebellious	Strong
Scared	Surprised	Playful
Important	Thankful	Tired
Safe	Understood	Trusting
Unsure	Uneasy	Uncomfortable
Lonely	Unhappy	Grieving
Tense	Worried	Sad

Color My Time in Counseling

Ages: Young (5-6), Middle (7-11), and Adolescents (12- up)

Materials

- Colored markers, crayons, Pencils, Pens, etc...
- Paper

> **How This Activity Builds Resilience:** Having strong emotional and cognitive regulation and self-control skills create building blocks for resilience. Reinforces goal attainment and personal competence.

Rationale:

The *Color My Time in Counseling* was adapted from the "Color Your Life" technique introduced by Kevin O'Connor (1983). In the traditional use of the technique, feelings are paired with colors (ie., red=angry; purple = rage; blue= sad; black = very sad; green = jealous; brown = bored; gray = lonesome; yellow= happy; orange = excited) to create a picture representing the client's internal feelings. The client is given a blank piece of paper and the treatment provider instructs the client to let the paper represent his or her life. The client then fills the page with colors that represent feelings the client has. The *Color My Time in Counseling* activity was adapted for termination and is appropriate for individual, family, or group treatment.

You may use this activity with young clients if the processing remains very concrete. Engaging a 5-7 year old in past, present, future processing is difficult because it calls for a level of cognitive development s/he may not have attained.

Family or group application: 1) The family or group members complete projects individually and share his/her individual projects with the group. Or, 2) Family or group members collaborate on a community project. The treatment provider processes the group experience and points out emerging themes.

Directions:

1. Fold one piece of paper in half. Unfold it and at the top on one side write, "The beginning of counseling" and on the other side write, "The end of counseling".

127

2. Treatment provider directs the client to start with the side of the page labeled "The beginning of counseling" and fill in that side of the page with colors, words or pictures representing feelings s/he recalls having about life at the beginning of treatment, including how it felt to begin treatment (If appropriate, provider completes a review to refresh client's memory.)

3. The client fills in the first half of the page following the directions given.

4. Treatment provider reviews same directions for the second half of the page labeled "The end of counseling." This side of the page is filled in with colors, words or pictures representing feelings s/he currently has about life, including how s/he feels about counseling ending.

5. Treatment provider processes both sides of the page- one at a time. Keep the focus on feelings.

 The goal is to process the client's range of feelings about treatment ending. Be mindful that it is not the time to discuss coping skills, strategies etc. When the client has fully processed his/her feelings, move on to Step 3.

My Story: Chapter 2

Ages: Young (5-6), Middle (7-11), and Adolescents (12- up)

Materials:

- Copy of My Story Chapter 2
- Use any activity from Step 2:
  Process the Range of Feelings
  about Treatment Ending.
  Insert activities after the Chapter 2 title page.

> **How This Activity Builds Resilience:**
> Having strong emotional and cognitive regulation and self-control skills are building blocks for resilience. Reinforces goal attainment and personal competence.

Rationale:

My Story has four chapters that you can use to process all 4 termination steps. It is best utilized with an individual to process the therapeutic experience (some treatment providers have used it successfully with families). Storytelling is a powerful clinical tool that is often used in evidenced-based practice models.
Constructing a creative narrative about the treatment experience gives the client the opportunity to process his/her thoughts and feelings in a concrete way with the support of a trusted treatment provider.

> **Though this is a narrative activity, engage the right brain with colors, symbols, pictures and other creative elements.**

To complete Chapter 2, select any activity in Step 2 (Process the range of feelings about treatment ending) to insert into the chapter. Which activity (and how many) to select is at the discretion of the treatment provider. If unsure which activity to choose or how many, you should seek the consultation of a licensed colleague or supervisor for assistance. If desired, combine the individual sections into one book and give it to the client during the last session.

Directions:

1. Select any activity in Step 2 and insert into the *My Story: Chapter 2* book.
2. The treatment provider supports the client to complete the activity with as much or as little involvement as is clinically appropriate.
3. Once the activity is completed, the treatment provider processes the activity with the client.

Below is a description of what each section in "My Story" contains:

Chapter One: Educates the client about treatment ending and puts supports in place to pre-empt early termination.

Chapter Two: Processes the client's range of feelings about treatment ending, including that addressing feelings may trigger previous losses.

Chapter Three: Prepares the client to manage life after treatment ends.

Chapter Four: Honors the relationship and brings treatment to an end.

My Story

Chapter 2

My feelings about counseling ending

STEP THREE

Prepare Client to Manage Life After Treatment Ends

21st Century Seminars

where professionals grow

132

STEP THREE

Prepare Client to Manage Life After Treatment Ends

Step 3, is the largest window of opportunity to enhance resilience before treatment ends. During this step, you will: 1) Address the remaining work to be done; 2) Prepare the client for set-backs, trauma reminders, and difficult anniversaries; and, 3) Ensure your client is connected to an resilience building support system (family, friends, community, school etc.) and asset-building activities.

Some treatment providers move immediately from Step 1 to Step 3, skipping over processing the client's feelings about termination. It is important step to process the client's feelings about termination. While it may be easier to focus on concrete skill building than the awkward feelings evoked by termination, if the client has not made sense of the range of feelings about treatment ending, his/her ability to emotionally invest in preparing for a life after treatment ends, may be compromised.

What to do:

1. Review treatment goals. Identify remaining work to be fine-tuned.

2. Build Resilience: Prepare client to maintain skills and manage future challenges, anniversaries, and trauma reminders.

3. Build Resilience: Encourage client to connect with caregivers, community supports and to participate in asset-building activities.

How to do it:

1. Review treatment goals, discuss progress made and remaining work to be done.

Reviewing treatment goals during termination involves balancing the goals and successes the client has already achieved with identifying the remaining work to be fine-tuned during termination.

Allow the client to lead the discussion about his/her own progress, versus you telling the client what s/he has achieved. If the client's feedback is accurate, validate and support the progress made and devise a plan to address the remaining work. If the client's assessment of his/her own progress is not accurate or s/he minimizes the progress made, you have the opportunity to address any self-defeating distortions, thinking errors or unhelpful thoughts.

Most evidence-based practice models include periodic goal reviews so if this process is up-to-date, move on to the next task of preparing the client to manage and maintain skill and supports after treatment.

Theme remaining work to termination.

After the goal review, you may have a list of issues your client wants to address prior to treatment ending (for example, anger management, refusal skills, bullying strategies, etc.). Frame the work in terms of how the client can be prepared to manage these issues if they arise after treatment ends. This way, termination remains alive during this very important skill-building phase.

Case Transfers and Premature Terminations

If your client is transferring to another treatment provider or has informed you s/he is terminating prematurely, you can still complete a goal review and coach the client on how to discuss the gains made and the remaining work to be completed with the new treatment provider. The worksheet *About Me* follows the goal review and is used with individuals or families who are transferring to a new treatment provider due to a case transfer or a premature termination. With premature terminations, you should use this worksheet even if you are uncertain whether or not your client will re-enroll in treatment elsewhere. It is typically best practice to recommend the client continue treatment and this is a helpful worksheet to facilitate this process. Use the completed worksheet to empower the client to articulate his/her needs to a future treatment provider in the event that s/he re-enrolls in treatment.

Once your client has the information for the new treatment provider, you have completed all of the relevant elements of Step 3 (including some coaching on how to maintain the gains made thus far and planning for future challenges). Move on to Step 4, to honor the therapeutic relationship and end treatment.

2. Build Resilience: Prepare client to maintain skills and manage future challenges, anniversaries, and trauma reminders.

After identifying the remaining work to be fine-tuned, use this information to prepare the client to manage and maintain the skills and supports needed to maintain success after treatment ends. This is the time to reinforce the asset-building factors promoting resiliency such as improved frustration tolerance, cognitive regulation, and behavior control. Focus on strengthening concrete coping skills, for example; deep breathing, cognitive reframing, thought stopping etc. Identify supports in your client's family, community, and school and any extra-curricular, recreational, or community activities that function as protective assets. And, prepare the client for set-backs, trauma reminders, and difficult anniversaries.

Before, during, and after treatment themes: Process what the client's life was like before treatment, how things have changed for the client during treatment, and how things will be different after treatment ends. Identify the client's strengths, skills, supports, and assets which helped the client work through the challenges that existed before the client entered treatment. Incorporate these strengths, skills, supports, and assets into a coping plan or a survival kit for the client to use as a reference after treatment ends.

The *Road to my Success; Color my Time in Treatment; Color my Future; Bag of Skills; Basketball; My Survival Kit,* contain before, during and after themes and facilitate identifying coping skills, strengths, safety plans, family and community supports. All of these interventions help address remaining work to be done by re-teaching concepts and reinforcing skills as needed. Additionally, many of these interventions encourage creating written plans the client can take with him/her after treatment ends.

What I Need for the Future themes: What I Need for the Future themes, include preparing the client for future disappointments, trauma reminders, losses, and challenges. Termination must involve asset-building problem solving, such as, how the client will get his/her needs met after treatment ends, building personal safety skills and identifying the skills to address future disappointments, trauma reminders, losses, and challenges. It is helpful for you to process fears of the future and normalize set-backs. Predict, plan, and prepare for how the client will cope with difficult anniversaries and trauma reminders. This work is important to building resilience. Having an internal locus of control, a sense of self-efficacy, and acquiring the skills to handle future challenges are asset-building skills that enhance resiliency across all developmental ages.

Use the *It Will Pass Calendar* to predict times of the year that may be emotionally difficult for the client. The calendar also prompts the client to put a plan in place to directly cope with the anticipated issue. Several other activities such as the *Bag of Skills, Basketball, My Survival Kit, Step-by-Step, Look for the Rainbow, Color my Future; What I Need for my Future; and, When I Look into my Future Visualization Exercise* contain what I Need for the Future themes and address set-backs, difficult anniversaries, and trauma reminders.

3. **Build Resilience: Encourage client to connect with caregivers, community supports and to participate in asset-building activities.**

A positive connection to supports such as, healthy adult and peer relationships; school staff; community resources; extended family and kinship relations, is highly correlated to building resiliency in children and adolescents. Relational work is best implemented at the beginning of treatment to allow time for important bonds to develop. You can be the agent of change that brings healing to a relationship or a referral source that connects a client to a coach, mentor, teacher, sibling, church member, big brother, or sister. If available, network with the professionals in the client's life to find mentoring programs or services for your client. Many probation officers, social workers, CASA (Court Appointed Special Advocates) workers, school counselors, drop out prevention specialists, or case managers, etc., are helpful resources to find programs for your client. Too often, high-risk clients have little to no family or extended family support. However, research shows, a safe, nurturing bond with a single person or having at least one close friend, are important to building resilience. Not all clients will have a plethora of family or community supports, but one relationship can make a powerful difference.

Chapter Summary: Step Three

- Step 3 is the **most important step** during termination to building resilience in your client.

- **In this step**, the treatment provider completes a treatment goal review, identifies and addresses the remaining work to be done, and prepares the client to adjust to what life will be like without the therapeutic relationship.

- Reviewing **treatment goals** involves balancing the goals and successes already achieved, with identifying the remaining work to be fine-tuned.

- Allow the **client to lead** the discussion about his/her progress versus you telling the client what you believe s/he achieved during treatment.

- **Theme** the remaining work to termination. For example, if the client wants to better address anger management skills, etc., frame this in terms of how the client can be prepared to manage his/her anger if the issue arises after treatment ends.

- For **case transfers or pre-mature terminations**, complete a goal review and coach the client how to discuss the gains made and the remaining work to be completed with the new treatment provider. Depending on the case, preparation for future challenges may be limited or not applicable so, you may move to Step 4 rather quickly with case transfers or premature terminations.

- **After identifying the remaining work**, use this information to prepare the client to manage and maintain skills after treatment ends. Pay particular attention to preparing the client for set-backs, trauma reminders and difficult anniversaries.

- **Themes** such as: Comparing life *before, during and after treatment* and, *what I Need for the Future* help the client identify his/her assets and to prepare for future challenges.

- **Reinforce concrete skill building and identify supports** in client's family, community, and school as well as any extra-curricular, recreational, or community activities that can function as protective assets.

- Create concrete **written coping plans and survival kits** for the client to use as a reference after treatment ends.

STEP THREE

Prepare Client to Manage Life After Treatment Ends

Interventions:

1. Guide to Promoting Resilience in Children and Adolescents
2. Goal Review
3. About Me
4. Bag of Skills
5. Basketball
6. Road to My Success
7. My Survival Kit
8. Clay Activity: For the Future
9. When I Look into my Future: Guided Imagery Exercise
10. It Will Pass Calendar
11. Look for the Rainbow
12. Step-by-Step
13. Color My Time in Counseling
14. Color My Future
15. Coping Word Search
16. My Story: Chapter 3

*The worksheets refer to the treatment provider as a "counselor". Feel free to change the worksheets to reflect your work as a counselor, case manager, social worker, psychologist, etc.

What to Do:

1. Review treatment goals and assess for remaining work to be fine-tuned.
2. Build Resilience: Prepare client to maintain skills and prepare for future challenges, anniversaries, and trauma reminders.
3. Build Resilience: Encourage client to connect with caregivers, community supports and to participate in asset-building activities.

STEP THREE
Prepare Client to Manage Life After Treatment Ends

#	Intervention	Goal	Age	M	Materials Needed
1	Guide to Promoting Resilience in Children and Adolescents	Information for Mental Health Professionals	5-18	N/A	Guide included
2	Goal Review	Rating sheets for client to track progress. Different rating sheets for older and younger clients	5-18	I F	Goal Charts included
3	About Me	Assists with transferring information from one provider to another during a case transfer or premature termination.	5-18	I F	Worksheet included. Pen, pencil or maker
4	Bag of Skills	Art activity. End result produces a "bag" of concrete skills for client.	5-18	I F G	2 sheets of paper, pens, pencils, markers. Paper bag
5	Basketball	Kinetic activity using Step 3 themes. Can be used for all 4 termination steps. Engaging and non-threatening. Great for all, especially kids with language or cognitive challenges.	5-18	I F G	Scissors, small container for basketball hoop, and ball for shooting. Includes basketball court and cards
6	Road to my Success	Creative activity. Uses theme of 'road to success' to identify coping skills and plan for future challenges. Engaging, interactive	5-18	I F G	Worksheet included. Colorful pens, crayons, markers
7	My Survival Kit	Concrete, cognitive activity. Client can develop written strategies to manage various topics.	7-18	I F	Scissors, pen, or pencil. Survival kit cards included
8	Clay Activity: For My Future	Clay activity. Expressive arts. Uses symbols to identify items needed to maintain success.	5-18	I F G	Clay. Pen, pencil, or marker. Activity Sheet Included.
9	It Will Pass Calendar	Calendar to list anniversaries and develop pre-emptive coping strategies.	5-18	I F G	Pen or pencil. Calendar included
10	Look for the Rainbow	Creative Activity. Uses the theme of the rainbow to prepare for life after treatment.	5-18	I F G	Colorful pens, pencils, and markers. Worksheet included
11	Step-by-Step	A kinetic game using Step 3 themes. Spans all 4 termination steps. Engaging and non-threatening. Great for kids with language or cognitive challenges.	5-18	I F G	Pen, pencil, marker. Scissors. Stepping Stone template included.
12	Color My Time in Counseling	A continuation from step 2. Creative, art activity to address Step 3 themes. Encourages processing. Can be used to complement *Color My Future*.	5-18	I F G	Paper. Colorful pens, pencils, and markers.
13	Color My Future	Art activity to prepare for future challenges. Can be used alone or to complement "Color My Time in Treatment". Expressive, interactive	7-18	I F G	Paper. Colorful pens, pencils and markers.
14	Coping Word Search	Problem solving game play. Uses a word search made of coping words to prepare for the future.	7-18	I F	Pen, pencil or marker. Word search included
15	My Story: Chapter 3	Narrative activity. Creative, expressive.	5-18	I F	Pen, pencil, crayons or markers. Book included

*The worksheets refer to the treatment provider as a "counselor". Feel free to change the worksheets to reflect your work as a counselor, case manager, social worker, psychologist, etc.

Guide to Promoting Resilience
In Children and Adolescents

Ages: Young (5-6), Middle (7-11), and Adolescents (12- up)

Materials:

- Guide to Promoting Resilience in Children and Adolescents

Rationale:

The *Guide to Promoting Resilience in Children and Adolescents* is a tool to help you understand the factors that build resilience. Research shows developmental assets:

- Build resilience in all young people regardless of their gender, socioeconomic status, race or ethnicity and are stronger predictors of success or failure than poverty or being from a single parent household.

- Protect youth from engaging in high risk and problem behaviors like illicit drug use, suicide attempts and anti-social behavior and promote thriving behavior such as valuing diversity, maintaining good health, and succeeding in school.

Developmental assets will help support your client to thrive in future challenges. This is empowering information for treatment providers as we can help develop and enhance these assets in our clients. Termination represents the last window of opportunity to ensure these factors are in place prior to treatment ending. Your client may not have ALL of the assets listed but remember, the more assets a client has, the greater the likelihood of thriving and not engaging in high-risk behaviors. Be advised this is a tool to use as a guide and is not for diagnostic purposes.

Directions:

- Use the following chart as a guide to determine how to best support resiliency in your client. This is a tool and not a one-size-fits-all cookbook. Your client may have individual and unique needs.

Guide to Promoting Resilience in Children and Adolescents

©21st Century Seminars

21st Century Seminars	What Builds Resilience by Developmental Age	What Builds Resilience in All Ages
Preschool Age Children	• A growing sense of autonomy • Capacity for successful social relationships • Able to manage emotions such as frustration • Able to seek and illicit support from others.	• Able to regulate frustration, has cognitive coping skills and impulse control strategies. • A safe, nurturing bond with a single person (i.e., grandparent, teacher, sibling).
School Age Children	• Self-perceived sense of efficacy, personal competency and self-esteem. Effectively uses a "think before reacting" problem solving style. • Developing an internal locus of control and believes s/he can influence her/his world. • Flexible coping strategies and has a range of ready skills, including the use of humor. • Positive relationships with peers and adults.	• Has at least one close friend and is able to maintain friendships over time. • Has adults/caregivers who communicate positive, age-appropriate expectations for roles and responsibilities. • Faith and religious practices • Reliable emotional support from caregivers who encourage emotional expressiveness.
Adolescents	• Sense of personal responsibility and social maturity. • Believe s/he has some control over her/his own fate and has a desire to control their destiny. • Somewhat achievement oriented • Has goals and can function independently. • Has internalized set of values and can use them to make decisions. • Socially perceptive and able to interact and build relationships with others.	• Positive school experience and feeling connected to the school community. • Feel connected to the larger community. Extended family and neighborhood supports. • Able to make a contribution to their community.

Goal Review

Ages: Young (5-6), Middle (7-11), and Adolescents (12- up)

Materials:

- Goal Chart
- Pen, Pencil, or Marker

> **How This Activity Builds Resilience:**
> Promotes self-efficacy, personal responsibility, autonomy, internal locus of control, personal competency, and self-esteem. Encourages goal orientation and achievement. Identifies a healthy range of coping skills.

Rationale:

Evidence-based practice models typically include periodic goal reviews. So, if this process is complete then move on to other Step 3 activities that focus on skill building. Completing a goal review is a concrete reminder that treatment is ending. It reinforces skills already acquired and identifies the remaining work to be fine-tuning before treatment ends.

 Reviewing goals for young children should primarily involve collaboration with the parents. Young children and those with reading or language issues may require assistance from the treatment provider.

Directions:

1. The treatment provider writes the client's goals on the chart. In general, the provider should be cautious to not overwhelm the client with too many goals and to word them in a positive, strength-based way. Goals for some agency or insurance requirements must be medically necessary, measurable, and observable, and related to improving the client's daily functioning. However, this goal chart is for your client's use and is not intended for insurance or agency purposes, so feel free to word goals in a client-friendly manner to facilitate the goal review.

142

2. **Treatment provider Says:** *Now that we have talked about ending counseling, this activity will help us look at the work we have done together and what work we still have left to do before services end.*

3. The treatment provider directs the client to rate his/her progress with his/her treatment goals. The answer will either be "met", "not met" or "so-so". For clarity, the provider may explain the meaning of these words to younger children.

4. Encourage honesty and give praise and encouragement. Remember to reinforce the idea that the client is ready to terminate because of the positive progress made in treatment. It is natural to still have some things to work on in the weeks leading to termination.

5. Feedback from the goal review is used to revisit strategies, coping skills strengths, and people in the client's world that can help him/her to be successful.

6. If the client underestimates or minimized the gains made, the provider has the opportunity to intervene and help the client to explore why this is, and to then embrace his/her success.

Sample Goal Chart for middle to adolescents:

My Goals	Met	Partially Met	Not Met
1. I learned ways to control my anger			
2. I learned about grieving			
3. I can make and keep friends			
4. I can use words to ask for what I need			
5. I can talk about my strengths			

Sample Goal Chart for young to middle:

My Goals	😊😊👍	SO-SO 😊	😞👎
1. I learned ways to control my anger			
2. I learned about grieving			
3. I can make and keep friends			
4. I can use words to ask for what I need			
5. I can talk about my strengths			

My Goal Chart

Name: _____

My Goals	Met	Partially Met	Not Met

My Goal Chart

Name: _____

My Goals	😊😊 👍	😊 SO-SO	☹ 👎

About Me

Ages: Young (5-6), Middle (7-11), and Adolescents (12- up)

Materials:

> **How This Activity Builds Resilience:** Promotes self-efficacy, personal responsibility, autonomy, internal locus of control, personal competency, and self-esteem. Encourages goal orientation and achievement. Reinforces age-appropriate expectations for roles and responsibilities, and supports building a positive relationship with an adult.

- About Me-Worksheet
- Markers, Pens, Pencils

Rationale:

The *About Me* activity follows the Goal Review and is used with individuals or families who are transferring to a new treatment provider due to a case transfer or a premature termination. Use this worksheet with premature terminations even if you are uncertain whether or not your client will re-enroll in treatment elsewhere. It is typically best practice to recommend the client continue treatment and this is a helpful tool to facilitate this process.

Once your client has completed the worksheet, you have completed all of the relevant elements of Step 3. Move on to Step 4, to honor the therapeutic relationship and end treatment.

Family application: 1) Complete worksheet with your client individually, then share the worksheet with the parent(s); Or, 2) Complete worksheet as a family activity and process the experience. Prepare the client and family for the transfer or, provide psychoeducation on why continued treatment will be beneficial.

Directions:

1. After you complete a goal review, you can use this worksheet to document the information the client wishes to share with the new treatment provider. If appropriate, coach your client on how to share the information with the new provider. Depending on the developmental and cognitive abilities, the client may share his/her thoughts in words, symbols or pictures...Be creative.

About Me

My Name Is:

My Favorite Things to do Are:

My Strengths Are:

My Goals Were:

I Want to Keep Working On:

Bag of Skills

Ages: Young (5-6), Middle (7-11), and Adolescents (12- up)

Materials:

- Paper bag
- 2 Sheets of paper
- Markers, Pens, Pencils

> **How This Activity Builds Resilience:** Helps client develop a healthy range of coping skills that can be applied to many scenarios. Promotes personal responsibility, social maturity, and internal locus of control. Reinforces ability to influence own fate. Encourages building healthy relationships with others. Connects clients to positive adults, caregivers, community members, and school supports.

Rationale:

The *Bag of Skills* is a common, art-based intervention that was adapted for termination. It can be used individually, with a family, or group. It encourages the client to identify the coping skills, affirmations, strengths, and people in their lives who helped him/her grow from the person s/he was at the beginning of treatment to person s/he is at the end of treatment. By the end of the intervention, the client will have a "bag of skills" that will help support his/her progress after treatment ends. Share the final product with caregivers as appropriate.

Family or Group application: Making a successful "bag of skills" may vary significantly between individual members. Smaller groups are more conducive to this intervention than larger groups. Encourage group processing as members can gain knowledge and skills from their common experiences. In family work, members discuss how the family unit can support one another with their skills. The family may also make skill cards specifically for issues the family unit will face (i.e., communication; the anniversary of a death, etc.)

Directions:

1. On a sheet of paper, the client writes statements, feeling words, or symbols that describe what he/she found challenging or wanted to change about his/her life before treatment began. These statements or feeling words should be cut into strips and placed inside of the decorated paper bag.

2. Decorate the outside of the bag with statements, feelings, or symbols that describe what the client likes about his/her life now or what has improved since treatment began.

3. The client reaches into the paper bag and takes out one statement or feeling word at a time and discusses what s/he has learned in treatment that has helped her/him move from "the person described inside of the bag to the person described on the outside of the bag".

4. Process Questions to Consider:

    *   What has changed in your life for the better since starting counseling?
    *   What are some skills you learned in counseling that will help you in the future?
    *   What are your strengths and how can these strengths help make your life better?
    *   What has not changed in your life as much as you wanted it to?
    *   What do you see as the biggest challenges you will face in the next few months or years after counseling ends?
    *   What are some times of the year when you may have some set-backs?
    *   How should you plan for difficult anniversaries or trauma reminders?
    *   How can you apply the skills you learned in counseling to deal with the challenges?
    *   Who are people in your home, school or community you can rely on to support you after counseling ends?

5. As each statement is processed, the treatment provider or client keeps a list on a separate sheet of paper, of the strategies, coping skills, strengths and supportive people that helped the client be successful on a separate sheet of paper. The treatment provider can add strategies, skills, and strengths with discretion. Strategies can be role-played or rehearsed if the client needs more work to solidify the skills.

6. Once all of the strips on the inside of the bag have been taken out, the list of strategies, coping skills, strengths, or supportive people, should be reviewed, and and placed inside of the paper bag. At the end of treatment, the client keeps the "bag of skills" to use as a support.

7. This intervention may take place over more than one session. The paper bag can be used as a transitional object on the last day of treatment.

Basketball

Ages: Young (5-6), Middle (7-11), and Adolescents (12- up)

Materials:

- Over-the-door Basketball Hoop Or, any container can be substituted for a basketball hoop.

- Basketball Cards and Game Board

- Small ball; or make a basketball using a crumpled piece of paper or foil.

- Treatment provider can mix in some, none, or all of the "fun" cards

Rationale:

Some clients are kinetic learners and make good use of activities that are combined with physical activity. *Basketball* can be played individually, with a family, or a group. *It* directs the client to shoot a ball into to a "hoop" and to draw termination-themed playing cards. There are basketball games for Steps 1, 2, 3 and 4. The cards in this activity were specifically designed to help the client work through the issues outlined in Step 3: Preparing the client to manage life after treatment ends. The game directions are the same but, the cards change based on the task. The basketball game can be used over several sessions to process the different tasks (just add on the appropriate cards) or the games can be played independently, depending on the needs of the client. Share the final product with caregivers as appropriate.

Family or group application: Each family or group member takes a turn shooting a basket and answering a question while the treatment provider facilitates a group discussion and points out emerging themes.

Part One: Educates the client about treatment ending and puts supports in place to pre-empt early termination.

Part Two: Processes the client's range of feelings about treatment ending, including that addressing feelings may trigger previous losses.

Part Three: Prepares client to manage life after treatment ends.

Part Four: Commemorates the relationship and brings treatment to an end.

Directions:

1. **Treatment provider says:** *Now that we have talked about ending counseling, there is a game I would like us to play together. It will help us talk about the skills you need to stay successful after counseling ends. We are going to shoot baskets. If you make it, take a 'hoop card' and if you miss a shot, take a 'brick card'.* **Optional:** Write the client's answers on the back of each card. Bind the cards together with a binder ring(s) to make a booklet or place the cards in a decorated container. Give the cards to the client on the last session as a transitional object.

2. Treatment provider draws and answers cards as well. Provider processes the client's answers or facilitates ideas as appropriate.

3. If one stack becomes depleted before the other, the provider can say something like, *"Let's see what the other cards say, just for the fun of it..."*

4. The cards can be photocopied and laminated for durability.

Step 3...Cards for Basketball:

Hoop: Before counseling ends, I want to work on these things…	**Brick:** How will you cope with future set-backs?
Hoop: What strengths have helped make things in your life better?	**Brick:** What has changed in your life for the better since you starting counseling?
Hoop: What has not changed in your life as much as you wanted it to?	**Brick:** When hurt happens in the future, how will you help yourself feel better?
Hoop: Name 5-7 strategies or coping skills you learned in counseling?	**Brick:** When you think about the future, what are some things that you worry about?
Hoop: What are the times of the year when you may have some set-backs?	**Brick:** Name people you can go to for support after counseling ends.

Fun Basketball Cards:

Hoop: Say something positive about yourself and take another turn	**Brick:** Lose a turn
Hoop: Make a trick shot	**Brick:** Make an over the shoulder shot
Hoop: Close your eyes and make a shot	**Brick:** If you could make a wish what would it be?
Hoop: Stand on one foot and make a shot	**Brick:** If you could change one thing about the world what would you change?
Hoop: Name one thing about yourself that you would never want to change	**Brick:** What one thing about your future you are looking forward to.

Basketball Board Game

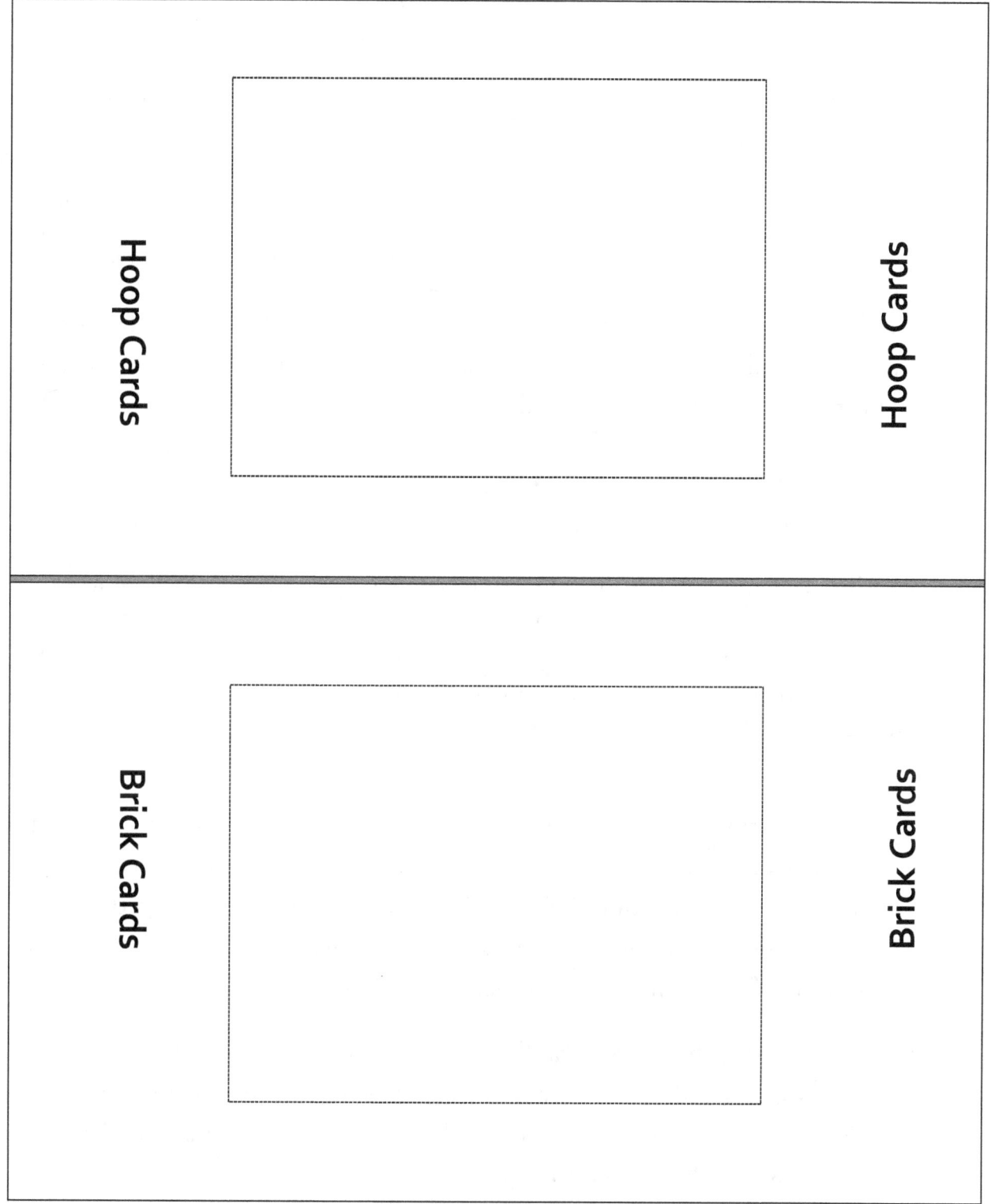

Hoop Cards

Hoop Cards

Brick Cards

Brick Cards

Basketball Game Board

Road to My Success

Ages: Young (5-6), Middle (7-11), and Adolescents (12- up)

Materials:

- "Road to My Success" Worksheet
- Markers, Pens, Colored Pencils

Rationale:

The *Road to My Success* can be used for individual, family, and group intervention and accomplishes several things. First, it supports the client to identify the strengths, coping skills, and other assets that helped the client reach his/her goals. Second, it helps the client understand the role these assets can play in maintaining forward progress once treatment ends. Finally, identifying "road blocks" supports the client to predict, plan, and prepare for future challenges. Share the final product with caregivers as appropriate.

Family or group application: 1) Family or group members complete worksheets individually and share them with the group. Or 2) A family completes one worksheet collaboratively and includes themes related to the family's future success. The treatment provider processes the group's experience and highlights emerging themes.

Directions:

1. Use the activity sheet to guide client. On the side of the sheet labeled "then," the client lists (in words, symbols or pictures) what he/she found challenging or wanted to change about his/her life before treatment began. In the area labeled "now," the client lists (in words, symbols or pictures) what s/he likes about his/her life now, as treatment is ending.

2. In the "Strengths/Coping Skills/People" area, the treatment provider and client discuss and list the strengths, coping skills, strategies, and people in the client's support system that assisted the client to move from "then" to "now." In the "Road Block" section, the treatment provider should work with the client to discuss and list (in words, symbols, or pictures) potential road blocks (including anniversaries and trauma reminders) to maintaining the success achieved and how to overcome the road blocks.

156

Road to My Success

Strengths / Coping Skills/ People

Road Blocks

My Survival Kit

Ages: Middle (7-11) and Adolescents (12- up)

Materials:

- "Survival Kit" cards
- Pen, Pencil, Scissors

Rationale:

> **How This Activity Builds Resilience:** Helps client develop a healthy range of coping skills that can be applied to many scenarios. Promotes personal responsibility, social maturity, and internal locus of control. Reinforces ability to influence own fate. Encourages building healthy relationships with others. Connects clients to positive adults, caregivers, community members, and school supports.

The *My Survival Kit* activity consists of 36 cards, labeled with a range of life issues (depression, strengths, anger, family, bullying, set-backs, etc.) This is a very personalized activity that is best used with individuals. Share the final product with the caregiver(s) as appropriate. The cards are used to make a survival kit that will help prepare the client for life after treatment ends. The treatment provider can work with the client to select the topics appropriate for the client's unique needs. There are blank cards to add life issues as needed. With each topic, identify and discuss the strengths, coping skills, people, and other assets the client has available to successfully manage each situation. This plan should be written on the back of each survival kit card. Place the completed cards in a container of choice or make a booklet with binder rings. Include strengths and words of encouragement. Be creative and decorate the container or make a personalized booklet. Experiment with different materials to cover the booklet (felt, foam, cloth, etc.).

Family or Group Application: N/A

Directions:

1. **Treatment Provider Says:** *As we prepare for you to end counseling, it is important to create a Survival Kit to plan for future situations. To make our survival kit, we will select feelings, situations or events that may be challenging for you in the future. We can also add topics if we need to. On the back of each card, we will write what you can say or do to cope with each situation. When you experience one of these situations after treatment ends, you can use the tips on these cards to help you cope until the feeling(s) or situation passes.*

Survival Kit Cards

Survival Kit

**Positive Thoughts
and Words of
Encouragement**

Survival Kit

Depression

Survival Kit

Self-Control

Survival Kit

Anger

Survival Kit

Stress

Survival Kit

Anxiety / Worry

Survival Kit Cards

Survival Kit **Self-Injury**	Survival Kit **Negative Thoughts**
Survival Kit **My Strengths**	Survival Kit **Grief**
Survival Kit **Sadness**	Survival Kit **Suicidal Thoughts**

Survival Kit Cards

Survival Kit **Nightmares**	Survival Kit **Fears**
Survival Kit **Alcohol Use**	Survival Kit **Drug Use**
Survival Kit **Trouble with my Parents**	Survival Kit **Trouble in School**

Survival Kit Cards

Survival Kit

Neighborhood Trouble

Survival Kit

People in my Support System

Survival Kit

Hearing Voices

Survival Kit

My Biggest Challenges

Survival Kit

Seeing Things that are Not There

Survival Kit

Anniversaries

162

Survival Kit Cards

Survival Kit **Running Away**	Survival Kit **Bullying**
Survival Kit **Internet Issues** **(Texting/Social Networking)**	Survival Kit **Upsetting Reminders**
Survival Kit **Gossip**	Survival Kit **Teasing**

Survival Kit Cards

Survival Kit **Healthy Thoughts**	Survival Kit **Self-Care**
Survival Kit **Sense of Humor**	Survival Kit
Survival Kit	Survival Kit

Clay Activity: For the Future

Ages: Middle (7-11) and Adolescents (12- up)

Materials:

- For the Future Activity Sheet
- Air-dry Clay
- Pen, Pencil, or Marker

> **How This Activity Builds Resilience:**
> Develops coping skills that can be applied to many scenarios. Promotes personal responsibility, social maturity, and internal locus of control. Reinforces ability to influence own fate. Encourages building healthy relationships with others. Connects clients to positive adults, caregivers, community members, and school supports.

Rationale:

Clay Activity: For the Future is a symbolic activity the client engages in with the treatment provider. It may be adapted for family or group sessions as well. It directs the client to make a symbol (out of clay or with a sandtray miniature) that represents him/herself, as well as symbols for items needed to have a successful future. Share the final product with the client's caregiver as appropriate.

Family or group application: Make a symbol that represents the family or group. Family or group members alternate turns, making items that will help the family unit or group members be successful after treatment ends. Members document items on the activity sheet. Treatment provider facilitates the group experience and highlights themes.

Directions:

1. **Treatment Provider Says:** *Today we will continue preparing for counseling to end by talking about things you want to take with you from your experience that will make your life successful after services end. For example, you may want to take some skills you learned, words of wisdom, your strengths, a positive statement, or even a person who you want to rely on to support you. I want you to first take a piece of clay and form it into a shape that represents you (or substitute a sandtray miniature for clay if that is your preference). Then, each of us will take a small piece of clay (or select different miniatures) and make it into something that symbolizes the item you will need to continue your success when counseling ends.*

2. Record the items and what the items symbolize on the activity sheet. Educate the client on how the activity can assist with future challenges.

For the Future Activity Sheet

Item	How It Will Help

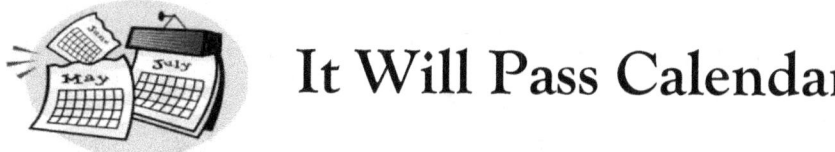

It Will Pass Calendar

Ages: Young (5-6), Middle (7-11), and Adolescents (12- up)

Materials:

> **How This Activity Builds Resilience:** Develops coping skills that can be applied to many scenarios. Promotes personal responsibility, social maturity, and internal locus of control. Reinforces ability to influence own fate. Encourages building healthy relationships with others. Connects clients to positive adults, caregivers, community members, and school supports.

- Will Pass Calendar
- Pens or pencils

Rationale:

The *It Will Pass Calendar* is appropriate for individual, family and group intervention. It supports the client to predict, plan and prepare for difficult anniversaries and trauma reminders such as holidays, places, songs, seasons, birthdays etc. The calendar encourages the client to write in coping thoughts and coping skills to manage the challenges. Remember to also add in positive anniversaries. Parent involvement is usually an important aspect of evidence base practice models. For younger children or older children with developmental disabilities, parent involvement is particularly important, as they may not fully understand the concept of time and anniversaries. Having a supportive, understanding caregiver during sensitive windows is vital.

Family or group application: 1) Family or group members complete worksheets individually and share them with the group. Or 2) A family completes one calendar collaboratively. The treatment provider processes the group experience and highlights emerging themes.

Directions:

1. **Treatment Provider Says:** *Now that we are planning to end counseling, it is important for us to talk about how some times of the year can be more difficult than others. Certain times of the year may bring up sad or difficult memories. Most people have times in their lives when they may feel more happy or sad and you will too. I want us to make a calendar of events that may remind you of sensitive times so we can make a coping plan. I want you to remember that the feelings you have during these times are normal and they will pass.*

It Will Pass Calendar

Month	January	February	March	April	May	June
What I will do to help myself						
Reminder and						

Month	July	August	September	October	November	December
What I will do to help myself						
Reminder and						

Look for the Rainbow

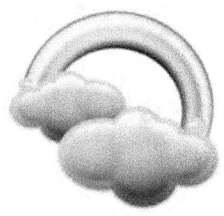

Ages: Young (5-6), Middle (7-11), and Adolescents (12- up)

Materials:

> **How This Activity Builds Resilience:** Develops coping skills that can be applied to many scenarios. Promotes personal responsibility, social maturity, and internal locus of control. Reinforces ability to influence own fate. Encourages building healthy relationships with others. Connects clients to positive adults, caregivers, community members, and school supports.

- Look for the Rainbow Activity Sheet
- Markers, Pens, Pencils

Rationale:

The *Look for the Rainbow* activity is appropriate for individual, family and group intervention. It uses the theme of the rainbow to help the client identify skills needed to help maintain success when treatment ends. Clouds represent future challenges (Including triggers, trauma reminders, and anniversaries). The rainbow represents the coping skills, assets, strengths, and supports that will help overcome the cloudy days. Share the final product with the client's caregiver as appropriate.

Family or group application: 1) Family or group members complete worksheets individually and share them with the group. Or 2) A family completes one activity sheet collaboratively. The treatment provider processes the group's experience and highlights emerging themes.

Directions:

1. **Treatment Provider Says:** *Today we are going to talk about how to prepare for life after counseling ends. I have an activity for us to do together. It's called Look for the Rainbow. What do you think about when you hear the word; cloud?...what about; rainbow?...Today we are going to think of clouds as the things that may make us sad, worried or upset in our lives and rainbows as all the good things that bring us our strengths, coping skills, and people to help us overcome the clouds.*

2. Encourage the client to write in the clouds, things s/he may worry about in the future or that may be challenging for him/her (anniversaries, triggers, reminders, etc.) after treatment ends. In the rainbow, the client writes the strengths, coping skills, or positive thoughts s/he may have to help overcome the challenges that may come on the cloudy days. Process the experience and connect the strengths, coping skills, etc., to managing the challenges

Look for the Rainbow...

170

Step-by-Step

Ages: Young (5-6), Middle (7-11), and Adolescents (12- up)

Materials:

- Copy "stones" as needed
- Optional: laminate "stone"

> **How This Activity Builds Resilience:** Develops coping skills that can be applied to many scenarios. Promotes personal responsibility, social maturity, sense of humor, and internal locus of control. Reinforces ability to influence own fate. Encourages building healthy relationships with others. Connects clients to positive adults, caregivers, community members, and school supports.

Rationale:

Step-by-Step is a kinetic play therapy game. Games involving physical challenges are fun and engaging for most people and are a good way to engage the client around a sensitive topic. In this game, the client moves from one "stone" to another to answer questions about termination. After stepping on a stone, the client (or treatment provider) picks up the stone, reads the question written on it, and answers the question. There are Step-by-Step activities for Steps 1, 2, 3 and 4. This section addresses Step 3 issues to prepare the client to manage life after treatment ends. This activity may be used independently or used over several sessions to work through the entire termination process. If used the latter way, the script should be altered to include: *Imagine this path is like your life and each step will take us closer to ending treatment and to you reaching your life goals. Each week we will lay out more stones to help us set goals, practice the things we have learned together, and prepare for your graduation from treatment.* Optional: Bind "stones" together or place in a notebook or envelope and give them to the client on the last session as a transitional object.

Family or Group Application: Members take turns stepping on the "stones" and answering questions. Treatment provider facilitates a discussion per the emerging themes. Add background music for fun. Play with various moves like: Do the chicken walk to your next answer. Walk like a monkey. Move like a snake. Hop like a rabbit. Do your coolest walk, etc. If office space is an issue, vary placement of the stones among the floor, walls and furniture...Be creative. If mobility is an issue due to physical disability or limitation, use a beanbag that the client can toss onto the answer sheets.

Directions:

1. Treatment provider writes one Discussion Question onto each "stone" (For example: if using 5 questions, there should be 5 stones.) Then, place each "stone" on the floor.

2. **Treatment says:** *We have talked about counseling ending and what it feels like to say good-bye. Now we are going to have some fun with preparing for when services end. The exercise is called "step-by-step." There is a question written on each stone. As you step on each stone, read and answer the question written on it.*

3. Treatment provider facilitates discussion and processes feelings as the client moves through the questions. For example, with the discussion question, "What has changed in your life for the better since you started treatment?" You may engage the client in a discussion about strengths, to reinforce client's readiness to end treatment.

Discussion Questions:

- What has changed in your life for the better since you started counseling?
- What have you learned from counseling that will help you in the future?
- What strengths can help make things better in your life?
- What has not changed in your life as much as you wanted it to?
- What are times of the year when you may have some set-backs?
- How will you cope with future set-backs or upsetting reminders of past trouble?
- When you think about the future, what are some things you worry about? What are some things that make you feel hopeful?
- When hurt or disappointment happens in the future, how will you help yourself feel better?
- Who are the people you can go to for support after counseling ends?

Fun Discussion Questions to mix in at treatment provider's discretion:

- If you could change one thing about the world, what would you change?
- Stand on one leg and give yourself a compliment.
- Name one thing about yourself that you would never want to change?

"Stone" for Step-by-Step Activity:

Color My Time In Counseling

Ages: Young (5-6), Middle (7-11), and Adolescents (12- up)

Materials

- Coloring utensils
- Paper

> **How This Activity Builds Resilience:** Helps client develop a healthy range of coping skills that can be applied to many scenarios. Promotes personal responsibility, social maturity, and internal locus of control. Reinforces ability to influence own fate. Encourages building healthy relationships with others. Connects clients to positive adults, caregivers, community members, and school supports.

Rationale:

The *Color My Time in Counseling* was adapted from the "Color Your Life" technique introduced by Kevin O'Connor (1983). In the traditional use of the technique, feelings are paired with colors (i.e., red=angry; purple = rage; blue= sad; black = very sad; green = jealous; brown = bored; gray = lonesome; yellow= happy; orange = excited), to create a picture representing the client's internal feelings. The client is given a blank piece of paper and the treatment provider instructs the client to let the paper represent his or her life. The client then fills the page with colors that represent feelings the client has. The *Color My Time In Counseling* activity in this manual was adapted for termination and can be used in individual, family, or group work.

You can use this activity with young clients if the processing remains very concrete. Engaging a 5-7 year old in past, present, future processing is difficult because it calls for a level of cognitive development s/he may not have attained.

Family or group application: 1) Family or group members complete activity individually and share them with the group. Or 2) A family may collaborate on a community project. Provider processes the group experience and emerging themes.

Directions:

1. Fold one piece of paper in half. Unfold it and at the top on one side write; "The beginning of counseling" and on the other side write; "The end of counseling".

2. Treatment provider directs the client to start with the side of the page labeled "In the beginning of counseling" and fill in that side of the page with colors (words, pictures) that represent feelings s/he had about life at the beginning of counseling. (If appropriate, consider a review first to refresh client's memory).

3. The client completes the first half of the page following the directions given.

4. Treatment provider reviews same directions for the second half of the page labeled "Now that counseling is ending." This side of the page is filled in with colors, words or pictures representing feelings the client currently has about his or her life now that treatment is ending.

5. Use the finished product to process and identify which coping skills, strategies, assets, family, and community supports helped support the client to move from the person s/he was in the beginning of treatment to the person s/he is now at end of treatment. For example, you might say, *I noticed you have less angry and sad feelings at the end of counseling than at the beginning. How do you think this happened? What have you learned in counseling that has helped your anger?*

6. Make a list of the coping skills, strategies, assets, family, and community supports for the client to use as a reference after treatment ends.

7. OPTIONAL: Complement this activity with the *Color My Future* activity to explore the client's hopes and fears of the future and to prepare for set-backs, trauma reminders, and anniversaries.

Color My Future

Ages: Young (5-6), Middle (7-11), and Adolescents (12- up)

Materials

- Coloring utensils
- Construction paper

> **How This Activity Builds Resilience:**
> Helps client develop a healthy range of coping skills that can be applied to many scenarios. Promotes personal responsibility, social maturity, and internal locus of control. Reinforces ability to influence own fate. Encourages building healthy relationships with others. Connects clients to positive adults, caregivers, community members, and school supports.

Rationale:

The *Color My Future* is an art-based activity that has two parts. The first part of the activity engages the individual, family, or group in a discussion about life after treatment. The second part of the activity, engages the client(s) in brainstorming which skills, strengths, and support systems are needed to continue forward progress. The treatment provider can also use the theme of this activity to predict, plan, and prepare for future challenges, anniversaries, and trauma reminders. This activity can be used as a complement to the *Color My Time In Counseling* exercise cited earlier in this manual. Or, the two activities can be done independently. Share the final product with the client's caregiver as appropriate.

As with it's predecessor, *the Color My Future*, activity was adapted from Kevin O'Connor's "Color Your Life" technique (1983). In the traditional use of the technique, feelings are paired with colors (ie., red=angry; purple = rage; blue= sad; black = very sad; green = jealous; brown = bored; gray = lonesome; yellow= happy; orange = excited) to create a picture representing the client's internal feelings. The client is given a blank piece of paper and the treatment provider instructs the client to let the paper represent his or her life. The client then fills the page with colors that represent feelings the client has.

You can use this activity with young clients if the processing remains very concrete. Engaging a 5-7 year old in past, present, future processing is difficult because it calls for a level of cognitive development s/he may not have attained. Simply ask the child to create a coping plan based on the issues (anger, anxiety, worries, nightmares, etc.,). The child colors his/her activity.

Family or group application: 1) Family or group members complete activity individually and share it with the group. Or 2) A family may collaborate on a community project. Provider processes the group experience and emerging themes.

Directions:

1. Provider writes: "How I feel about the Future," on the top of a piece of paper.

2. The provider directs the client to color in the page with colors that represent how the client feels about the future after counseling ends. Sometimes treatment providers draw a 5-6 inch circle in the center of the page because coloring the entire page can be overwhelming.

3. The processing should include what client can do to address any worries or concerns about the future and identify family or community supports the client will need to maintain his/her forward progress. Use this information to create a written coping plan for the client to use after treatment ends.

4. **Consider these discussion prompts:**

- What has changed in your life for the better since you started counseling?
- What have you learned from counseling that will help you in the future?
- What strengths have helped make things better in your life?
- What has not changed in your life as much as you wanted it to?
- What are times of the year when you may be difficult for you?
- How will you cope with future set-backs or upsetting reminders of past troubles?
- When you think about the future, what are some things you worry about?
- When you think about the future, what are some things that make you feel hopeful?
- When hurt or disappointment happens in the future, how will you help yourself feel better?
- Who are the people you can go to for support after counseling ends?

Coping Word Search

Ages: Middle (7-11) and Adolescents (12- up)

Materials:

> **How This Activity Builds Resilience:**
> Reinforces the client's coping skills, assets and supports. Honors ability to influence own fate. Encourages building healthy relationships with others. Connects clients to positive adults, caregivers, community members, and school supports.

- Coping Word Search Worksheet
- Coping Word Search Answer Key
- Markers, Pens, Colored Pencils

Rationale:

Coping Word Search is a puzzle game that challenges the client to search for 16 skills and concepts that will help prepare him/her for a life after treatment. It is appropriate for individual or family use. Introducing a puzzle game into a treatment group may evoke the element of competition and take the focus off of termination. The goal of this intervention is to process what will be helpful for the client after treatment ends. It is okay if your client says an item may not apply to his/her situation. For example, your client may not be anxious. Already having mastery over anxiety can be identified as a strength, or you can take the opportunity to discuss the how the client can use the skills learned in treatment, if faced with anxiety in the future. After all, feeling anxious is a normal part of life; we all encounter some form of anxiety from time to time. You can also tailor the word search to your client's unique needs by saying; *"Hmmmm, cutting is not on the list but if you have an urge to cut in the future..."* It is important to connect the coping skills to what the client has learned about healthy thoughts, feelings and behaviors. The directions encourage the client to create a written coping plan for future challenges. Share the final product with the client's caregiver as appropriate.

Family application: Family members alternate turns finding the coping words. The treatment provider facilitates a family discussion and observes themes as they emerge.

Directions:

1. **Provider Says:** *Today we will continue preparing for counseling to end. Here is a word search puzzle that has 16 items for you to find. After you solve the puzzle, we can discuss how the various items can be a part of helping maintain success after services end.*

2. The provider supports as needed, depending on the developmental, cognitive and language ability of the client. Hint: The first letter of each word in the puzzle is in bold (ie. **H**INT). Shhh...Use this hint at your discretion!

COPING WORD SEARCH

Directions: Using the list below, circle the items hidden in the word search chart. When complete, discuss how the items can be apart of helping you prepare for counseling to end. Some kids/teens find it helpful to use the words to make a written coping plan for the future.

P	R	F	S	P	C	D	Y	V	F	I	X	N	H	E	N	C	W	C	X	S	G	N	M	F
S	Q	F	U	K	O	M	E	W	Q	A	A	N	X	I	E	T	Y	O	H	A	V	W	P	R
U	S	F	P	M	P	X	V	P	K	T	M	E	I	H	L	M	U	M	N	F	I	A	R	I
U	V	E	P	N	I	M	K	X	R	Z	G	I	N	G	C	K	W	M	W	E	D	N	C	E
I	B	Y	O	T	N	U	C	S	B	E	B	N	L	O	W	B	W	U	O	T	D	G	S	N
S	I	W	R	F	G	C	F	E	T	J	S	T	L	Y	M	E	H	N	I	Y	I	E	K	D
R	J	O	T	I	P	K	E	L	M	R	G	S	Y	A	C	A	X	I	R	V	P	R	J	S
E	U	R	S	M	L	K	Z	W	D	K	E	I	I	S	R	R	T	C	I	A	L	T	H	
F	W	R	F	M	A	V	G	P	V	D	G	I	Q	O	T	P	U	Y	O	C	E	N	Y	I
I	Y	I	G	R	N	Q	X	I	T	G	J	E	S	Z	N	O	B	E	B	W	L	Q	R	P
O	W	E	I	H	P	R	E	D	I	C	T	P	L	A	N	P	R	E	P	A	R	E	M	S
D	W	S	P	I	J	N	R	H	U	I	Y	S	R	R	Z	A	W	Y	P	Y	D	R	U	O
H	M	D	E	V	K	Q	I	T	W	I	L	L	P	A	S	S	Z	H	G	H	Q	T	Z	Y
O	I	X	H	S	E	L	F	C	A	R	E	Z	P	G	A	S	T	R	E	N	G	T	H	S
M	E	Q	K	I	H	F	X	P	S	E	T	B	A	C	K	S	S	A	T	N	L	K	M	S

COPINGPLAN	STRESS	ANGER	SETBACKS
DEPRESSION	ANXIETY	ITWILLPASS	SAFETY
COMMUNITY	WORRIES	STRENGTHS	SUPPORTS
FRIENDSHIPS	FAMILY	PREDICTPLANPREPARE	SELFCARE

Coping Word Search: ANSWER KEY

		S		C	D			F								C	S			F
		U		O		E		A	A	N	X	I	E	T	Y	O	A			R
		P		P		P		M								M	F	A		I
		P		I		R		I								M	E	N		E
		O		N		S	E	L								U	T	G		N
	W	R		G		T		S			Y					N	Y	E		D
	O	T		P		R		S								I		R		S
	R	S		L			E		I							T				H
	R			A				S		O						Y				I
	I			N					S		N									P
	E	P	L	A	N	P	R	E	D	I	C	T	P	R	E	P	A	R	E	S
	S																			
					I	T	W	I	L	L	P	A	S	S						
			S	E	L	F	C	A	R	E		S	T	R	E	N	G	T	H	S
					S	E	T	B	A	C	K	S								

© 21st Century Seminars

180

My Story: Chapter 3

Ages: Young (5-6), Middle (7-11), and Adolescents (12- up)

Materials:

- Copy of My Story Chapter 3
- Use any activity from Step 3: Prepare Client to Manage Life After Treatment. Insert activities into Chapter 3.

Rationale:

The *My Story* has four chapters that you can use to process all 4 Termination Steps. It is best used with an individual to process the therapeutic experience (some treatment providers have used it successfully with families). This section focuses on Step 3 themes: Prepare client to manage life after treatment ends. Storytelling is a powerful clinical tool that is often used in evidence-based practice models. Constructing a narrative about the treatment experience gives the client opportunity to process his or her thoughts and feelings in a concrete way with the support of a trusted treatment provider. Share the final product with the client's caregiver as appropriate.

Below is a description of what each section of "My Story" contains:

Chapter One: Educates the client about treatment ending and puts supports in place to pre-empt early termination.

Chapter Two: Processes the client's range of feelings about treatment ending, including that addressing feelings may trigger previous losses.

Chapter Three: Prepares client to manage life after treatment ends.

Chapter Four: Honors the relationship and brings treatment to an end.

My Story
Chapter 3

Preparing to Leave Counseling

My Goals, Skills, and Supports

Survival Kit

It is important to leave counseling with a plan for your future. List the goals you had and the skills you will take with you after counseling ends.

Survival Kit

On the road of life, it is normal to have up's and downs. During the up times we may feel happy, upbeat and confident. During the down times we may feel sad, hurt, and unsure of ourselves. We may even come across reminders or anniversaries of past hurt. We call these things trauma reminders. When these reminders cross our path, we may feel upset or confused all over again. On this page, write or draw what trauma reminders you may come across.

Survival Kit

Healthy thinking is something that everyone can use. Thoughts can change our feelings and how we feel can change our behavior. Healthy thinking can also help us cope with upsetting and confusing trauma reminders. Write or Draw how you will keep your thoughts healthy after counseling ends.

Survival Kit

Now, create a plan for how you will cope and stay relaxed when upsetting or confusing trauma reminders pop up in the future. Make sure to list your coping skills, strengths, and people in your support system that you can go to for support.

STEP FOUR

Honor the Therapeutic Relationship and End Treatment

21st Century Seminars

where professionals grow

STEP FOUR

Honor the Therapeutic Relationship and End Treatment

As each termination step progresses, the client becomes gradually more exposed to the idea of ending the therapeutic relationship. Step 4 begins the process of saying good-bye. This final task involves bringing closure to the client's clinical work by honoring the therapeutic relationship, making meaning out of the therapeutic experience, and ending treatment.

Be ever conscious of ending treatment in a planned, sensitive manner. Research tells us that youth report feeling a stronger bond with their treatment providers toward the middle to end of treatment than at the beginning. Moreover, the quality of the therapeutic relationship is a strong predictor of therapeutic outcome for youth, particularly for those with a history of maltreatment, juvenile delinquency, and externalizing behaviors. You want to transition your client out of treatment with the care and sensitivity with which it began. You also want to end treatment in a way that leaves your client open to future relationships. An unsuccessful ending can potentially impact the treatment outcome and impact how your client manages future relationships.

What to do:

- Support client to make an enduring connection to the treatment provider and the therapeutic relationship.

- Build Resilience: Encourage making meaning out of the treatment experience through altruism and corrective activities.

- Have a final celebration and end treatment.

- Client leaves treatment with skills that promote resiliency and remains open to future relationships.

How to do it:

1. Support client to make an enduring connection to the treatment provider and the therapeutic relationship.

You make an enduring connection when you and your client mutually engage in making rituals, creating namesakes, and making keepsakes that can be used as transitional objects on the last day of treatment. The two of you decide the way you remember your relationship. Activities can include anything from creating a special handshake, word, nickname, or symbol, to making a poem, writing a play, or creating an art project. The two of you can make key chains, necklaces, bracelets, picture frames, hand prints, treasure chests, message bottles, etc., that contain brief, positive messages using strength words, positive affirmations, and wishes for the future. Whatever you decide, it is important to create the object together. Sometimes, due to the excitement of the moment, treatment providers will make the item outside of session to give to the client as a gift. Or providers will observe the client making the object during the session. The goal in this step is to make an item collaboratively that represents the relationship the two of you have built together; thus, the importance of the two of you creating the item together. The product itself can be given to the client, as a transitional object, when treatment ends. This object validates that the therapeutic relationship was real and meaningful.

 When creating commemorative messages for your client, "You" messages to the client are preferred over "I" messages from the treatment provider (i.e., "You deserve the best" vs. "I think you deserve the best"). Treatment is to support the client to discover his/her own strengths and is less about the opinion of the treatment provider.

2. Encourage making meaning out of the therapeutic experience through altruism and corrective activities.

Jacobs (1999) believes that working through childhood traumatic grief includes an existential component. He recommends treatment providers encourage their clients to make meaning out of their experience and find meaning in life after the trauma and or loss. Giving back to others is a powerful way to do this. Resiliency research lends further support for Jacobs' recommendation, as children and adolescents who feel connected to and are able to make a contribution to their community are more resilient than those who do not. Giving back also promotes a belief in a positive future and encourages youth that they can influence their world. There are various ways, large and small, to accomplish this.

Encourage the client to engage in corrective activities, like writing a letter to future clients, with the goal of helping other young people understand mental health treatment, depression, grief, healing, surviving, etc. Or you can help the client understand how impactful being a positive role model can be. Other clients may volunteer in their local community or find ways to adopt an agency or raise money for charitable events. This activity is about helping the client discover what will work for him/her, and is not about what the treatment provider feels the client should do.

 Be aware that finding meaning in the treatment experience is not the same as asking the client to explore "why" s/he became a victim or "why" s/he experienced their trauma. This discussion may not be helpful to your client. A better approach is to explore "how" s/he can use the therapeutic experience to make a contribution to others and the community.

3. Have a final celebration and end treatment

Loss is a real and a profound experience. The treatment provider's goal must be to make termination a different kind of loss; and one that the client is an active participant in rather than a helpless bystander of. For this reason, it is important to include your client in the planning of some kind of celebration to end treatment. This is an empowering process and will support your client to know therapeutic endings can be different than previous painful ones.

Celebrations are a positive way to provide closure to the treatment process. Celebrations vary from provider to provider and agency to agency and do not necessarily involve planning a party for the client or spending money. Celebrate means *to have fun, to have a good time, or to enjoy yourself.* In other words, plan something fun and enjoyable to do with your client. See Appendix A for guidelines on celebrations (use of food and beverages, inviting others, taking pictures, etc.).

4. **Client leaves treatment with skills that promote resilience and remains open to future relationships.**

When set up properly from the beginning, the termination process can yield powerful results. Following the guidelines of this manual, you have the knowledge and skills to include resiliency-building interventions into each step of the termination process. This supports your client to leave treatment feeling confident about his/her ability to thrive and manage future challenges.

Ending treatment in a planned, sensitive manner helps the client terminate in such a way that s/he can remain open to new relationships in the future. Treatment is a process and may continue in the future. If clients can generalize the mistakes of one relationship to future relationships, then they can also learn to generalize the successes of one relationship to future relationships.

The termination process allows us, mental health providers, a unique opportunity to give this life-changing gift to our clients.

Chapter Summary: Step Four

- As each termination step progresses, the client becomes gradually more exposed to the idea of ending the therapeutic relationship.

- Step 4 begins the process of saying good-bye, by honoring the therapeutic relationship, making meaning out of the therapeutic experience, and ending treatment.

- Be ever conscious of ending treatment in a planned, sensitive manner.

- Youth report feeling a stronger bond with their treatment providers toward the middle to end of treatment than at the beginning. The quality of the therapeutic relationship is an especially strong predictor of treatment outcome for youth with a history of maltreatment, juvenile delinquency, and externalizing behaviors.

- An unsuccessful ending can potentially impact treatment outcome and impact how your client perceives future relationships with other treatment providers.

- Honor the therapeutic relationship by engaging in rituals, creating namesakes, and making keepsakes that can be used as transitional objects. Create the object together to symbolize the relationship the two of you built together.

- When making commemorative messages for your client, "You" messages to the client are preferred over "I" messages from the treatment provider. Treatment is to help the client discover his/her own strengths and is less about the opinion of the provider.

- Make meaning out of the therapeutic experience through altruism and corrective activities. Giving back to others is a powerful way to do this.

- When set up properly from the beginning, the termination process can yield powerful results.

- Following the 4-steps to termination in this manual, will support your client to leave treatment feeling resilient and confident about his/her ability to thrive and manage future challenges.

STEP FOUR

Honor the Therapeutic Relationship and End Treatment

Interventions:

1. Hand Prints
2. Positive Affirmation Activities
3. Strength Word Activities
4. Fortune Teller
5. The Power of Positive Words Crossword Puzzle
6. Blow it into the Future
7. Clay Activity: Hand Me the Future
8. Planting a Seed
9. Step-by-Step
10. Basketball
11. Message Book
12. When I Look Into My Future: Guided Imagery Exercise
13. Letter to My Future Self
14. My Story: Chapter 4

*The worksheets refer to the treatment provider as a "counselor". Feel free to change the worksheets to reflect your work as a counselor, case manager, social worker, psychologist, etc.

The Above Activities:

1. Support client to make an enduring connection to the treatment provider and the therapeutic relationship.

2. Build Resilience: Encourage making meaning out of the therapeutic experience through altruism and corrective activities.

3. Confirm final termination celebration.

4. Support client to leave treatment with skills that promote resilience and remaining open to future relationships.

STEP FOUR

Honor the Therapeutic Relationship and End Treatment

#	Intervention	Goal	Age	M	Materials Needed
1	Hand Prints	Art activity. Uses symbolism of the hand to make a keepsake. Theme: how hands can heal. Engaging	5-18	I F G	Paper, colored pens, pencils, pencils, paint or large ink pad
2	Positive Affirmation Activities	Several activities that incorporate positive affirmations into projects. Process how positive words can help others. Creative, interactive	5-18	I F G	Paper. Colorful markers, pens, pencils. Optional craft items, see instructions
3	Strength Word Activities	Several activities that incorporate strength words into projects. Process how the client's strengths can help others. Interactive, creative	5-18	I F G	Paper, markers, pens, colored pencils. Optional craft items, see instructions
4	Fortune Teller	Uses the fortune teller for commemoration and finding meaning. Playful, engaging.	5-18	I F G	Paper. Pen, pencil or marker
5	The Power of Positive Words Crossword Puzzle	Uses a crossword puzzle to encourage discussion of strengths, successes, support system and helping others. Problem solving fun, engaging	7-18	I F	Pen, pencil or marker. Crossword puzzle included
6	Blow It Into the Future	Uses bubble blowing to honor and find meaning. Expressive, creative, engaging, playful	5-18	I F G	Bubbles. Index cards. Binder rings or container for cards
7	Clay Activity: Hand Me the Future	Memorialize hand and finger prints. Encourages theme of using hands to help others. Interactive, engaging, creative, playful	5-18	I F G	Clay. Writing tool for clay.
8	Planting a Seed	Plant a fast-growing seed. Use plant theme as a metaphor for future growth	5-18	I F G	16 oz. plastic cup. Soil. 3-4 sunflower seeds. Water
9	Step-by-Step	A kinetic game using Step 4 themes. Engaging and non-threatening. Great for kids with language or cognitive challenges.	5-18	I F G	Pen, pencil, marker. Scissors. Stepping Stone template included.
10	Basketball	A kinetic game using Step 4 themes. Engaging and non-threatening. Great for all, especially language or cognitive challenges.	5-18	I F G	Scissors, small container for basketball hoop and ball for shooting. Includes basketball court and cards
11	Message Book	Narrative Activity. Creative, expressive	5-18	I F G	Paper. Binder. Colorful writing utensils
12	When I Look Into My Future: Guided Imagery	Relaxation and visualization. Culminates in an art activity. May also be used with the *Letter to My Future Self* activity	7-18	I F G	Paper. Pen, pencil or marker. Optional magazine pictures. All scripts included
13	Letter to My Future Self	Client writes a letter to be mailed to client @ 6 weeks after termination. Narrative, creative, expressive	5-18	I F G	Paper. Pen, pencil or marker. Optional magazine pictures
14	My Story: Chapter 4	Narrative Activity. Creative, expressive	5-18	I F	Pen, pencil, crayons or markers. Book included

Hand Prints

Ages: Young (5-6), Middle (7-11), and Adolescents (12- up)

Materials:

- Paper
- Colored pens, colored pencils, paint, or large ink pad

Rationale:

Handprints are a fun and meaningful way to honor the therapeutic relationship and make meaning out of the treatment experience. It can be adapted for individual, family or group use. In many cultures, hands symbolize work, productivity, or a binding agreement ("let's shake on it"). In some religions the hand represents a blessing or the conduit for healing. Theme the project to remember the work done, how productive the client was in reaching his/her goals, an agreement the treatment provider and client will make about the future, the blessings the client is grateful for, or the healing that the client has done and will continue to do.

Family or group application: 1) Family or group members make individual projects (handprints). Then, each family or group member adds his/her own hand print, positive statement, word, or symbol to each project. Or 2) A family collaborates on one project. Treatment provider facilitates a group discussion and points out emerging themes.

To make the activity commemorative: Treatment provider adds his/her own hand or finger prints, words of encouragement, strength words, and well wishes for the future.

To make meaning out of the treatment experience: Discuss how the client will use his/her hands to help others, make the world a better place, or help other youth with similar experiences.

Directions:

1. Client and treatment provider each trace one or both of their hands on a piece of paper (you can also make hand prints using ink or paint). Then, each writes positive good-bye messages and well wishes for the client's future success.

2. Or impressions of the hands can be made after coating hands with paint or ink and placing hands on paper. Each writes positive good-bye messages and the treatment provider writes well wishes for the client's future success.

3. Use different colors and handprint patterns for creativity.

Sample Hand Prints:

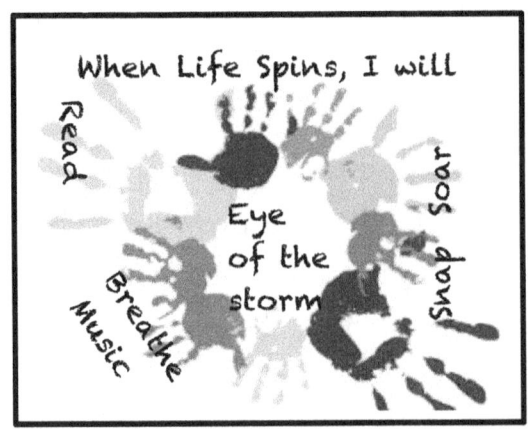

Positive Affirmation Activities

Ages: Young (5-6), Middle (7-11), and Adolescents (12- up)

Materials:

- 8 ½ x 11 piece of paper
- Colored Markers, Pens, Pencils

> **How This Activity Builds Resilience:** Encourages emotional expressiveness and maintaining a positive relationship with an adult. Reinforces positive self-esteem, self-competence, and client's ability to influence others and make a positive contribution to the community.

Rationale:

Using affirmations complements many evidence-based practice goals to enhance cognitive coping skills such as reframing, thought stopping, keeping thoughts in perspective, and embracing true, healthy thoughts. The following activities incorporate affirmations to help the client rehearse his/her strengths, successes, support system, and timeless truths that will endure even after treatment ends. As evidenced by brain research, when rehearsed sufficiently, information transfers into long-term memory. Any of the art activities from this intervention can be given to the client on the last session as a transitional object. They may also be incorporated into family and group work as well.

Family or group application: 1) Family or group members make individual projects. Each family or group member adds a positive word, affirmation, or symbol to each project. Or 2) A family collaborates on one project. Treatment provider facilitates a group discussion and points out emerging themes.

To make the activity commemorative: Provider adds his/her own words of encouragement, strength words and well wishes for the future.

To make meaning out of the treatment experience: Discuss how the client will use what s/he has learned about thinking positively that will help others heal, help make the world a better place, or help other kids/teens with similar experiences.

Directions:

1. **The treatment provider** discusses the purpose of positive affirmations, the reasons they are useful, and how saying and thinking positive things will help the client maintain forward progress.

2. To honor the termination process and honor the therapeutic relationship, the provider can write one or two brief, positive statements to the client. "You" messages to the client are preferred over "I" messages from the treatment provider (i.e., "You deserve the best" vs. "I think you deserve the best"). Treatment supports the client to discover his/her own strengths and is less about the opinion of the provider.

3. A variety of activities, including affirmations are included. The provider selects the activity that best matches the client's developmental level and clinical needs.

Affirmations can be written onto:

- Wooden coins
- Craft sticks
- A Journal
- Strips of paper
- Index cards
- Poker Chips
- Rocks or glass stones
- A Collage

Note: If a client is likely to use a rock or glass stone to injure themselves or someone else, these items should be substituted for a safer item such as wooden tokens, poker chips, or paper strips for safety. Client safety is priority.

Affirmations can also be:

- Made into key chains, bracelets, necklaces using alphabet beads
- Written around hand prints
- Used in a fortune teller
- Written onto strips or paper and placed in a bag or keepsake box
  (Be creative-place affirmations in a take out box to make a Hope in a Box or, Secret Agent or Military "black box").

Sample Affirmations for the Client:

- I'm getting there
- I am not alone
- I will get through this
- I can do it
- I have strengths that will get me through any challenge
- I am loving
- I deserve the best
- Time heals
- I deserve the best
- I can overcome anything
- I will treat myself with love and care
- I can help others

- I am a good person who has the right to be happy
- I'm stronger, wiser, better
- Life is worth living
- Tough times come but they also go
- I've been through worse and will survive this too
- Things will get better
- I am a good person
- I am stronger than my problems
- I can decide how I want to be treated

Sample Affirmations from the Treatment Provider to the Client:

- Your gifts and talents will help you do well in life.
- You deserve the best
- You can reach your goals
- You have everything you need, believe in yourself
- Remember your support system is there to love and support you
- You are a good role model

- You have people in your life who love and care about you
- Be encouraged, you can do it!
- You are a good person
- Remember you have many strengths
- You are strong and will do well in life

Strength Word Activities

Ages: Young (5-6), Middle (7-11), and Adolescents (12- up)

Materials:

- 8 ½ x 11 piece of paper
- Markers, Pens, Colored Pencils
- Various materials- see suggestions for activities

> **How This Activity Builds Resilience:** Encourages emotional expressiveness and maintaining a positive relationship with an adult. Reinforces positive self-esteem, self-competence, and client's ability to influence others and make a positive contribution to the community.

Rationale:

This activity uses *Strength Words* as mnemonic memory devices to help the client recall information learned while in treatment. In brain research, a mnemonic memory device is a learning technique that increases memory retention. The technique pairs information we want to remember with an image, color, movement, sentence, or word that makes the information easier to recall. This activity pairs words with statements to help the client remember strategies learned while in treatment. Pairing information this way helps the information "stick" in the brain longer and makes the information easier to remember. Strength Words may also be incorporated into family and group work as well.

Family or group application: 1) Family or group members make individual projects. Each family or group member adds a strength word or symbol to each project. Or 2) A family collaborates on one project. Treatment provider facilitates a group discussion and points out emerging themes.

To make the activity commemorative: Treatment provider adds his/her own words of encouragement, strength words, and well wishes for the future.

To make meaning out of the treatment experience: Discuss how the client can use what s/he has learned about strengths, coping and empowerment to help others, make the world a better place, or help other youth with similar experiences.

Strength Word	Symbolizes
Humor	I have a good sense of humor
Creative	I am creative
Artistic	I am artistic

Coping Skill Word	Symbolizes
Breathe	I can use deep breathing to calm down
Music	I will listen to music when I feel upset
Snap	I will snap my rubber band to avoid cutting

Empowerment Word	Symbolizes
Dream	I will follow my dreams
Hope	I will hold onto hope
Courage	I have the courage to live a full life

Directions:

1. **Treatment Provider Says:** *Today we are going to continue preparing for counseling to end. Let's look at this list of strength words...when you use the word 'strong' what will that word represent to you?*

2. Educate the client on the purpose of strength words and how strength words can be used outside of treatment and once services end.

3. To honor the termination process and if clinically appropriate, the treatment provider can personally write one or two strength words to the client as well wishes and hopes for the future. "You" messages to the client are preferred over "I" messages from the treatment provider (i.e., "You are strong and will survive," vs. "I think you are a survivor,") as treatment is to support the client to discover his/her own strengths and is less about the opinion of the provider.

4. Any of the final art projects can be used as a transitional object in the termination process. A variety of sample activities are suggested in this section. The treatment provider selects the activity that best matches the client's developmental level and clinical needs.

Sample Activities Include:

Draw or paint strength words onto paper, wooden coins, rocks, or glass stones, craft sticks (metallic colored markers work well on glass or rock surfaces).

 If a client is likely to use a rock or glass stone to injure themselves or someone else, these items should be substituted for a safer item such as wooden tokens, poker chips, or paper strips for safety. Client safety is priority.

Clay: Flat stones can be formed using air-dry clay. A strength word can be written onto the stone. Optional: Once dry, the stone can be painted or decorated.

Strength word reminders: Strength words can be written onto strips of paper and placed in a paper bag or keepsake box, or taped to pens or pencils for the client to keep as reminders.

Alphabet and colored beads can be used to make key chains, bracelets, or necklaces. Adolescents can use colored beads to symbolize words (i.e., blue=stay calm; green = reminds me to breathe when I am upset...; yellow= remember to think positive thoughts).

Strength ball: Write strength words onto a small vinyl ball (soccer ball, football, baseball...)

Strength Words

Strengths	Coping Skills	Empowerment
Humor	Breathe	Dream
Creative	Music	Hope
Artistic	Snap	Courage
Trustworthy	Grounding	Dream
Unique	Laugh	Live
Athletic	Think	Serenity
Passionate	Visualize	Acceptance
Strong	Relax	Patience
Giving	Distract	Respect
Quiet	Focus	Love
Loving	Sing	Joy
Smart	Poetry	Wisdom
Independent	Exercise	Forgiveness
Stylish	Walk Away	Passion
Generous	Read	Own-It
Hard-working	Bubbles	Smile
Dedicated	Draw	Peace
Mature	Support System	Powerful
Kind	Calm	Tried and True
Thoughtful	Positive Thinking	Thinker
Street-wise	Education	Doer
Easy-going	Plan	Overcomer
Friendly	Rest	Bold
Helpful	Nutrition	Future

Fortune Teller

Ages: Young (5-6), Middle (7-11), and Adolescents (12- up)

Materials:

> **How This Activity Builds Resilience:** Encourages emotional expressiveness and maintaining a positive relationship with an adult. Reinforces positive self-esteem, self-competence, and client's ability to influence others and make a positive contribution to the community.

- 8 ½ x 11 piece of paper
- Markers, Pens or Colored Pencils

Rationale:

A *Fortune Teller* is a fun paper contraption that children of all ages have used for generations to send messages back and forth. It can be incorporated into individual, family and group sessions and is a perfect item to imbed strength words, coping reminders, empowering statements, positive affirmations, and wishes for the future. The Fortune Teller can be given to the client at the end of treatment as a transitional object.

Family or group application: 1) Family or group members make individual projects. Each family or group member adds a positive word or symbol to each project. Or 2) A family collaborates on one project. Treatment provider facilitates a group discussion and points out emerging themes.

To make the activity commemorative: Provider adds his/her own words of encouragement, strength words, and well wishes for the future.

To make meaning out of the treatment experience: Discuss how the client will take what s/he has learned about healing to help others, make the world a better place, or help other kids/teens with similar experiences.

Directions:

1. **Make a perfect square from an 8 ½ " x 11" piece of paper.**
   a. Fold a bottom corner of the page to the opposite edge.
   b. Cut off the excess strip to the right of the triangle.
   c. Unfold the page to reveal a square.

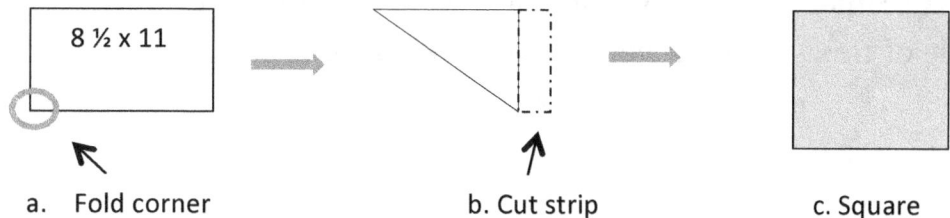

a. Fold corner b. Cut strip c. Square

2. **Fold each of the four corners of the square so that the four corners meet in the center. The corners should not overlap.**

Fold each corner toward the center   The corners should not overlap

3. **Turn the paper over (folds should face down). Fold each corner back toward the center, just as you did in step 2. You will end up with a smaller square.**

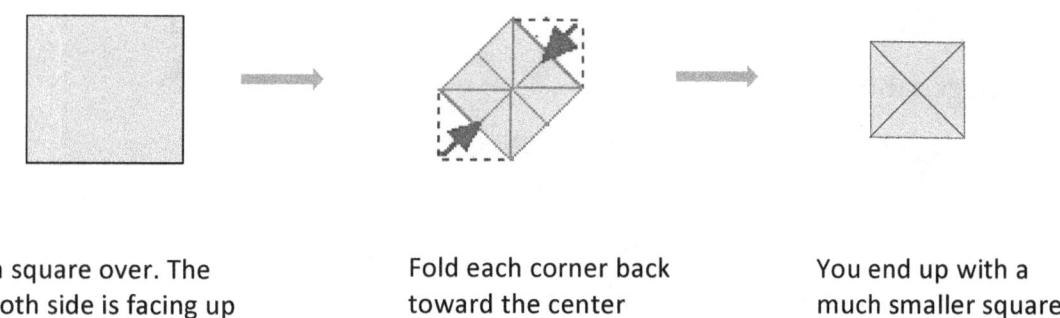

Turn square over. The   Fold each corner back   You end up with a
smooth side is facing up   toward the center   much smaller square

4. Fold the square in half. Unfold and fold in half the other way. Do this a couple of times to make your fortune teller flexible.

5. Keep fortune teller folded in half (crease side down) and slide your fingers in the pocket folds. As you slide your fingers in the folds, the tips will flare out like an umbrella and you will be able to open and close the fortune teller.

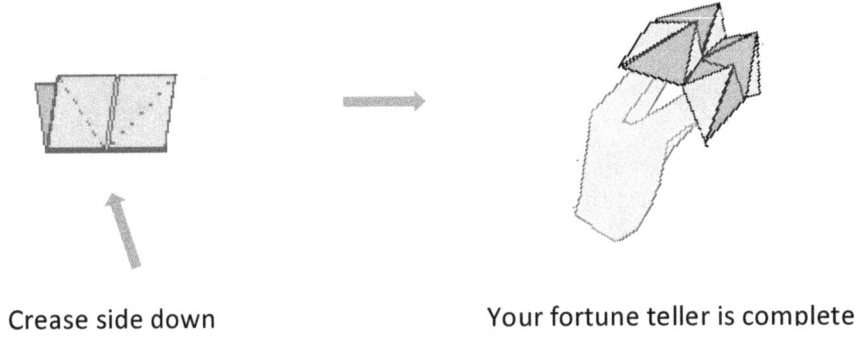

Crease side down

Your fortune teller is complete

6. Suggestions:

- Write words or sayings on the 4 outside squares, the 8 inside triangles and on the innermost flaps.
- Suggestions:
- The 4 outside flaps - colors or feeling words
- The 8 triangles in the inside - coping skill words, strength words (if not used earlier), or empowering words.
- The innermost flaps - positive affirmations or wishes for the future (written by both the client and treatment provider).

The Power of Positive Words
Crossword Puzzle

Ages: Middle (7-11) and Adolescents (12- up)

Materials:

- The Power of Positive Words Crossword Puzzle
- Pen, Pencil, Marker
- Answer Key

> **How This Activity Builds Resilience:** Encourages emotional expressiveness and maintaining a positive relationship with an adult. Reinforces positive self-esteem, self-competence, and client's ability to influence others and make a positive contribution to the community.

Rationale:

The *Power of Positive Words: Crossword Puzzle* is a fun commemorative activity that combines strength words, coping reminders, positive affirmations, and reminders of the client's support system in the same exercise. It can be included into individual and family sessions but is contraindicated for use in a group due to the element of competition that may take the focus off of termination. Affirmations can be used to remind the client of his/her strengths, past successes, support system and timeless truths that will endure with him/her even after treatment ends. **Family members** alternate turns finding positive words. Treatment provider processes the experience with the family.

To make the activity commemorative: Leave an inspirational message on the puzzle. Give the puzzle to the client on the last session as a transitional object.

To make meaning out of the treatment experience: Discuss how the client will take what s/he has learned about healing to help others, make the world a better place, or help other kids/teens with similar experiences.

Directions:

1. **Treatment Provider Says:** *Today we will continue preparing for counseling to end. Here is a crossword puzzle that has 14 positive statements for you to complete. Afterwards, we can talk about how the positive statements can help you continue the positive progress you have made after services end.* The provider supports as needed depending on the developmental, cognitive, and language ability of the client.

2. Provider discusses the purpose of positive affirmations, the reasons they are useful and how saying positive things about his or herself will help the client maintain forward progress.

The Power of Positive Words
Crossword Puzzle

Directions: Complete the sentences below and use the missing words to complete the crossword puzzle.

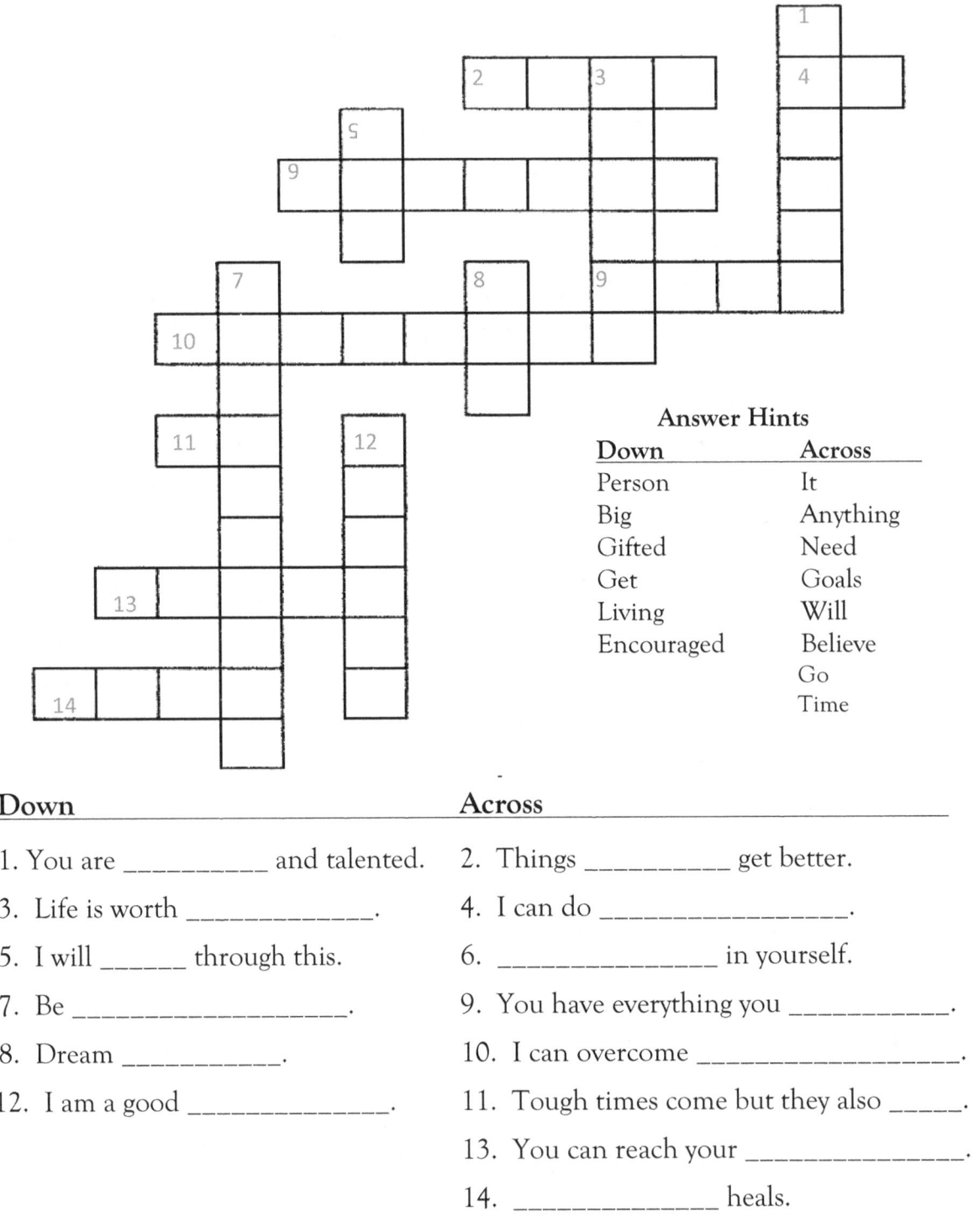

Answer Hints

Down	Across
Person	It
Big	Anything
Gifted	Need
Get	Goals
Living	Will
Encouraged	Believe
	Go
	Time

Down

1. You are _____ and talented.

3. Life is worth _____.

5. I will _____ through this.

7. Be _____.

8. Dream _____.

12. I am a good _____.

Across

2. Things _____ get better.

4. I can do _____.

6. _____ in yourself.

9. You have everything you _____.

10. I can overcome _____.

11. Tough times come but they also _____.

13. You can reach your _____.

14. _____ heals.

208

The Power of Positive Words
Crossword Puzzle Answer Key

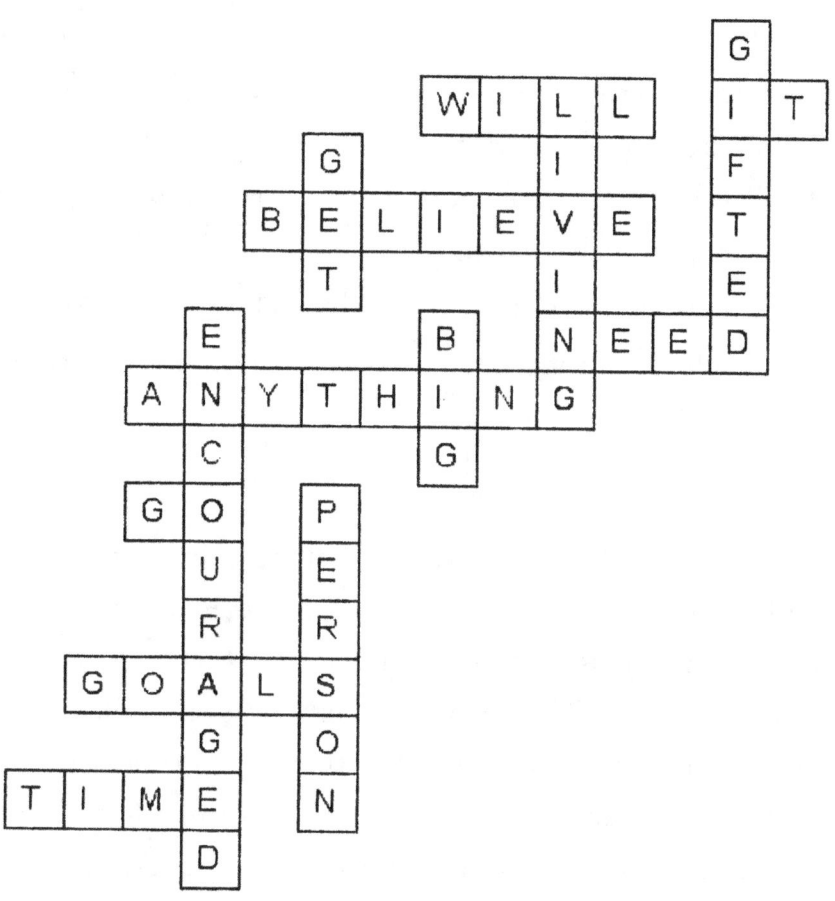

Blow It Into The Future

Ages: Young (5-6), Middle (7-11), and Adolescents (12- up)

Materials:

> **How This Activity Builds Resilience:** Encourages emotional expressiveness and maintaining a positive relationship with an adult. Reinforces positive self-esteem, self-competence, and client's ability to influence others and make a positive contribution to the community.

- Index Cards
- Pens, Pencils, or Markers
- Bubbles (or bubble gum*)
- A bag, pouch, case, box, or small binder rings to make the index cards into booklets

*Confirm that your client is not allergic to gum, sugar, or food coloring. Sugared gum is contra-indicated for diabetic clients.

Rationale:

Blowing bubbles is a fun, relaxing activity for all ages and can be incorporated into individual, family, and group sessions. *Blow it into the Future* is a commemorative activity that directs the client and treatment provider to make a wish or hopeful statement about the future. The wish or statement is then blown into a bubble to symbolically launch it into the future. Whether the bubble pops on its own or is popped by the client or treatment provider, the popping of the bubble represents how the wish is released into the world...it can never be returned or cancelled.

Family or group application: 1) Family or group members blow wishes and hopeful statements into bubbles. Treatment provider decides if it is feasible for each member to have an individual bottle of bubbles. Sharing is also fun. Treatment provider facilitates a group discussion and points out emerging themes.

To make the activity commemorative: Provider blows wishes or hopeful statements into bubbles. Feel free to write the wishes down in a creative way and give them to the client.

To make meaning out of the treatment experience: Discuss ways the client can make his/her wishes or hopes for a positive future help others, make the world a better place, or help other kids/teens with similar experiences.

Directions:

1.   The provider educates the client on the meaning and importance of wishes. Some ideas are: Wishes celebrate work well done or a fresh start. In many cultures, wishes are like blessings that are passed from one person to another (like when people send cards or say nice things about others at birthday parties). Wishes can also symbolize a fresh start the individual wants (like when one is asked to make a birthday wish for oneself).

2.   Provider or client (as appropriate) writes down the wishes on index cards. Encase the cards in a bag, box, pouch, or other container and give them to the client. The index cards can also be bound with two small binder rings.

3.   Suggestions of what to blow into the future. Be creative and encouraging...

Sample Strength Words:
- Hope
- Courage
- Sensitivity
- Patience

Sample Coping Skills:
- The power to dream
- The will to live
- I will use my survival kit

Sample Positive Affirmations:
- My family and friends love and support me
- I believe I can do it
- I can control my anger
- Fear will not stop me

Sample Discussion Questions:
- Talk about the success your adult self will have and blow it into the future
- Think of a word or phrase that only you and your treatment provider will know and blow it into the future.
- Talk about what you will do from here forward to make the world a better place to live in. Blow it into the future.

Strength Words

Strengths	Coping Skills	Empowerment
Humor	Breathe	Dream
Creative	Music	Hope
Artistic	Snap	Courage
Trustworthy	Grounding	Dream
Unique	Laugh	Live
Athletic	Think	Serenity
Passionate	Visualize	Acceptance
Strong	Relax	Patience
Giving	Distract	Respect
Quiet	Focus	Love
Loving	Sing	Joy
Smart	Poetry	Wisdom
Independent	Exercise	Forgiveness
Stylish	Walk Away	Passion
Generous	Read	Own-It
Hard-working	Bubbles	Smile
Dedicated	Draw	Peace
Mature	Support System	Powerful
Kind	Calm	Tried and True
Thoughtful	Positive Thinking	Thinker
Street-wise	Education	Doer
Easy-going	Plan	Overcomer
Friendly	Rest	Bold
Helpful	Nutrition	Future

Clay Activity: Hand Me the Future

Ages: Young (5-6), Middle (7-11), and Adolescents (12- up)

Materials:

> **How This Activity Builds Resilience:** Encourages emotional expressiveness and maintaining a positive relationship with an adult. Reinforces positive self-esteem, self-competence, and client's ability to influence others and make a positive contribution to the community.

- Air-dry Clay
- Writing tool for clay

Rationale:

Clay handprints are a fun and meaningful way to honor the therapeutic relationship. In the *Hand Me the Future* activity, the treatment provider and client both lay down prints of their hands and write well wishes to one another. This activity can be adapted for family and group intervention as well.

Family or group application: 1) Family or group members make individual projects. Each member adds a positive word or symbol to each project. Or, 2) Family makes one collaborative project. Provider processes the experience.

To make the activity commemorative: Provider adds his/her own words of encouragement, strength words, and well wishes for the future.

To make meaning out of the treatment experience: Process how the client will take what s/he has learned about healing to help others, make the world a better place, or help other kids/teens with similar experiences.

Directions:

1. Use a handful of clay to form a base for the handprints.
2. Client and treatment provider each leave a handprint in the clay.
3. Provider and client can leave their initials, well wishes, symbols or a strength word in the clay.

It was so nice knowing you...Hope, Dream and Live I deserve the best!

Planting a Seed

Ages: Young (5-6), Middle (7-11), and Adolescents (12- up)

Materials:

- 16 ounce plastic cup
- Enough planting soil to fill ¾ of the plastic cup
- 3-4 Sunflower seeds, water and bright direct sunlight

> **How This Activity Builds Resilience:**
> Encourages emotional expressiveness and maintaining a positive relationship with an adult. Reinforces positive self-esteem, self-competence, and client's ability to influence others and make a positive contribution to the community.

Rationale:

Planting a Seed is a powerful way to honor the therapeutic relationship and help the client look forward to the future. It can be used in individual, family, and group work and is a wonderful metaphor for life, growth, and the termination process. Sunflower seeds are fast growing and can produce plants in 1-2 weeks (this does not imply that the termination process will take 1-2 weeks). The treatment provider must keep this in mind and carefully time this intervention with the termination process. If you have limited time, plant the seeds the same day you make the termination announcement. This will allow time for the plant to grow. The plant can be given to the client on the last session as a transitional object.

Family or group application: 1) Group members make individual plants. At the beginning of each group, members speak positive words over each plant. Or, 2) Each family member plants one seed into the same cup. Each week, family speaks positive words over their plant. Provider processes the experience.

To make the activity commemorative, you and the client can make up secret wishes, empowering words, or positive statements to speak to the plant. The treatment provider can also write positive statements or wishes for the future onto a popsicle stick or a ½ inch plastic strip (plastic is more durable in wet soil) and place it into the soil.

To make meaning out of the treatment experience, process how and in what ways the client can help others grow.

Directions:

1. **Treatment Provider Says:** *Let's honor your graduating from treatment by planting some sunflower seeds and watching them grow over the next few weeks before we end treatment. You remind me of a plant growing because...Each week we will check on the plant's progress.*

2. Provider and client fill the cup with soil and plant the seeds together.

3. Each week, the two of you can check on the growth of the plant.

4. Some plant experts believe plants grow better when kind words are spoken over them so it certainly wouldn't hurt to use the "check in" as a time to practice positive affirmation or speaking strength words out loud.

5. Provider processes the parallel between the plant's growth and the client's growth (it sometimes takes a while to see but the work will show if given enough time and nurturance. What seeds have we planted during treatment? How can you continue to nurture these seeds?).

Directions for Planting:

- Fill 16 ounce cup ¾ full of planting soil.
- Moisten soil with 2-3 tablespoons of water.
- Plant 3-4 sunflower seeds 2 inches into the soil.
- Expose to direct sunlight.
- Water soil with @ 2 tablespoons of water every 4-5 days.

See pictures on the next page...

*The pictures below are of 3 sunflower seeds planted in a 16 oz. plastic cup. The seeds were given 2 tablespoons of water every 4-5 days and daily bright light.

Planting **Day 1**	
Week 1 **7 days after planting**	
Week 2 **14 days after planting**	
Week 3 **21 days after planting**	

Step-by-Step

Ages: Young (5-6), Middle (7-11), and Adolescents (12- up)

Materials:

> **How This Activity Builds Resilience:** Encourages emotional expressiveness and maintaining a positive relationship with an adult. Reinforces positive self-esteem, self-competence and client's ability to influence others and make a positive contribution to their community.

- Pen, Pencil or Marker. Scissors
- Copy "stones" as needed
- Optional: laminate "stone"

Rationale:

The *Step-by-Step* can be used as an individual, family, or group intervention. The activity spans all 4 steps of the termination process. This section transforms the Step-by-Step exercise into a commemorative activity and supports processing making meaning out of the treatment experience. This activity can be a continuation of previous sessions or be used independently as a stand-alone activity. Feel free to refer to previous sections as a reference.

Family or Group Application: Family or group members alternate taking turns advancing on the "stones." Treatment provider processes the group experience.

To make the activity commemorative: Items are already imbedded into the activity; follow discussion questions.

To make meaning out of the treatment experience: Items are already imbedded into the activity; follow discussion questions.

Directions:

1. Before the session, the treatment provider writes one strength word, coping skill, empowerment word, positive affirmation, question or wish onto a "stone." (For example: if using 5 words or wishes, there should be 5 stones). Because this is a commemorative activity, the provider should participate to honor of the therapeutic relationship. Provider's answers are tailored to meet the needs of the client (i.e., "You are brave and courageous"; "you have a bright future"). See page 192 for samples.

2. **Treatment Provider says:** *Today we are going to do an exercise called "Step-by-Step" that will help us celebrate all the work you have done in counseling and the bright future you have ahead of you. I want you to think of the stones as a pathway that will lead you out of counseling and into your life. We have traveled some of this journey together and you are ready to move on into your life. There is a path of stones on the floor. There is a word or a wish written on each stone. As you step on a stone, pick it up and read what is written on it. If it is a word, talk about how you are like that word. If it is a statement or question, you can read it aloud and go from there.*

3. If space is limited, the stones can be alternated between the floor and the wall. The client can have fun moving between each stone, jumping up to touch the stones off of the wall or doing a "cool" move to step on the stones on the floor. Treatment provider makes the activity engaging by giving the client high-fives, fist bumps, or a special handshake with each answer.

4. **If this is a last session**, the provider can place the stones leading to the door as a concrete way to end the session. At the end of the road, the provider may give the client a token [bookmark, certificate, plant, handprints, (see Appendix A for more ideas)] and say good-bye. The stones can also be collected, bound together, and given to the client as a transitional object.

5. **Sample strength words, positive affirmations or wishes:** (There are many options, be creative and sincere.)

- Brave...talk about how you are brave.
- Say out loud, "I am a good person who deserves to be happy."
- Artistic...talk about why you are artistic.
- Make one wish for your future.
- (name of provider) wishes you a life full of happiness
- Dream...talk about your future dreams.
- (name of provider) says, "Remember your support system is there to love and support you."
- In what ways will your life be successful when you are an adult?
- What will you do from here forward that will make the world a better place to live in?
- On the back of this stone, write a special word, which represents you that only you and your counselor will know.
- Leave a message of hope with your counselor that will help other young people in the future. (You and the client can determine the theme)

"Stone" for Step-by-Step Activity:

Basketball

Ages: Young (5-6), Middle (7-11), and Adolescents (12- up)

Materials:

- Over-the-door Basketball Hoop or, any container can be substituted for a basketball hoop.
- Small ball or make a basketball out of a crumpled piece of paper or aluminum foil.
- Commemorative Basketball Cards and Game Board
- A bag, pouch, box, or 2 small binder rings to hold the cards

Rationale:

Some clients are kinetic learners and make good use of activities that are combined with physical activity. *Basketball* directs the client to shoot a ball into to a "hoop" and draw cards that ask termination-themed questions. It can be used for individual, family and group intervention. There are basketball games for Steps 1, 2, 3 and 4. The cards in this activity were specifically designed to help the client work through the issues outlined in Step 4. The game directions are the same but, the cards change, based on the task. The basketball game can be used over several sessions to process the different tasks (just add on the appropriate cards) or the games can be played independently, depending on the needs of the client.

Family or group application: Each family or group member takes a turn shooting a basket and answering a question while the treatment provide facilitates a group discussion and points out emerging themes.

To make the activity commemorative: Items are already imbedded into the activity; see basketball cards. The commemorative set of cards can be given to the client at the end of treatment.

To make meaning out of the treatment experience: Items are already imbedded into the activity; see basketball cards.

Part One: Educates the client about treatment ending and puts supports in place to pre-empt early termination.

Part Two: Processes the client's range of feelings about treatment ending, including that addressing feelings may trigger previous losses.

Part Three: Prepares the client to manage life after treatment ends.

Part Four: Commemorates the relationship and brings treatment to an end

Directions:

1. **Treatment Provider says**: *As you know we are getting ready to end counseling. Today we are going to honor all the work you have done and to celebrate the bright future you have ahead of you. We are going to shoot baskets. If you make it, take a 'hoop card' and if you miss a shot, take a 'brick card'. The cards will tell us what to do.*

2. Provider draws and answers cards as well. Provider processes the client's answers or facilitates ideas as appropriate.

3. If one stack becomes depleted before the other, the provider can say something like, "*Let's see what the other cards say, just for the fun of it...*"

4. The cards can be photocopied and laminated for durability.

Step 4...Basketball Cards:

Hoop:

Let your counselor write a message to you on the back of this card.

Brick:

Take a slow, deep breath and say: I am not alone and I will get through tough times

Hoop:

Say this out loud: I am a good person who deserves to be happy.

Brick:

What has changed in your life for the better since you started counseling?

Hoop:

In what ways will your life be successful when you are an adult?

Brick:

Leave a message of hope with your counselor that will help other kids in the future.

Hoop:

How will your adult self be different than who you are now?

Brick:

Your counselor believes you are a special person who will do well in life.

Hoop:

Your counselor says: You have everything you need; believe in yourself.

Brick:

On the back of this card, write a special word that represents you, which only you and your counselor, will know.

222

Step 4...Basketball Cards:

Hoop: Which word describes you best: Hopeful, Dreamer, Survivor	**Brick:** Remember how to forgive
Hoop: Make a trick shot and say: I deserve the best	**Brick:** Make an over the shoulder shot and say: I am loving
Hoop: Which word describes you best: Poetry, Drawing, Relaxing	**Brick:** Take a slow deep breath and say: Time Heals
Hoop: Stand on one foot and say: I am stronger than my problems	**Brick:** Say out loud: Tough times come but they also go.
Hoop: What word describes you best: Giving, Smart, Hard-working	**Brick:** What will you do from here forward to make the world a better place to live in?

Message Book

Ages: Young (5-6), Middle (7-11), and Adolescents (12- up)

Materials:

> How This Activity Builds Resilience: Encourages emotional expressiveness and maintaining a positive relationship with an adult. Reinforces positive self-esteem, self-competence, and client's ability to influence others and make a positive contribution to the community.

- A sheet of paper (lined or blank) (Provider may also create a message on a computer)
- 3- ring binder

Rationale:

The *Message Book* activity encourages clients to embrace the concept of paying it forward and to commemorate the therapeutic relationship. Individual, family or group members create a message that the treatment provider will place into a "message book" for future clients to read. The message is one of encouragement, helpful hints, and words of wisdom from past clients to future clients. The message can be in words, symbols, or pictures depending on the developmental and cognitive levels of the client. Clients can dictate their message through the provider if this will aid the message writing process.

Family or group application: Each family or group member writes a message of hope and encouragement on their "family" or "group" page in the message book.

To make the activity commemorative: Items are already imbedded into the activity.

To make meaning out of the treatment experience: Items are already imbedded into the activity.

Directions:

1. **Treatment Provider Says:** *You are graduating from counseling because of your progress. Let's do something that will help other young people in the future. You are such an example for others. Will you leave a message with me that will help other young people who have troubles in the future? You can give advice, suggestions, words of*

wisdom, draw a picture or make a symbol...anything that you believe will help them feel hopeful that things in their lives can get better.

2. Provider supports client to complete a message. Sharing past works of clients has pros and cons. This is best done at the beginning of treatment to inspire hope. However, showing past work samples during termination, can give the client ideas but it may also cause some clients to feel intimidated or pressure to do the same thing. You know your client the best but allowing the client to develop his/her own product is usually a good idea.

3. When the message is complete, the provider and client may place their thumbprints, or a symbol representing their name, on it. The client should avoid using his/her name to honor confidentiality.

4. The provider and client place the message in the message book together. The provider may give the client as copy of the message at the end of treatment as a transitional object.

When I Look Into My Future: Guided Imagery Exercise

Ages: Middle (7-11) and Adolescents (12- up)

Materials:

> **How This Activity Builds Resilience:** Encourages emotional expressiveness and maintaining a positive relationship with an adult. Reinforces positive self-esteem, self-competence, and client's ability to influence others and make a positive contribution to the community.

- 8 ½ x 11 piece of paper
- Markers, Pens, Colored Pencils

Rationale:

When I Look Into My Future is a powerful termination exercise. It directs the client to imagine his/her future, in which the trauma experience is in the past. It also encourages the client to consider activities to give back to others. This activity can be used for individual, family, or group intervention. The exercise reinforces that the client is not defined by the trauma experience and will have other, more positive, experiences through her/his lifespan. Once the exercise is complete, the client writes down the strengths, strategies, and people in his/her support system that can help the client grow into her/his future self. Client may also write a *Letter to My Future Self,* which follows this intervention, as a complement to this exercise. Feel free to alter any part of the script to your client's unique experience.

Family or group application: Each family or group member participates in the relaxation, visualization activity, and discussion. Treatment provider follows discussion prompts.

To make the activity commemorative: Items are already imbedded into the activity.

To make meaning out of the treatment experience: Items are already imbedded into the activity.

Directions:

1. The client should be told the activity involves closing his/her eyes while listening to the treatment provider's voice. Expect some giggles, especially if the client is new to visualization. Your tone of voice and body language will help model appropriate behavior for the client. You should use the relaxation script

first to help client relax. Use a soft, even tone of voice. For ease of use, familiarize yourself with the script first.

2. **Treatment Provider Says:** *Let's take a journey into a future time where you are going to imagine yourself as a happy, successful adult. To do this, I want you first to relax yourself and clear your mind by closing your eyes and taking a few deep breaths. Let's take a few minutes to relax your body; then I will start the story.*

Relaxation Script: (5 minute script)

Close your eyes and take three big, slow, deep breaths. (Pause and coach the client to breathe properly if needed)...*Good...As you breathe out, begin to relax and let go of the tension or tightness in your body. Let go of anything that is bothering or worrying you. As you breathe, imagine the air is warm and soothing. Breathe in deeply* (watch client breathe) *and then imagine breathing out any worry, sadness, distraction, or bothersome thought. Send it far away from your body. Good, let's do that again...breathe in peace and quiet and breathe out tension and stress.* (Make sure the client is breathing well before moving on.) *As you breathe in this nice, warm air, imagine it floating to the top of your head and turning into a soft, warm, glowing light. Let the warm light spread slowly over your entire head and down to your face. Let your face relax. Feel the tension melt away as you breathe in* (pause) *and breathe out all tension; imagine it floating away. Now, let the warm light relax your eyes. Let your mouth open just a tiny bit so your jaw can relax. Focus on the soothing, warm light as you feel it move over your neck and shoulders. Hold the warm light there as it softly rocks back and forth helping you to relax and let go. Continue to breathe and relax. Good. Let the warm light move slowly from your neck down to your shoulders. Imagine the light separating and moving down both of your arms, filling them with light and warmth. The light melts into your elbows and into your hands. Now, squeeze your hands tightly* (short pause), *then release your grip and feel them fall. With this next breath, imagine breathing in the two waves of light from your hands into your nose and down into your chest. You feel warmth and light around your heart. Hold the light there while you relax and breathe in. Your face, shoulders, chest, and arms are relaxed and calm. With this next deep breath, imagine pulling the light from your chest into your belly...softening and relaxing it. Now, let the warm light slide down each hip, relaxing your thighs and legs. The light relaxes you as it slides further into your ankles and feet. Imagine*

227

the light wrapped around your feet like a warm, soft blanket. Your entire body is calm and relaxed.

Keep your eyes closed as we begin imagining your future life. (Provider pauses and moves on to the "When I look into my Future" Visualization Script)

When I look Into My Future: Guided Imagery Script: (5 minute script)

Use your imagination to travel into the future. Imagine you are much older than you are now. You have family and people around you that you are proud of and who treat you well. You are happy with your life. You have a successful career and have accomplished many things. You are in the stage of your life where you have all the money you need. You have traveled to many places. Although you are much older than you are now, your body is active and healthy. You have good friends that you enjoy being around. Today you are visiting with some of them. Keep your eyes closed and keep breathing while you imagine where you meet your friends and what time of day it is (short pause to allow client to visualize)...Good. You are with your friends and each of you will be talking about your lives when you were growing up. After listening to your friends, soon it will be your turn to talk about what you were like growing up.

Every few minutes I will give you another topic to discuss with your friends. When you hear me pause, this means it is time for you to imagine what you are saying to your friends. When you are ready to move on, nod your head or lift your finger. Ready? (Wait for the head nod or finger signal.)

First, you are going to talk about what it was like growing up and dealing with the problems you had. (Pause until client nods head to continue.)

Now, one of your friends asks you to talk about the things and the people in your life that helped support you when you were growing up. (Pause and wait for signal.)

Excellent, now imagine talking about how you went on with your life and became successful. Describe your job, if you married, if you had children, your hobbies, the places you traveled to, the kind of home you lived in. (Pause and wait for signal.)

Great, now discuss how different you are now as an older person than you were growing up. (Pause and wait for signal.)

Now imagine yourself talking about how it feels to have your past so far behind you. The hurt you had growing up only lasted a short time. You grew up and had a life filled with many other wonderful, fun and positive things. (Pause and wait for signal.)

Keep your eyes closed as you imagine how your conversation with your friends ends and how you all say good-bye to one another. (Pause and wait for signal.)

Good, keep your eyes closed. Let's take a few slow, deep breaths. When you are ready, and only when you are ready, slowly open your eyes. (Allow the client to take his/her time. Have the client take a few deep breaths after his/her eyes are open.)

Discussion Prompts:

- Draw a picture of your future self.
- What did you say to your friends about how you felt growing up?
- What did you imagine your future life to be like?
- What were you successful in?
- How were your older self and younger self different?
- How were they the same?
- How did your older self say you got stronger?
- How will you make the future not only better for yourself but also for others?
- How did it feel to look back as your older self and know that your hurts were so far behind you? What is the message to be learned from this?
- How did you say goodbye to your friends?
- What was helpful about this exercise?

Letter to My Future Self

Ages: Young (5-6), Middle (7-11), and Adolescents (12- up)

Materials:

- Paper (lined or blank)
- Envelope and stamp
- Writing utensil of choice
  (Provider may also use a computer
  to create the letter)

> **How This Activity Builds Resilience:**
> Encourages emotional expressiveness
> and maintaining a positive relationship
> with an adult. Reinforces positive self-
> esteem, self-competence, and client's
> ability to influence others and make a
> positive contribution to the
> community.

Rationale:

Letter writing is a powerful tool that can be used in many ways. The *Letter To My Future Self*, directs the client to write a letter to himself/herself that the practitioner will mail to the client at a later time. This activity may follow the *When I look Into My Future Guided Imagery Exercise* or may be used as a stand-alone activity. It may be adapted for family and group work. The letter contains a positive message, words of encouragement, reminders to use coping skills or other strategies the client wants to send to him/herself. The letter does not have to be written, it can include pictures or symbols – anything that will be helpful to the client. The client can dictate his/her words through the treatment provider if this will aid the letter writing process.

Family or group application: Each family or group member writes a personal letter.

To make the activity commemorative: Treatment provider adds words of encouragement to the letter.

To make meaning out of the treatment experience: N/A. This is a personal letter

Directions:

1. The letter should be sealed in an envelope and addressed in the presence of the client. Mail the letter in 4-6 weeks after the client ends treatment.

2. If the client's residence is likely to change, the provider should send the letter to a residence where the client is most likely to receive it. For example, to a foster care agency, close relative, long-time friend, social worker, adoption worker, court appointed special advocate (CASA), attorney, or to the counselor or principal at the client's school (with an appropriate release of information.)

My Story: Chapter 4

Ages: Young (5-6), Middle (7-11), and Adolescents (12- up)

Materials:

- Copy of *My Story Chapter 4*
- Use any additional activities from Step 4: Honor the Therapeutic Relationship and End Treatment. Insert activities into Chapter 4.

> **How This Activity Builds Resilience:**
> Encourages emotional expressiveness and maintaining a positive relationship with an adult. Reinforces positive self-esteem, self-competence, and client's ability to influence others and make a positive contribution to the community.

Rationale:

The *My Story* has four chapters that you can use to process all 4 Termination Steps. It is best used with an individual to process the therapeutic experience (some treatment providers have used it successfully with families). This section focuses on Step 4: Honor the therapeutic relationship and end treatment.

To make the activity commemorative: Items are already imbedded into the activity.

To make meaning out of the treatment experience: Items are already imbedded into the activity.

Below is a description of what each section of "My Story" contains:

Chapter One: Educates the client about treatment ending and puts supports in place to pre-empt early termination.

Chapter Two: Processes the client's range of feelings about treatment ending, including that addressing feelings may trigger previous losses.

Chapter Three: Prepares the client to manage life after treatment ends.

Chapter Four: Honors the relationship and brings treatment to an end.

My Story

Chapter 4

Celebrating Counseling

and

Saying Good-Bye

My Counselor and I

You and your counselor should use the space below to create something together to remind you of your time in counseling. Be creative and work together!

Making Meaning

Most items in nature (sun, water, plants, animals, and so on...) give back to the world we live in and play a part in making the world a better place. Use the space below to show how you will use the life and experiences you have had so far, to give back to those around you. How will you make the world a better place?

Congratulations

Appendix

21ˢᵗ Century Seminars

where professionals grow

Appendix A

Ideas for the Last Session

Celebrations
Hand Prints
Gift Bags
Certificates
Bookmarks
Letter from the Treatment Provider
Speeches
Graduation Picture

*The worksheets refer to the treatment provider as a "counselor". Feel free to change the worksheets to reflect your work as a counselor, case manager, social worker, psychologist, etc.

Note: This is not an exhaustive list of what to do on your last session. Use these activities as examples and be creative. Your options are endless.

Celebrations

Ages: Young (5-6), Middle (7-11), and Adolescents (12- up)

Materials:

- Varied (see below)

> **How This Activity Builds Resilience:** Termination celebrations encourage emotional expressiveness, use of humor, and maintaining a positive relationship with an adult. Reinforces goal attainment, sense of self-efficacy, social skills, and personal competence. **Optional:** Open terminations support building relationships with family, school, and community supports.

Rationale:

Celebrations are a positive way to provide closure to the treatment process. Celebrations vary from provider to provider and agency to agency and do not necessarily involve planning a party for the client or spending money. Celebrate means *to have fun, to have a good time, or to enjoy yourself.* In other words on the last day, plan something fun and enjoyable to do with your client.

Celebrations may include any of the activities listed below. The treatment provider can select one or more activities depending on how long the session is scheduled for.

A sample session may look like:

Greetings and check-in
Explain the session
Letter from the Treatment Provider
Hand Prints
Gift bag
Presentation of Certificate
"Good-bye" and client leaves the office

Caution Regarding Food and Beverages

Providing food and beverage is entirely up to you or your agency's policy and should be weighed carefully and done with parent consent. **Food allergies** can be deadly so the treatment provider must be extremely careful about food choices and clear all food options with the client and parent before allowing the client to consume anything. Food and beverages are a plus but not necessary. Your

238

termination celebration can be very meaningful without food. It is always a treat if there is an agency budget for snacks, but neither the provider nor a parent should feel pressure to provide food for a termination celebration. Whatever the budget, avoid over spending on treats. The purpose of the celebration is to have fun, not to over-indulge the client with treats.

Paying it forward for other treatment providers

Not all treatment providers serve food during or sponsor elaborate parties for their clients. Keep your fellow providers in mind when planning termination celebrations. Consider what future impact on your client if you give him/her a grand termination celebration and their future provider does not? Consider while you want your client to leave treatment with a sense of success and confidence, you do not want to leave your clients with unrealistic expectations that all providers end treatment with elaborate celebrations.

An open termination vs. a closed termination

An **open termination** celebration involves the treatment provider working with the client to have outsiders included in the termination celebration. A **closed termination** celebration involves the provider having a private celebration with the client and/or parent. Deciding to have an open or a closed termination celebration should be a well-thought out decision. Because of staff availability, open celebrations in residential treatment, school-based or inpatient settings, may be more manageable than agency-based celebrations.

Open termination sessions may potentially support resiliency by connecting the client to his/her family, school, and community supports. However, an open termination celebration has greater ethical and legal considerations involved. 1) For confidentiality reasons, inviting others is at the consent of the client and/or parent as appropriate.; 2) To minimize complications, those invited should be people the provider and client have reasonable access to.; 3) If inviting other minor children, the parents of those children need to be involved. And, the client would need to be comfortable with his/her peers, teachers, neighbors, or family members knowing s/he was involved in treatment. If all of these issues can be worked through, then having an open termination celebration can be very enjoyable for the client.

Hand Prints

Ages: Young (5-6), Middle (7-11), and Adolescents (12- up)

Materials:

- Paper
- Colored pens, colored pencils, paint or large ink pad

> **How This Activity Builds Resilience:**
> Termination celebrations encourage emotional expressiveness, use of humor, and maintaining a positive relationship with an adult. Reinforces goal attainment, sense of self-efficacy, social skills, and personal competence.

Rationale:

Including *handprints* in your termination celebration is a fun and meaningful way to honor and end the therapeutic relationship. In many cultures hands symbolize work, productivity, or a binding agreement ("let's shake on it"). In some religions the hand represents a blessing or the conduit for healing. Theme the handprint project to honor the therapeutic relationship and to celebrate termination.

Directions:

1. Client and treatment provider each trace one or both of their hands on a piece of paper or fabric. Then, each writes positive good-bye messages, words of encouragement, and well wishes to each other. Include the client's strengths. Remember to use "you" messages, over "I" messages (see page 196 for samples.)

2. Make impressions of the hands after coating them with paint or ink and placing hands on paper. (Be aware of drying time.) Each writes positive good-bye messages and well wishes to each other.

3. Use different colors and handprint patterns for creativity.

240

Sample Hand Print Ideas:

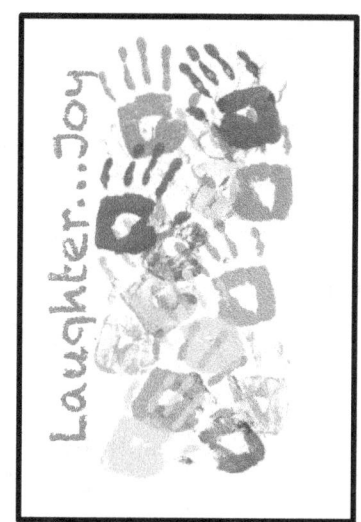

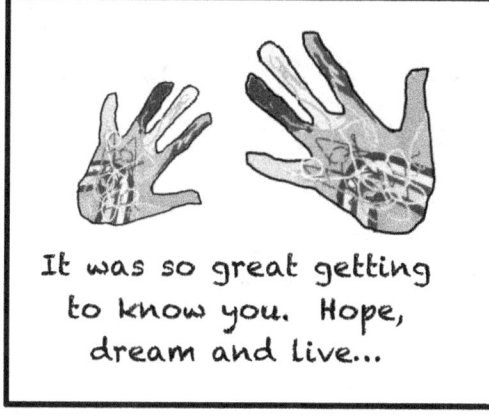

Gift Bags

Ages: Young (5-6), Middle (7-11), and Adolescents (12- up)

Materials:

- Gift Bags, Gift pouches, Decorated Paper Bag
- Miscellaneous items, note cards

> **How This Activity Builds Resilience:** Termination celebrations encourage emotional expressiveness, use of humor, and maintaining a positive relationship with an adult. Reinforces goal attainment, sense of self-efficacy, social skills, and personal competence.

Rationale:

Gifts bags are often given out at the end of celebrations to show guests appreciation for attending. Similarly, your ending celebration may include giving a gift bag to your client to honor the therapeutic relationship. It will also serve as a transitional object. The gift bag can be filled with various items and note cards with well wishes, hopes for the future, or affirmations. You do not have to spend a lot of money on the gift bag. Items commonly found in an office can be used. See examples below. Your gift bag should be unique to and age-appropriate for your client.

Directions:

Treatment provider writes a message on the bag or the gift tag: (Sample message) *Congratulations! You have worked hard and can be proud of yourself. Here are some special items for you to take with you.*

- *A bottle of bubbles for you to keep breathing and blowing life into your dreams*
- *Your favorite sandtray miniature to remind you that you can overcome anything*
- *A pencil with happy faces to remind you to smile*
- *The crisis line number in case you need someone to talk to*
- *My business card- just in case*
- *Star stickers to remind you that your potential is as limitless as the stars in the sky.*

242

Sample Gift Bag Items:

- Small toy, sandtray miniature, book or other item the client played with in treatment.

- Bottle of bubbles

- Small container of clay

- Pens, pencils with affirmations taped to them

- New journal or coloring book

- Stickers

- Wooden coin, stone, or token with strength word written on it

- Beaded bracelet with strength colors or strength word.

- Symbolic items such as hearts, flowers, animal pictures or figures, stars (Attach a note explaining what each item symbolizes).

- Provider's business card (be clear about your policy regarding ongoing contact with the client)

- Crisis line number (if appropriate)

Certificates

Ages: Young (5-6), Middle (7-11), and Adolescents (12- up)

Materials:

- Paper
- Certificates can be made using:

  o Online templates
  o Pre-printed certificates

> **How This Activity Builds Resilience:**
> Termination celebrations encourage emotional expressiveness, use of humor, and maintaining a positive relationship with an adult. Reinforces goal attainment, sense of self-efficacy, social skills, and personal competence.

Rationale:

Certificates are a meaningful keepsake item. Ideally, termination is framed as the culmination of work well done, so it seems appropriate to provide the client with a certificate to celebrate the client's progress. Presenting your clients with a certificate is in keeping with most graduation celebrations.

Directions:

Create a certificate to honor the client's work. To protect confidentiality, avoid putting private information like the client's goals, reason for treatment, or other confidential information on the certificate.

Sample statements:

- *Congratulations on reaching your goals...well done!*
- *This certificate is in honor of all of the hard work and tremendous progress you have made.*
- *To honor your strength and courage*

Bookmarks

Ages: Young (5-6), Middle (7-11), and Adolescents (12- up)

Materials:

- Paper
- Laminate for durability
- Embellish as appropriate.

> **How This Activity Builds Resilience:**
> Termination celebrations encourage emotional expressiveness, use of humor, and maintaining a positive relationship with an adult. Reinforces goal attainment, sense of self-efficacy, social skills, and personal competence.

Rationale:

Bookmarks are a keepsake item and a terrific way to leave the client with a personal message, words of encouragement, or well wishes from the treatment provider.

Directions:

Create a bookmark to honor the client's work. To protect confidentiality, avoid putting private information like the client's goals, reason for treatment or other personal information on the certificate.

Suggestions:

- Client's name
- List strength words, words that represent coping skills or empowerment words.
- Positive Affirmations
- Wishes
- A poem

Letter from the Treatment Provider

Ages: Young (5-6), Middle (7-11), and Adolescents (12- up)

Materials:

As appropriate to compose a letter

> **How This Activity Builds Resilience:**
> Termination celebrations encourage emotional expressiveness, use of humor, and maintaining a positive relationship with an adult. Reinforces goal attainment, sense of self-efficacy, social skills, and personal competence.

Rationale:

A letter from the treatment provider to the client can be a powerful tool. The letter should focus on the client and highlighting the client's progress and strengths. Providers should guard against emoting about how the client will be missed. Remember to use "you" messages, over "I" messages (see page 192 for samples).

Directions:

Summarize the main accomplishments and highlight strengths. To respect confidentiality, be cautious about disclosing details of why the client came to treatment and what the client did during services. Avoid lengthy letters. You may use the following letter as a guide.

Dear Susie,

> *When we first met, I remember seeing that big, bright smile of yours. You were quiet at first but as we talked some, played some games and drew pictures, you opened up and shared your feelings. You taught me about your strengths. You learned some things that will help you face any challenge that may come your way. Now, you are stronger and better and have so much to be proud of. Thank you for sharing with me and for letting others see your strengths. If times get tough in the future, you already know what to do. You can handle it. You have so much to offer the world and have all the gifts and talents you need to do well. It has been my pleasure getting to know you. Be well and remember; you deserve a good life.*

Speeches

Ages: Young (5-6), Middle (7-11), and Adolescents (12- up)

Rationale:

If inviting outside attendees to your graduation (per the wishes of your client and with proper parent consent), speeches can work very well. Attendees say a short speech of congratulations during the celebration. Screen the speeches ahead of time to ensure appropriate content. Caution guests to maintain confidentiality.

> **How These Two Activities Build Resilience:** Termination celebrations encourage emotional expressiveness, use of humor, and maintaining a positive relationship with an adult. Reinforces goal attainment, sense of self-efficacy, sociability, and personal competence. **Optional:** Open terminations support building relationships with family, school, and community supports.

This intervention tends to work well with clients in school-based, inpatient, or residential settings. These clients tend to be in closer proximity to their treatment team or staff members, who can step into a termination celebration with relative ease, versus clients receiving treatment via community mental health clinics or private practice offices.

Graduation Picture

Ages: Young (5-6), Middle (7-11) and Adolescents (12- up)

Rationale:

A picture with the treatment provider and client (or any attendees), is very special and a wonderful memento of the therapeutic relationship and/or graduation celebration. *Do not ever photograph a minor without written permission from the parent.* The client's image should be deleted from your memory card or computer for protection.

Directions:

Mount the picture on a piece of paper. The provider (and attendees if appropriate) can write a personal message, well wishes, and words of encouragement to the client.

Appendix B

Frequently Asked Questions

I am a mental health professional but I do not provide therapy. Will this model of termination work for me?

Yes it will! Mental health services extend beyond individual therapy and includes treatment provided by a variety of professionals who work in a broad variety of settings. The four steps in this training manual can be applied to clinical case management, behavior therapy, supportive counseling, life skills coaching, and so forth. These services are as impacted by the quality of the treatment relationship as individual therapy and providers can certainly use these 4 steps as a guide to end their treatment relationships in a planned and sensitive manner.

My client's case hasn't been open that long. I don't think termination means that much to him. We are stopping just when it seems we are starting. What is a proper termination in this case?

Treatment providers must remain highly aware of three important points: 1) Children and adolescents build a stronger therapeutic alliance with their treatment providers toward the middle to end of treatment. 2) Traumatized children may overgeneralize the mistakes of one relationship to all future relationships. And, 3) A goal of termination must be to end the therapeutic relationship in a way that keeps the client open to future relationships. Because children and adolescents bond differently to their treatment providers than adults, you cannot gage the importance of termination to a client on whether the client seems attached to you. Not taking the time to end the relationship in a planned, sensitive manner may impact how your client views future treatment relationships and may impact whether the client seeks out and is able to make good use of treatment in the future. While you also may not feel "invested" in the relationship, termination is about taking care of the client's feelings and needs. To address the awkwardness of ending treatment shortly after a case opens, process what it is like to start and stop treatment so quickly, whether the client has experienced abrupt endings before and whether and how this abrupt experience may impact his/her willingness to participate in treatment in the future. Do not ignore or minimize the issue. If you are thinking about it, chances are the client is too. Bring it up and theme the discussion to the termination process.

How long should the termination process last?

In researching termination, recommendations varied widely from 2 weeks to one year. In her book, "Blending Play Therapy with Cognitive-Behavior Therapy: Evidence-based and Other Effective Treatment and Techniques", author Athena Drewes recommends that "...termination occurs as a gradual process, so that preparation for completion of therapy takes place over several sessions " (pg. 339). In this day of evidence-based practice, mental health contracts and insurance limitations, the number of sessions to devote to termination may vary according to one's training, the model practiced or work setting (ie., private practice vs. a mental health contracted agency). This 4-step guide is effective regardless of the model, agency setting, or insurance contract. The number of sessions is less important than ensuring that treatment ends in a planned, sensitive manner.

The reality is some settings have more flexibility than others. In short-term models, termination may wrap-up over a couple of sessions. For example, the entire Trauma-Focused Cognitive Behavior Therapy (TF-CBT) treatment model occurs over 12 to 20 sessions. In this case, termination may occur over 2 to 3 sessions. However, it is ethically important to note that while TF-CBT is a short-term model, the authors indicate that the number of sessions, including the time devoted to termination, is flexible to the client's needs. No matter what the setting, the authors recommend that treatment be "terminated in a planned and sensitive manner " (pg. 203) and caution how the loss of a trusted treatment provider may trigger previous loss and abandonment issues in clients with complex trauma histories. (Cohen, Mannarino and Deblinger, 2006.)

This 4-step guide allows for flexibility. Termination can be addressed in a few sessions or over several sessions. How many sessions is not as important as how thoroughly the 4 termination tasks are covered. For example, if your client informs you s/he will be moving out of the area in 1-2 weeks, while you do not have control over the timeframe, this manual helps you understand the information that should be covered. You can use this 4-step guide to cover termination effectively in your allotted timeframe. Be sure to use the *About Me* worksheet to encourage your client to re-enroll in treatment at their new location.

What if I have only a couple of sessions to terminate?

Without adequate preparation, terminating over 2 or 3 sessions is challenging. If you know ahead of time that you will be working with limited sessions, it is important to set up the appropriate treatment expectations with your client from the beginning. Termination must be discussed at the onset of treatment. The treatment should be framed as a relationship that will end once goals are reached. Conduct regular goal reviews so the client remains up-to-date on his/her progress in treatment and termination remains present in the treatment process. Finally, the treatment provider should follow the 4 steps to termination outlined in this manual to optimize the likelihood of a successful termination process. If a move, transfer of providers, or other event interrupts treatment prematurely, use the 4-step guide to help you to complete termination in the allotted time frame. The worksheet *About Me* is a helpful tool for case transfers and premature terminations.

Counting down termination each week feels awkward. What if my client drops out of treatment because we are so focused on termination?

40% to 60% of mental health treatment cases end prematurely. Some studies suggest premature termination is related to the client having different expectations of treatment than the treatment provider. However, studies also support that a strong therapeutic alliance and psychoeducation about role expectations and the treatment process can mitigate early termination. So counting down sessions each week ensures you and your client remain on the same page regarding termination. However, being aware of the possibility of premature termination is important because other clients may avoid facing the loss of the therapeutic relationship by exiting from treatment early. The first task of "Educating the client about treatment ending," must address this issue. The handout entitled *Common Reactions as Treatment Ends*, the *Parent Letter* and several Step 1 activities address the issue of premature termination. You should address the likelihood of early termination openly and honestly and put supports (contracts, verbal agreements, check-ins, parent, or treatment team support) in place to pre-empt early termination.

My client was inconsistent throughout treatment. I do not want her thinking she did something inappropriate to cause treatment to end. How do I address this?

This is a common feeling and concern for treatment providers because some clients may believe they have done something inappropriate to cause termination (especially if there were attendance or compliance issues during treatment). The provider can address this issue by focusing on the client's progress and strengths as a reason for termination. Also, many activities in the first task of "Educating the client about treatment ending," address this issue directly, allowing the provider and client to process distorted or unhelpful thoughts openly and honestly.

Termination is inevitable. It is unethical to not adequately prepare your client for it. It is important that treatment providers are honest and direct. You do not want to model avoidance for your client or by your avoidance, send your client the message that s/he cannot handle the termination process.

My client started opening up after I told him it was time to end. I'm afraid if I talk too much about termination he will stop sharing. How do I address this?

A common error is to avoid talking about termination when you observe a change (whether that change is positive or negative), in your client after talking about termination. Rather than avoiding talking about termination because of the change, consider the change may have occurred because of termination. Some clients withdraw and some continue on unscathed. Other clients, who previously did not make good use of treatment, begin to open up and become the model client. A treatment provider may be very confused about what to do with this dynamic if not clear that this can be a normal part of the termination process. In these cases, the provider should spend time helping the client sort out these feelings and how to cope with them as a part of preparing the client to end treatment. It is important to process the change in the client and connect the change to termination. (I notice this is the first time you are talking about...why do you think this is coming up for you now that we have...sessions/weeks left?)

May I offer extra sessions, accept a gift or see a client at unscheduled times during termination?

A supervisee once said she never really believed in counter-transference until she went through the termination process. Until it was pointed out to her, she had let sessions run long, saw clients at unscheduled times, avoided counting down sessions out loud, and accepted gifts. As we processed her feelings in supervision, she discovered underlying feelings of guilt and feeling like she was abandoning her clients. Learning about counter-transference and the possible impact on treatment is a good start. Being under a good supervisor or working in consultation with an objective, licensed colleague is helpful. Once the issues are identified, then you can be more present in treatment with your client and actively bring termination into your sessions.

After beginning termination, my client sent me a "friend" request on my social media page. How shall I address this?

Social media, text, and video messaging, email, and cell phone capabilities makes termination more challenging than in a pre-internet culture. Clients may be able to locate their providers via social media sites and request ongoing contact. It is important to clarify your policy on social media exchanges with clients at the beginning of treatment so role expectations are clearly defined from the onset. In our culture of technology, it is more common for human beings to sustain contact through social media. So, this may be a very normal and innocent request from clients who are unfamiliar with the staunch traditions of our mental health profession. However, termination may revive this issue for others, who may be struggling with the ending of the therapeutic relationship. If your policy was not clear from the beginning of treatment address this issue with care and sensitivity. You want to avoid your client ending treatment feeling rejected or embarrassed by their seemingly innocent request. If you have conflicted feelings about this issue, it is important to consult with a licensed supervisor or an objective, licensed colleague for support and guidance.

May I hug my client on the last session? What if my client hugs me?

Physical contact with clients should always be weighted against what is in the client's best interest; cultural and developmental implications; ethical considerations, and the treatment provider's own style and possible counter-transference or transference feelings. Some treatment providers are comfortable having physical contact with clients because of experience, training, and good supervision. Other providers are innately and naturally comfortable touching their clients. Yet, many treatment providers have treated clients very successfully without including touch in the therapeutic relationship. If you do not typically touch your clients or have shied away from touching a particular client, it is ill advised to alter your routine simply because you are terminating. You run the risk of telegraphing your discomfort and the show of affection may be misinterpreted as contrived and insincere. With that being said, the provider should be prepared that termination brings up many issues that did not surface in the earlier phases of treatment; including hugs from the client or our own unexpected desire to hug the client. <u>Whatever you decide, remember the goal of your termination is to end your treatment in a way that the client remains open to future relationships.</u> Plan ahead and decide how you will respond if your client asks for a hug or spontaneously attempts to hug you.

Here are some guidelines that may help:

Side hugs: Stop about a foot from your client. Bend sideways from the waist so your chest and hips never make contact with the client's body. When you hug your client, your hand should touch the top of the client's shoulder.

Front hugs: Stop about a foot from your client. Bend forward at the waist and fold your shoulders in a concave position so your shoulders lead the hug and your chest does not make contact with the client's body. When you hug your client, your hands should touch the top of the client's shoulder blades.

Appendix C

Managing Counter-transference Feelings During Termination

Counter-transference is a professional term mental health professionals use to describe our own personal feelings that are triggered in response to the emotions, experiences, or problems our client faces. More simply stated, it is when our own feelings interfere with treatment. Counter-transference can be positive, neutral, or negative. Counter-transference feelings serve a purpose and are often triggered by our own personal feelings that may be unconscious, unresolved, or deeply personal. Self-aware treatment providers are skilled at using counter-transference to aid the treatment process and others may be overwhelmed by it. These issues are very common in termination and are more subtle and insidious than most treatment providers realize. Counter-transference can easily cloud our judgment, create biases and influence our decision-making. Counter-transference is different for everyone but some common examples include:

- Avoiding speaking directly to the client about termination.
- Allowing sessions to run over the allotted time.
- Having strong feelings before, during or immediately after treatment (such as feeling unusually anxious before session, dreading talking about termination, feeling emotionally drained, guilty or sad after termination.)
- Rescheduling make-up sessions when the client misses a session, when you usually do not.
- Not charging for "no shows" when you customarily charge.
- Wanting to hug or touch a client when you customarily do not.
- Wanting to give a gift when you customarily do not or, giving gifts that are above and beyond what you typically give.

This list is not exhaustive, but are common red flags that you may be experiencing counter-transference feelings around termination. It is our ethical responsibility to identify and monitor these feelings to minimize interference with treatment. You must remember that the overarching goal of termination is to help the client experience endings in a healthy way so that clients are more open to future relationships. To avoid dealing with the loss by prolonging sessions, giving excessive gifts, allowing sessions to run long, etc., gives a subtle message that the client cannot survive without you or cope with the loss of treatment ending. It also models that avoiding feelings is better than coping with them.

5 Tools to Manage Counter-transference Feelings

1. *Are you changing your routine?* Counter-transference influences treatment providers to act out of his/her routine. This is why self-monitoring provides protection against counter-transference. If you find yourself changing your routine (i.e., allowing make-up sessions when you did not before; not charging for missed sessions when you did before; calling the client to give reminders about attending session, when you did not before); these are clues that you may be experiencing counter-transference.

2. *Identify the underlying thought or feeling and monitor it.* It is important that you take the time before and after sessions to process your thoughts and feelings about the treatment and identify the feelings that are being triggered. Ask yourself the following questions:
   * *Does this client or situation remind me of someone or some event from the past?*
   * *What have endings been like for me in my own past? Am I trying to avoid triggering those feelings?*
   * *What is it that is keeping me from following the agency guidelines or staying within my own boundaries?*

   Once the feelings are brought to the conscious level, you can equip yourself to monitor them. Some tools to consider are: journaling, positive self-talk during session, or writing a coping word or thought that you put in the corner of your office to help remind you to stay aware and grounded.

3. *Remember counter-transference is normal.* Give yourself permission to have the thoughts and feelings, just don't succumb to them. New treatment providers, give yourselves permission to be new and inexperienced. Even the most

seasoned providers were green once upon a time. While you are growing your skills, give your clients the most valuable gift of all; the experience of having a warm, trusting, reliable adult with whom they can build a genuine relationship.

4. *Self-Care.* Termination can be an emotional experience for you as well as your client. If you are experiencing a challenging termination or having several terminations simultaneously it is important to consciously take care of yourself. Make sure you are eating healthy meals, exercising, and getting enough rest. Fully disengage when not at work and enjoy your hobbies, friends and family.

5. *Seek Support.* If you find yourself feeling challenged, confused, or overwhelmed by counter-transference issues, feel free to consult with a clinical supervisor or an objective licensed colleague for feedback and support. One of our greatest clinical tools is consultation. You and your client will only benefit from your seeking the wisdom of a seasoned practitioner, who can offer you the support and guidance to manage a very common experience.

Appendix D

Managing Transference Feelings During Termination

Transference is a professional term mental health professionals use to describe the feelings the client has about issues in treatment. Transference feelings may be positive, neutral, or negative and may arise at any point during treatment. However, it is common for strong feelings to arise during termination. The feelings the client may have are sometimes powerful enough to impact the therapeutic process or become projected onto the treatment provider. Sometimes a treatment provider may pick up on transference issues by listening to the client's themes in session. Other times the provider's gut reactions to a client's disclosures or behaviors provide clues to the transference feelings. These client-driven issues are also natural in termination and are different with each client. Some clues to identifying transference issues are if the client:

- Who was typically quiet and disengaged, begins to disclose more sensitive material after the termination announcement is made.
- Misses, is late to, or seems less engaged when in session.
- Regresses or decompensates in behavior outside of treatment.
- Brings gifts or asks to take items home from the treatment room.
- Wants to hug you, when hugs were not customarily given.
- Discloses termination related themes (betrayal, anxiety, fears, anger, abandonment, disappointment) during their treatment sessions.
- Denies that treatment will end.
- Asks repeat questions about where you will be going, or doing when treatment ends and if they can continue treatment at your new agency (if you are leaving) or return to services after the case closes.

While not an exhaustive list, these red flags indicate that a client may be experiencing transference feelings around termination. It is important that you take the time to process these feelings with the client, answer the client's questions honestly and help the client resolve any underlying feelings (fear of failure, anxiety about opening themselves to new supports, triggered loss issues, etc.). Terminating the case without addressing these issues may undermine the work done in treatment, as the client will be left vulnerable to his/her fears or misperceptions.

5 Tools to Manage Transference Feelings

1. *Utilize available interventions.* Review Task 1 and Task 2 Interventions that have questions around what the client may feel or think about the termination process. These tools will serve as a guide to help you explore and address the underlying thoughts and feelings and allow for a corrective experience.

2. *Normalize feelings and do not rush the process.* Honor and validate the client's feelings. Take time to explore the client's thoughts and feelings about termination and past good-byes. Doing so will support your therapeutic "good-bye" to be different than other experiences the client has had.

3. *Deal directly with the client's feelings and behaviors.* (For example: "I notice you seem quiet in session today and I am wondering how you are feeling about ending treatment?..."). It is important to listen to themes emerging during termination. So, if a client is speaking of a friend who disappointed him/her then you may choose to ask the client if he/she also feels disappointed in you somehow (ie., "I hear you talking about feeling disappointed, what has been disappointing about termination?").

4. *Build on strengths and instill hope.* Refer to the client's coping skills that will help manage feelings. ("What have you learned in treatment that will help?").

5. *Seek Support.* If you are feeling challenged, confused, or overwhelmed by these issues from your client, it is advisable to consult with a clinical supervisor or an objective licensed colleague. One of our greatest clinical tools is consultation. You and your client will only benefit from your seeking the wisdom of a seasoned practitioner, who can offer you the support and guidance to manage experiences that arise quite often between a treatment provider and a client.

References

Armbruster, P., & Kazdin, A. E. (1994). Attrition in child psychotherapy. *Advances in Clinical Child Psychology, 16*, 81–108.

Applegate, J. S., & Shapiro, J. R. (2005). *Neurobiology for clinical social work: Theory and practice.* New York, NY: Norton.

Barrett, M. S., Chua, W. J., Crits-Christoph, P., Gibbons, M. B., & Thompson, D. (2008). Early withdrawal from mental health treatment: Implications for psychotherapy practice. Psychotherapy: Theory, Research, Practice, Training, 45, 247-267.

Benson, P. L., Scales, P. C., Hamilton, S. F., & Sesma, A., Jr. (with Hong, K. L., & Roehlkepartain, E. C.). (2006, November). Positive youth development so far: Core hypotheses and their implications for policy and practice. Search Institute Insights & Evidence, 3 (1) 1–13.

Bickman L. A common factors approach to improving mental health services. Mental Health Services Research 2005;7(1):1–4. [PubMed: 15832689]

Blaustein, M. E., Kinniburgh, K. M. (2010). Treating traumatic stress in children and adolescents. New York: Guilford Press.

Bolger, K.E., Patterson, C.J., & Kupersmidt, J.B. (1998). Peer relationships and self-esteem among children who have been maltreated. *Child Development, 69*(4), 1171-1197.

Brady, J.P., Davison, G. C., Dewald, P. A., Egan, G., Fadiman, J., Frank, J. D., Gill, M. M., Hoffman, I., Kempler, W., Lazarus, A., Raimy, V., Rotter, J., & Strupp, H. H., (1980). *Some views on effective principles of psychotherapy.* Cognitive Therapy and Research, 4, 269-306.

Campbell-Sills, L., Cohan, S., & Stein, M. (2006). Relationship of resilience to personality, coping and psychiatric symptoms in young adults. *Behavior Research and Therapy, 44,* 585-599.

Carter, R. (2009). *The human brain.* New York, NY: DK Publishing.

Chandy, J. M., Blum, R. W., & Resnick, M. D. (1996). Female adolescents with a history of sexual abuse: Risk outcome and protective factors. Journal of Interpersonal Violence, *11*(4), 503-518.

Cicchetti, D., & Curtis, W. J. (2007). Multilevel perspectives on pathways to resilient functioning. *Development and Psychopathology, 19*(3), 627-629.

Cicchetti, D., & Rogosch, F., (2009). Adaptive coping under conditions of extreme stress: Multilevel influences on the determinants of resilience in maltreated children. *New Directions in Child and Adolescent Development, 124,* 47-59.

Cicchetti, D., & Rogosch, F. A., Lynch, M., & Holt, K. D., (1993). Resilience in Maltreated Children: Processes leading to adaptive outcome. *Development and Psychopathology, 5,* 629-647.

Cicchetti, D., Rogosch, F. A., & Toth, S. L., (2006). Fostering secure attachment in infants in maltreating families through preventive interventions. *Development and Psychopathology,* 18(3), 623-649.

Cohen, J. A., Mannarino, A. P., & Deblinger, E. (2006). *Treating Trauma and Traumatic Grief in Children and Adolescents.* New York: Guilford Press.

Dexheimer, M., Pharris, M., Resnick, M. D., & Blum, R. W. (1997). Protecting against hopelessness and suicidality in sexually abused American Indian adolescents. *Journal of Adolescent Health,* 21(6), 400-406.

Drewes, A. (Ed.) (209). *Blending play therapy with cognitive behavioral therapy.* New Jersey: John Wiley & Sons, Inc.

Eltz, M. J., Shirk, S. R., & Sarlin, N. (1995). Alliance formation and treatment outcome among maltreated adolescents. *Child Abuse and Neglect, 19,* 419–431.

Flores, E., Cicchetti, D., & Rogosch, F., (2005). Predictors of resilience in maltreated and nonmaltreated Latino children. *Developmental Psychology, 41,* 338-351.

Florsheim, P., Shotorbani, S., Guest-Warnick, G., Barratt, T., Hwang, W. C. Role of the working alliance in the treatment of delinquent boys in community-based programs. Journal of Clinical Child Psychology 2000;29(1):94–107. [PubMed: 10693036]

Goldfried, M. (1998). A comment on psychotherapy integration in the treatment of children. *Journal of Clinical Child Psychology, 28,* 49–53.

Gould, M., Shaffer, D., & Kaplan, D. (1985). The characteristics of dropouts from a child psychiatry clinic. *Journal of the American Academy of Child and Adolescent Psychiatry, 24,* 316–328.

Guthiel, I.A. & Congress, E. (2000). Resiliency in older people: A paradigm for practice. In R.R. Green (Ed.), *Resiliency: An integrated approach to practice, policy, and research* (pp. 40-520. Washington, DC: NASW Press.

Haggerty, R., Sherrod, L., Garmezy, N., & Rutter, M. (1996). *Stress, risk, and resilience in children and adolescents: Processes, mechanisms, and interventions.* New York: Cambridge University Press.

Hellige, J. B. (1993). *Hemispheric asymmetry: What's right and what's left.* Cambridge, MA: Harvard University Press.

Hogue, A., Dauber, S., Stambaugh, L. F., Cecero, J. J., Liddle, H. A. Early therapeutic alliance and treatment outcome in individual and family therapy for adolescent behavior problems. Journal of Consulting and Clinical Psychology 2006;74(1):121–129. [PubMed: 16551149]

Jaffe, S., Caspi, A., Moffitt, T., Polo-Thomás, M., & Taylor, A. (2007). Individual, family, and neighborhood factors distinguish resilient from non-resilient maltreated children: A cumulative stressors model. *Child Abuse and Neglect*, 31, 231-253.

James, B. (1989). *Treating traumatized children new insights and creative interventions.* New York: Lexington Press.

Karver, M.S., Handelsman, J.B., Fields, S., Bickman, L. Meta-analysis of therapeutic relationship variables in youth and family therapy: The evidence for different relationship variables in the child and adolescent treatment outcome literature. Clinical Psychology Review 2006; 26(1):50–65. [PubMed: 16271815]

Kazdin, A. E., Holland, L., & Crowley, M. (1997). Family experience of barriers to treatment and premature termination from child therapy. *Journal of Consulting and Clinical Psychology*, 65, 453–463.

Kazdin, A. E., Marciano, P. L., Whitley, M. K. The therapeutic alliance in cognitive-behavioral treatment of children referred for oppositional, aggressive, and antisocial behavior. Journal of Consulting and Clinical Psychology 2005;73(4):726–730. [PubMed: 16173860]

Kendall, P. C. (Ed.). (1991). *Child and adolescent therapy: Cognitive– behavioral procedures.* New York: Guilford Press.

Kim, J., & Cicchetti, D. (2003). Social self-efficacy and behavior problems in maltreated children. *Journal of Clinical Child and Adolescent Psychology*, 32(1), 106-117.

Kramer, S. (1990). *Positive Endings in Psychotherapy : Bringing Meaningful Closure to Therapeutic Relationships.* Wiley, John & Sons, Incorporated.

Lipschitz-Elhawi, R., & Itzhaky, H. (2005). Social support, mastery, self-esteem and individual adjustment among at-risk youth. *Child and Youth Care Forum*, 34(5), 329-346.

MacNeilage, P. F., Rogers, L. J., & Vallortigara, G (2009). Origins of the left and right brain. Scientific American, 301, 60-67.

Masten, A. S., Best, K. M., & Garmezy, N. 1990. Resilience and development: Contributions from the study of children who overcome adversity. *Development and Psychopathology*, 2(4), 425-444.

Masten, A. S., & Coatsworth, J. D. (1998). The development in competence in favorable and unfavorable environments. *American Psychologist*, 53(2), 205-220.

McGilcrest, I. (2009). *The master and his emissary: The divided brain and the making of the Western world.* New Haven, CT: Yale University Press.

McKay, M., Wood, J. C., & Brantley, J. (2007). *The Dialectical Behavior Therapy Skills Workbook.* California: New Harbinger Publications, Inc.

Mendez, J., Fantuzzo, J., & Cicchetti, D. (2002). Profiles of social competence among low-income African American preschool children. *Child Development, 73,* 1085-1100.

Mischel, W., Shoda, Y., & Rodriguez, M. L. (1989). Delay of gratification in children. *Science, 24,* 933-938.

Norman, E. (2000). Introduction: The strengths perspective and resiliency enhancement-a natural partnership. In E. Norman (Ed.,) *Resiliency enhancement: Putting the strengths perspective into social work practice* (pp 1-16). New York: Columbia University Press.

O'Connor, K. (1983). The Color-Your-Life Technique. In C. E. Schaefer & K. J. O'Connor (Eds.), *Handbook of play therapy* (pp. 251–258). NewYork: Wiley.

Porges, S. W. (2011). *The polygaval theory: Neurobiological foundations of emotions, attachment, communication and self-regulation.* New York, NY: Norton.

Rauktis, M. E., Vides de Andrade, A. R., Doucette, A., McDonough, L., Reinhart, S. Treatment foster care and relationships: Understanding the role of therapeutic alliance between youth and treatment parent. International Journal of Child and Family Welfare 2005;8(4):146.

Reis, B. F., & Brown, L. G. (2006). Preventing therapy dropout in the real world: The clinical utility of videotape preparation and client estimate of treatment duration. Professional Psychology: Research and Practice, 37, 311-316.

Resnick, M., Bearman, P., Blum, R. W., Bauman, K., Harris, K., Jones, J., et al. (1997). Protecting adolescents from harm: Findings from the National Longitudinal Study on Adolescent Health. *Journal of the American Medical Association, 278,* 823-832.

Robbins, M.S., Turner, C.W., Alexander, J.F., Perez, G. A. Alliance and dropout in family therapy for adolescents with behavior problems: Individual and systemic effects. Journal of Family Psychology 2003;17(4): 534–544. [PubMed: 14640803]

Russell, R. L., & Shirk, S. R. (1998). Child psychotherapy process re- search. *Advances in Clinical Child Psychology, 20,* 93–124.

Scamardo, M., Bobele, M., & Biever, J. L. (2004). A new perspective on client dropouts. Journal of Systemic Therapies, 23, 27-38.

Schore, A. N. (2003a). *Affect dysregulation and the disorders of the self.* New York, NY: Norton.

Schore, A. N. (2003b). *Affect regulation and the repair of the self.* New York, NY: Norton.

Semrud-Clikemn, M., Fine, J. G., & Zhu, D. C. (2011). The role of the right hemisphere for processing of social interactions in normal adults using functional magnetic resonance imaging. *Neuropsychobiology, 64,* 47-51.

Sesma, A., Jr., & Roehlkepartain, E. C. (2003). Unique strengths, shared strengths: Developmental assets among youth of color. *Search Institute Insights & Evidence,* 1(2) 1-13.

Shirk, S. R. (2001). The road to effective child psychological services: Treatment process and outcome research. In J. Hughes, A. LaGreca, & J. Conoley (Eds.), *Handbook of psychological services for children and adolescents* (pp. 43–59). New York: Oxford University Press.

Shirk, S.R., Karver, M. Prediction of treatment outcome from relationship variables in child and adolescent therapy: A meta-analytic review. Journal of Consulting and Clinical Psychology 2003;71(3):452– 464. [PubMed: 12795570]

Shirk, S. R., & Russell, R. L. (1996). *Change processes in child psychotherapy: Revitalizing treatment and research.* New York: Guilford Press.

Shirk, S. R., & Saiz, C. (1992). The therapeutic alliance in child therapy: Clinical, empirical, and developmental perspectives. *Development and Psychopathology, 4,* 713–728.

Shoda, Y., Mischel, W., & Peake, P.K. (1990). Predicting adolescent cognitive and self-regulatory competencies from preschool delay of gratification: Identifying diagnostic conditions. *Developmental Psychology,* 26(6), 978-986.

Southam-Gerow, M., Kendall, P. C., & Weersing, V. R. (2001). Examining outcome variability: Correlates of treatment response in a child and adolescent anxiety clinic. *Journal of Clinical Child Psychology, 30,* 422– 436.

Swift, J. K., & Callahan, J. L. (2008). A delay discounting measure of great expectations and the effectiveness of psychotherapy. Professional Psychology: Research and Practice, 39, 581-588.

Swift, J. K., Callahan, J. L., & Levine, J. C. (2009). Using clinically significant change to identify premature termination. Psychotherapy: Theory, Research, Practice, Training, 46, 328-335.

Tracey, T. J. (1986). Interactional correlates of premature termination. Journal of Consulting and Clinical Psychology, 54, 784-788.

Walitzer, K. S., Dermen, K. H., & Conners, G. J. (1999). Strategies for preparing clients for treatment: A review. Behavior Modification, 23, 129-151.

Werner, E. E., & Smith, R. S. (2001). *Journeys from childhood to midlife: Risk, resilience, and recovery.* Ithaca, NY: Cornell University Press.

Wierzbicki, M., & Pekarik, G. (1993). A meta-analysis of psychotherapy dropout. Professional Psychology: Research and Practice, 24, 190-195.

Worden, W. J. (2009). *Grief counseling and grief therapy: A handbook for the Mental Health Practitioner.* 4th edition. New York: Springer Publishing Company, LLC.

Wyman, P. A., Cowen, E. L., Work, W. C., Hoyt-Meyers, L., Magnus, K. B., & Fagen, D. B. (1999). Caregiving and developmental factors differentiating young at-risk urban children showing resilient versus stress-affected outcomes: A replication and extension. *Child Development, 70,* 645-659.

Wyman, P. A., Cowen, E. L., Work, W. C., & Parker, G. R. (1991). Developmentally and family milieu correlates of resilience in urban children who have experienced major life-stress. *American Journal of Community Psychology, 19*, 405-426.

Zastrow, C.H., & Kirst-Ashman, K.K. (2010). *Understanding Human Behavior And The Social Environment* (8th ed.). United States: Books/Cole.

Zelazo, P. D. (2001). Self-reflection and the development of consciously controlled processing. In P. Mitchell & K. J. Riggs (Eds.), *Children's reasoning and the mind* (pp. 169-189). London: Psychology Press.

Zwick, R., & Attkisson, C. C. (1985). Effectiveness of a client pretherapy orientation videotape. Journal of Counseling Psychology, 32, 514-524.

Course Description and Objectives

Course Description: Most mental health practitioners agree that termination is vital to the treatment process, but it can be difficult to know what to do each step of the way to make termination successful. This continuing education course offers a step-by-step guide to help practitioners navigate the termination process. It separates termination into four easy-to-follow steps designed to prepare children and adolescents to leave treatment hopeful about the future and with enough protective assets to support them to thrive in future challenges. Play therapy interventions were designed utilizing research from resiliency, brain development and evidence-based practice areas.

Course Objectives: At the end of this course, the practitioner will be able to:

- Understand the 4-steps of a successful termination so treatment ends in a planned, sensitive manner.
- Immediately implement at least 20 creative, developmentally and culturally sensitive interventions that enhance resiliency and strengthen protective assets in children and adolescents.
- Cultivate a deeper understanding for how to use the ending of the therapeutic relationship to bring healing to a traumatized client.
- Acquire tools to pre-empt a client's early termination from treatment during the termination process.
- Learn to identify and manage transference and counter-transference issues that may be triggered during the Termination process.
- Boost your confidence to end treatment successfully with challenging populations.

Continuing Education Instructions

1. Take CE examination on-line at 21stcenturyseminars.com (available Fall, 2014).

2. Or complete self-study exam using the CE examination included in this training manual.

3. Return the payment, completed answer sheet, AND the course evaluation to 21st Century Seminars via US mail or email (21stcenturyseminars@gmail.com). Include a copy of check or money order with email.

4. Keep a copy of your completed answer sheet. 21st Century Seminars is not responsible for materials lost via mail or email.

5. Please include a $49.00 check, cashier's check, or money order payable to 21st Century Seminars, for processing your materials. Your exam will be scored within 7 business days of receipt of **all** your materials and payment. Refunds will be honored less a $15.00 administrative fee when received in writing. There are no refunds once an answer sheet is scored.

6. You must answer a minimum of 80% (32 items) correctly to obtain your Certificate of Continuing Education. If you do not pass, you will be allowed to review the material and re-test until you achieve a passing exam score. There is a $10.00 administrative fee for re-tests when the tests are submitted via fax or email. Free unlimited re-tests are available at 21stcenturyseminars.com (available Fall, 2014). There is a $30.00 returned check fee. All fees must be paid before a CE Certificate will be issued.

Social Workers, Marriage and Family Therapists, Educational Psychologists and Professional Clinical Counselors: This course has been approved for 8.0 hours of continuing education self-study by the California Board of Behavior Sciences for LCSWs, MFTs, LEPs and, LPCCs. Provider # PCE 5317. Non-California residents must contact the licensing board in their respective states to determine if that state will honor the CE units earned through this course.

Play Therapists: This course meets the criteria for 8.0 hours of non-contact continuing education and training (Play Therapy Applications) for Registered Play Therapists (RPT) and Supervisors (RPT-S) through the Association for Play Therapy (APT) Approved provider 02-122. Our APT Play Therapy hours are approved in the United States, Alaska, Hawaii, and where Association for Play Therapy CE credit is accepted.

Registered Nurses: This course qualifies for 8.0 hours of continuing education contact hours by the California Board of Registered Nursing. Provider #: 16196. Non-California residents must contact the licensing board in their respective states to determine if their state will honor the CE units earned through this course.

Non-licensed Professions and Non-California Residents: Non-licensed and non-California professionals will receive a certificate of completion for 8.0 hours of training. Our Play Therapy training hours are approved in the United States, Alaska, Hawaii, and where Association for Play Therapy CE credit is accepted.

266

Continuing Education Instructions
Two easy ways to receive credit for 8.0 hours of training:

	1. On-Line at 21stcenturyseminars.com	2. Mail or Email
2 Ways to Test	Review training and test on-line at: 21stcenturyseminars.com (Interactive website launches Fall, 2014)	Copy and complete CE Answer Sheet and: 1. Mail to 21st Century Seminars. Address: 1590 W. Rosecrans Avenue, Suite D-130 Manhattan Beach, California 90266. 2. Email: Use included Email Cover Sheet to: 21stcenturyseminars@gmail.com
CE Credits	Reviewing course and taking exam on-line qualify for regular CE units. Website launches, Fall 2014	CE Exams that are mailed or emailed qualify for Self-Study CE units. If you prefer regular CE units, see instructions for the online option. Some states have a limit on the number of Self-Study CE units accumulated per renewal cycle.
CE Approval	Approved for 8.0 hours of continuing education for California LCSWs; LMFTs; LEPs, LPCCs and California Registered Nurses	8.0 Self-Study hours approved for California LCSWs, LMFTs, LEPs and LPCCs. 8.0 CE contact hours approved for California Registered Nurses.
CE for Non-Licensed and Non-California Residents	Non-licensed and non-California professionals will receive a certificate of completion for 8.0 hours of training. Non-California residents must contact the licensing board in their respective states to determine if that state will honor the CE units earned through this course.	
Play Therapy Training	APT Approved provider (02-122) for 8.0 hours of non-contact Play Therapy training. (RPT and RPT/S hours gained).	APT Approved provider (02-122) for 8.0 hours of Play Therapy training. Mail or email is considered non-contact. (RPT and RPT/S hours gained)
Course Evaluation	Completed on-line	Evaluation MUST accompany CE Answer Sheet. Complete and mail or email with copy of CE Answer Sheet
Test results	Immediate results. You must score at least 80% or 32 correct items to pass.	Will be scored within 7 business days. Notification via email. You must score at least 80% or 32 correct items to pass.
If you do not Pass the test	Re-test for free until you pass	Re-test until you pass. $10.00 administrative fee for each re-test.
Payments	Accepted on-line. Course costs $49.00	Mail in $49.00 Check or money order. $30.00 fee for returned checks.
CE Certificate	Downloaded instantly and stored 5 years	Will be sent to you via email and stored for 5 years.
Refund Policy	No refunds once test is taken	Refunds will be honored, less a $15.00 administrative fee, when received in writing. There are no refunds once an answer sheet has been scored.
Customer Service	Telephone: 213-761-8171 office Email: 21stcenturyseminars@gmail.com	

EMAIL COVER SHEET

Date: _____

TO: 21ˢᵗ Century Seminars

Email: 21stcenturyseminars@gmail.com

PRINT NEATLY - PRINT NEATLY - PRINT NEATLY

Name:_____

Phone: Day:(   )_____Cell: (   )_____

Email: _____@_____

You Must Include ALL 3 Items:

1. ☐ Completed CE Self-Study Course Evaluation

2. ☐ Completed CE Self-Study Answer Sheet

3. ☐ Include copy of Check, Cashier's Check or, Money Order with email.

Mail Payment To:

Mail $49.00 check, cashier's check, or money order to 21ˢᵗ Century Seminars, 1590 W. Rosecrans Avenue, #D-130. Manhattan Beach, California. 90266.

CE Policy:

21ˢᵗ Century Seminars will score your answer sheet and review your course evaluation within 7 business days after **ALL** materials and fees are received. A passing exam score is 80% or 32 correct answers. There is a $10.00 administrative fee for each re-test. Refunds will be honored, less a $15.00 processing fee, when received in writing. There are no refunds once an answer sheet is scored. It is advisable to keep a copy of your completed answer sheet. 21ˢᵗ Century Seminars is not responsible for materials lost via mail, fax or email. We will email your CE training certificate to the email address provided on your answer sheet.

CE Self-Study Course Evaluation 21st Century Seminars

(TYPE or PRINT NEATLY)

Dear Participant: Photocopy, then return this completed course evaluation **AND** a copy of your Continuing Education Answer Sheet to 21st Century Seminars to receive your Self-Study Certificate of Continuing Education. Include the $49.00 check or money order to pay for the course. A passing score is 80% or 32 correct items. There is a $10.00 administrative fee for re-tests. Refunds will be honored, less a $15.00 processing fee, when received in writing. No fees will be refunded once the answer sheet is scored. It is advisable to keep a copy of your completed answer sheet. 21st Century Seminars is not responsible for materials lost via mail or email. We will email your CE training certificate to the email address provided on your answer sheet.

Please complete the following statements by circling the number under the word that best describes your rating.

Name (optional):_____ Phone# _____

☐ Check here if you want 21st Century Seminars to contact you regarding your comments (Requires you to fill in your name and phone # above)

Course: _Termination That Works With At-Risk Children and Adolescents__ Self-Study Course__

Please rate this course on the following items:	Strongly Disagree	Disagree	Neutral	Agree	Strongly Agree
The information in this course improved my knowledge of the subject matter	1	2	3	4	5
The course was taught at the appropriate level	1	2	3	4	5
The course was the appropriate length	1	2	3	4	5
The course was interesting and easy to read	1	2	3	4	5
The authors were knowledgeable about the subject	1	2	3	4	5
The CE exam was appropriately challenging	1	2	3	4	5
The CE process was relatively easy and user-friendly	1	2	3	4	5
I would take another course from 21st Century Seminars	1	2	3	4	5

Comments or recommendations for this program:

Suggestions for future live classroom seminars, self-study programs or on-line trainings:

CE Self-Study Answer Sheet 21st Century Seminars
Termination That Works With At-Risk Children and Adolescents
(TYPE or PRINT NEATLY)

Name: _____

Address: _____

City: _____ State: _____ Zip: _____

Lic. Type: _____ Lic. No.: _____ RPT or RPT-S #: _____

☐ I am a registered Associate, Trainee or Intern #: _____ ☐ I am not licensed or registered

Tel No.: _____ Cell Phone: _____

Email (to receive your certificate): _____

Continuing Education Policy: 21st Century Seminars will score your answer sheet and review your course evaluation within 7 business days after all materials and fees are received. The $49.00 payment can be 1) mailed or, 2) Made through PayPal.com for faster processing. A passing score is 80% or 32 correct answers. There is a $10.00 administrative fee for re-tests. Refunds will be honored, less a $15.00 processing fee, when received in writing. No fees will be refunded once the answer sheet is scored. 21st Century will email your CE training certificate to the email address provided. It is advisable to keep a copy of your completed answer sheet. 21st Century Seminars is not responsible for materials lost via mail, fax or email.

Directions: Circle the letter corresponding to your answer.

#	Answer				#	Answer			
1	A	B	C	D	21	A	B	C	D
2	A	B	C	D	22	A	B	C	D
3	A	B	C	D	23	A	B	C	D
4	A	B	C	D	24	A	B	C	D
5	A	B	C	D	25	A	B	C	D
6	A	B	C	D	26	A	B	C	D
7	A	B	C	D	27	A	B	C	D
8	A	B	C	D	28	A	B	C	D
9	A	B	C	D	29	A	B	C	D
10	A	B	C	D	30	A	B	C	D
11	A	B	C	D	31	A	B	C	D
12	A	B	C	D	32	A	B	C	D
13	A	B	C	D	33	A	B	C	D
14	A	B	C	D	34	A	B	C	D
15	A	B	C	D	35	A	B	C	D
16	A	B	C	D	36	A	B	C	D
17	A	B	C	D	37	A	B	C	D
18	A	B	C	D	38	A	B	C	D
19	A	B	C	D	39	A	B	C	D
20	A	B	C	D	40	A	B	C	D

Continuing Education Self-Study Examination

Termination That Works With At-Risk Children and Adolescents

SELF-STUDY DIRECTIONS: Place your answers on the ANSWER SHEET. Return your completed answer sheet AND the course evaluation to 21ˢᵗ Century Seminars via mail or email. It is advisable to keep a copy of your completed answer sheet. 21ˢᵗ Century Seminars is not responsible for materials lost via mail or email. A passing score is 80% or 32 correct items. There is a $10.00 administrative fee for re-tests.

Do not mail this Examination. Keep it in case you must re-test.

1. Select the **BEST** answer. Research shows that developmental assets build
   _____ in young people.
   a. Resilience b. Developmental Factors c. Positive Assets d. Coping Skills

2. The number of developmental assets is a greater predictor of success or failure than gender, socio-economic status, race or ethnicity, or being from a single parent household.   a. True b. False

3. The more developmental assets a young person has, the _____ likelihood of thriving and not engaging in high-risk behaviors.   a. Less b. More

4. Research shows the **BEST** predictor of mental health treatment outcomes is the_____
   a. Treatment model   b. Counselor's training
   c. Therapeutic relationship   d. Client's age

5. Factors such as, developmental levels, age, gender, and ethnicity of the client have a stronger impact on treatment outcome than the quality of the therapeutic relationship.   a. True b. False

6. The therapeutic alliance for youth tends to grow stronger in the middle to latter stages of treatment, compared to adults, who form alliances more easily in the early stages of treatment.

a. True b. False

7. The quality of the therapeutic alliance has no impact on treatment outcomes for youth with histories of maltreatment, juvenile delinquency, or externalizing behaviors.

a. True b. False

8. Traumatized clients may overgeneralize the mistakes of one relationship to all future relationships.   a. True   b. False

9. A goal of termination must be to end the therapeutic relationship in such a way that supports the client to remain open to future relationships. a. True   b. False

Step One: Educate the Client About Termination

10. Which is **NOT** included in a typical termination announcement? _____
    a. Informing the client treatment is ending   b. Using clear, honest language
    c. Give a concrete ending date   d. None. All are a part of the announcement

11. (Select the **BEST** answer) If you find yourself avoiding the termination countdown each week and not talking about termination, this is an indication you may be experiencing _____.
    a. Avoidance   b. Depression   c. Counter-transference   d. Denial

12. It is important to focus on strengths and progress as the reason for termination because:_____
    a. It reinforces that the client is leaving the counselor versus the counselor leaving the client.
    b. It communicates that the client cannot manage without the counselor.
    c. It helps the counselor feel like s/he has done a good job.
    d. None of the above.

13. After processing the termination announcement, some clients may feel less motivated to attend treatment where as others may seem more motivated.

a. True   b. False

14. Even if not articulated initially, some clients may believe treatment is ending because s/he did something inappropriate or upsetting to the counselor.

    a. True   b. False

15. Some clients may benefit from a return to treatment because cognitive maturation may allow them to process past trauma differently.   a. True   b. False

16. If you clarified at the onset of treatment whether or not a client can continue a relationship with you after services ends, you do not need to revisit this again during termination.   a. True   b. False

17. A treatment provider should **NOT** give special consideration when terminating with clients in involuntary, inpatient or residential treatment centers.

    a. True   b. False

18. During termination, a treatment provider should address his/her policy about remaining in contact with clients via social media, text and video messaging, email or cell phone after treatment ends   a. True   b. False

19. It is important to have the client involved in planning the termination celebration.

    a. True   b. False

Step Two: Process the Range of Feelings About Termination

20. A treatment provider should fully process the range of feelings about treatment with a client before working on the concrete skills to prepare for life after treatment.

    a. True   b. False

21. Strong emotional regulation and self-control skills build resiliency in youth.

    a. True   b. False

22. Encouraging a client to express the full range of feelings about treatment means accepting that at times, they client may have sometimes felt bored or uncomfortable.

    a. True   b. False

23. If a client has a set-back during the termination process, you should stop working on termination to address the set-back.   a. True   b. False

24. A student saying good-bye to a teacher at the end of the school year, is an example of how sometimes good-byes are a normal part of life.

a. True   b. False

25. When should termination be discussed?
    a. At the very beginning of treatment.
    b. Periodically during treatment goal reviews.
    c. When the case is ready for termination.
    d. All of the above.

Step Three: Prepare Client to Manage Life After Termination

26. During the treatment goal review your client minimizes her progress and displays self-defeating distortions and thinking errors. According to this 4-step guide for termination, you should accept the client's point of view unconditionally.

a. True   b. False

27. With case transfers and pre-mature terminations, you should complete a goal review and also work to prepare the client for set-backs and future challenges.

a. True   b. False

28. If your client wishes to improve their frustration tolerance in the remaining weeks before treatment ends, you should: _____
    a. Refer out to another counselor
    b. Move the termination date back
    c. Tell the client it is too late, termination has already begun
    d. Honor the request and theme the remaining work to termination

29. Improving frustration tolerance, cognitive regulation, and behavior control builds resilience in youth.   a. True   b. False

30. Identifying and strengthening the client's connection to family, community and school does very little to build resilience in youth.   a. True   b. False

31. Using *Before, During, and After Treatment* themes and *What I Need for the Future* themes are effective ways to prepare a client for life after treatment ends.

a. True   b. False

Step Four: Honor the Therapeutic Relationship and End Treatment

32. Youth report feeling a stronger therapeutic alliance with their counselor during ____ of treatment:

    a. The beginning
    b. The beginning to middle
    b. Middle to the end
    d. The end

33. An unsuccessful ending can potentially impact the treatment outcome and impact how your client views future relationships.   a. True   b. False

34. The **BEST** activity to honor the therapeutic relationship includes the counselor:

    a. Giving a gift to the client
    b. Mailing a keepsake to client
    c. Observing client making a keepsake
    d. Making a keepsake with the client

35. Which represents the **BEST** commemorative message from a counselor to a client?____

    a. I wish you the best
    b. You deserve the best
    c. A and B
    d. A only

36. Children and adolescents, who make a contribution to their community, are more resilient than those who do not:

    a. True   b. False

37. Giving back to others does **not** promote a belief in a positive future and does **not** encourage youth that they can influence their world.

    a. True   b. False

38. Altruistic activities may include: _____

    a. Fund raising for a charitable cause
    b. Volunteering at a library
    c. Writing a positive message to a future client
    d. All of the above

39. Finding meaning in the treatment experience includes asking a client to explore "why" s/he experienced past trauma.   a. True   b. False

40. A celebration includes spending lots of money on food and gifts for a client.

    a. True   b. False

21st Century Seminars

where professionals grow